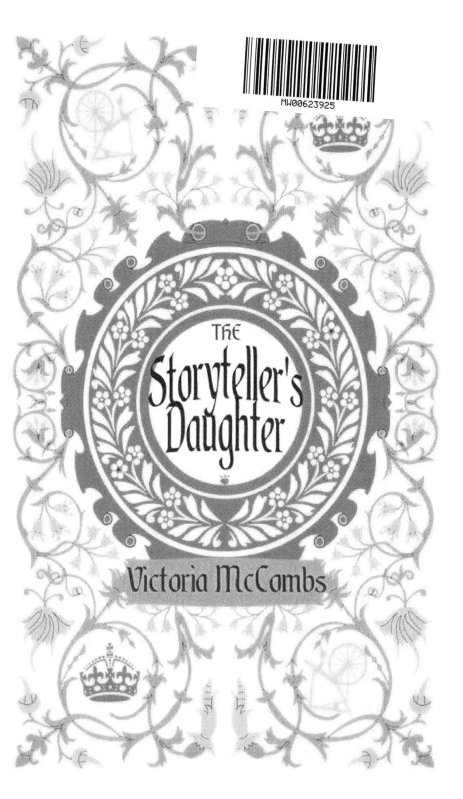

THE
Storyteller's Daughter

Victoria McCombs

J, I love you a lottle

Chapter One

IF I COULD CHOOSE my Gift, I'd want it to be practical like
making bread or shoes to provide for my struggling family. If I
couldn't have a practical Gift, then I'd want something
extravagant that people would pay to see, and then I'd use the
money to buy provisions so we'd never go hungry again. If the Gift
wasn't practical or brilliant, then it held little value in the eyes of
the merry folk of Autumn Leaf Village.

Futile, they said. There was no point in wishing for things I'd
never have.

The elder ladies gathered under the thick oak tree at the start
of the day to whisper about the Gifts behind their large hats, and I
caught snippets of their chatter when I heard my name roll from

their tongues. Each carried their own tale passed down from their grandmothers of how the Gifts came to be: sometimes it was a foolish wizard, sometimes a sorceress in training, once it was a beggar girl who made a wish. Whatever way Westfallen stumbled into the Gifts was unknown for certain, but everyone had one. Every child born showed signs of a special talent that set them apart from each other. Everyone had a piece of magic in their souls.

Everyone except me.

Somehow, out of all the children born in Westfallen over the past hundred years, I was the first to be born Giftless, and while I didn't know why my soul held no magic, I often wondered if it was because I was unworthy. The elder ladies seemed to think so.

Without a Gift to guide me, most folks believed I'd spend the rest of my days working in my parents' tavern.

It wasn't that I particularly disliked working here. In fact, there were many things I loved about the Riverfront Tavern: the smell of Lolly's cinnamon cakes, the warm glow from the two fires, the jovial laughter that could be heard from outside. But my favorite was when Papa got out his old barstool and leaned into it, and the whole tavern fell into a hush to hear his stories. Those were my favorite times.

That was Papa's Gift: storytelling, and he was the best storyteller Autumn Leaf Village had come by in years. He learned to talk before he was one year old and had been weaving mesmerizing tales ever since. After fifty years of storytelling, people said that his stories kept getting better each year, but they were wrong—his stories had always been this good.

Years ago, numerous taverns thrived in Autumn Leaf Village. But times grew hard and people's taste for such establishments dwindled, until now only two taverns remained—ours and Haystack Hallow, which sat out north behind the farms. Haystack Hallow was closer for many folks, but it didn't have Papa's stories. Mama stood tall as she served the customers, quick to tell any that my father was her husband. It was her one true claim to fame: being married to Papa.

Mama's Gift wasn't so special. She could turn any apple into a peach, but only on Saturdays. We'd eaten every dish with peaches imaginable, and I didn't have the heart to tell her I preferred apples.

At least she had a Gift, though. I'd eat a million peaches if it meant I had a Gift. There was nothing I could do about it; the years had passed and taken all hope of a Gift with it.

Tonight, the Riverfront Tavern was filled with customers. Our tables were set up in a wide W-shape in the winter months to share the heat from the fireplaces, and Papa would sit in the corner between the two as he told his stories. The conversations and laughter could always be heard from outside, along with Aiden's singing, and tonight was no exception. Papa, with his trouser pants rolled around his thick socks, sat perched on the edge of his old stool, bent forward with one hand on his knee as he told a tale of a dragon and a girl who could control fire. That would be quite a Gift, to wield fire. I'd never met someone with that Gift before, and I didn't know if I believed there to be such a person.

Sometimes I approached Papa after one of his stories to ask if the tale was true, and he'd get this gleam in his eye, lean forward, and say with a wink, "If the story lives in our hearts, then that makes it true." He wasn't answering my question, but he knew I didn't really want to know. I wanted to pretend all the stories were true.

I moved my broom toward the front, where old boots lay in a stack by the door. With the winter months upon us the folks' shoes were dirtier than a stable's ground, and we encouraged them to take off their shoes and warm their feet by one of our crackling fires. Sometimes I came down to sleep by one of the fires on the nights that my room wouldn't hold heat. Papa would hear and usually come out to join me, and we would cuddle up with blankets on the warm floorboards and fall asleep to one of his stories.

No matter how old I got, I was never too old to fall asleep to his stories.

Aiden sat at the far end of the bar in the corner, half-masked by shadows. Besides Papa's stories, Aiden was my next favorite thing about the tavern.

"You wouldn't keep missing spots if you weren't looking at him so often." My sister, Anika, threw a rag at me, which I avoided, and for a moment I thought about swinging my broom toward her feet in retaliation, but Mama walked by between us and I thought better of it. Anika didn't understand my courtship. It wasn't that she was too young, as at seventeen she was certainly old enough to be romantically inclined, but she seemed set on avoiding such feelings.

"Hush now." Mama retrieved the thrown rag and sent us both a look with lowered eyebrows, sending me back to work with my broom. "If Cosette has fallen in love, she isn't to be blamed for that."

My cheeks flushed at the comment, and I moved the broom faster.

"She can't be in love already. Are you in love?" There was a noticeable tinge of disgust in Anika's voice.

"I'd rather not be pestered about it, if you don't mind."

Mama huffed as she whirled herself around and wagged her long finger at me. "I most certainly do mind! Hanna's daughter was married just last week, and she's a year younger than you! Oh, the questions I got about when you would settle down!"

I put up my hands defensively at her sudden outburst. "It's only been six months of courtship. I'm still working things out."

Her hands mounted on her hips. "Cosette, tell me you aren't planning on running off that nice boy."

I straightened my back and drew my lips into a thin line. "No. If you must know, I like him quite a lot."

She smiled then, as if she won some sort of battle.

I thought I would have another year before Mama mentioned marriage. I *knew* I had a few years until Papa did. My hands couldn't move the broom away from this conversation fast enough. "I think I should focus on my new apprenticeship before I jump into a marriage."

If Mama replied, I was too far away to hear it.

The friendship between Aiden and me took me by surprise. He was the sort of man that everyone noticed: loud and cheerful and always around. If he was in the room, you'd know it, because you'd hear his laughter above all others. I was the opposite of him in that way; I was the girl that no one saw, usually because my face was hidden behind a book. Aiden had a word for me. Simple, he had said. I had taken offense to that until I realized he meant it as a compliment. He found me refreshing, and after years of friendship, it was no surprise to anyone when he asked to court me half a year ago.

After my chore and his song were over, I weaved my way back to him, sitting on the nearest stool and taking back the book he had been holding for me.

"What's this one about?"

I showed him the cover as I searched for my place among the pages. "A boy who trades places with his dead brother. He's a spy, you see, and the brother is a knight."

Aiden feigned interest by nodding his head. "Does he get caught?"

I grinned. "Not yet."

Aiden let me be as I read. His usual pullover shirt and trousers were paired with a single-breasted vest and shawl collar tonight, making him look very grown-up. He hadn't shaved this morning, and I could see a hint of dark hair stretching down toward his chin. Even though we sat near the kitchen, I could smell the garden on Aiden. His family grew one of the largest plots of vegetables in the village, and the smell of it clung to him. They had a greenhouse to work in when the winter brought its frost.

After a few moments of silence, Aiden prodded me again with a gentle nudge under the bar, but when I looked up, I was surprised to find his eyes weren't focused on me, but rather on something over my shoulder. "I think your mother is going to have a meltdown if you don't get up. She's glared at you three times now."

With a groan, I folded my book back up. "But I only just sat down!" As I glanced behind to Mama, she lowered her eyebrows at me. Though excited at the prospect of my courtship, Mama still prioritized the tavern over anything. She grew up here, and as result, she loved the tavern as much as she loved Papa. As she caught my eye, she pointed a sharp finger toward the counter, to which I nodded, replacing the book in my hand with a rag that I half-heartedly drew across the bar.

Aiden studied my book in his hand. "If you knew how to write, I'd say you could write some beautiful stories, and maybe we'd find your Gift after all."

For a moment my eyes closed, and my chest fell just enough that he wouldn't see. He was just being helpful, I had to remind myself. He wanted me to find my place in the village. People are defined by their Gifts. Who you marry, what job you have, it all depended on your Gift. Those with a special Gift were treated well, married nicely, and lived happily. There was a man who, if given stalks of cotton, could turn them into fine clothes overnight. His family was always dressed nicely, and he was given the hand of a count's daughter. Another man could conjure up bread. He also married a count's daughter.

But me? I was overlooked. I had no skills to help me, no talent to impress with. I knew all hope of finding a Gift was gone, but Aiden wasn't as convinced.

"I've tried to think up a few stories in my mind, but they aren't very good." The corners of my mouth lifted up to mimic a smile, but my lips felt as tight as my chest. I'd never tell him I couldn't bear being constantly reminded of my shortcoming. I knew it was thoughtfulness that drove him to search for my Gift, but his consideration blinded him to my pain.

Aiden's Gift was music, and while it wasn't a rare Gift, since four others in our village had it, his voice was my favorite. Mama agreed and paid him better than the rest. Soon, he became the only one she paid at all.

Still hopeful, Aiden shrugged one shoulder. "It's fine, we'll find your Gift one day."

My back leaned against the bar as I folded the rag in my hand. "I was waiting to tell you after I knew it would go well, but I might as well tell you now," I said. "I've been offered to train under Seamstress Kira."

Aiden's eyes grew as wide as his smile and he dropped my book. "Seamstress! That's splendid! When did you find out?"

"Just last night. Mama arranged it, if you can imagine that. They've planned to send Oria here to work while I train there, starting tomorrow." The smile on my face was real this time. Life as a seamstress wasn't much better than a tavern owner, but it was steady work, and a respected job. Seamstress Kira had acquired the task from her parents, and she managed to marry into a comfortable life with a baker. I could be happy with a life like that.

Seamstress Kira was known to be a kind woman with a gentle voice and a knack for making fine pies. I'd enjoy working alongside her. More importantly than that, I was finally going to have a way to identify myself. I would be a seamstress. It was an important step that I needed to take if I ever wanted to be my own person away from this tavern.

Maybe, just maybe, I wouldn't be the plain girl with no Gift anymore. I would be more than the Storyteller's Ungifted daughter.

Aiden lept from his seat to embrace me tightly. "This will be great," he breathed into my hair. "One day, I'll build you a shop so we will have a proper place for you to work and for us to live."

He'd never mentioned a future between us before.

I wish I could have taken the comment in stride or said something reaffirming back to him. Instead, when he pulled back, I strained a smile. If he noticed my unease, it didn't show.

Before I could come up with something to say, Anika came over to tell Aiden that he could sing now. He thanked her, then turned to me. "I'll see you after?"

I simply nodded.

Aiden moved away but Anika stayed and examined me for a moment. "Are you okay?" She was more perceptive than I gave her credit for. The things that Aiden never noticed, she picked up on in a matter of seconds. As I grabbed my rag, I nodded to her and moved on, unwilling to share my confused heart with my habitually mocking sister.

"You should know." Anika's hand caught mine, and her eyes shifted to both sides before she pulled me toward the bar and leaned her head in. Her voice lowered and dripped with intrigue as if she were sharing a spy's secrets with me. "I shouldn't be telling you this, but that's never stopped me before. Knowing you, you'll want to think about this for a while. Aiden's planning to ask for your hand in marriage."

My mouth fell open and Anika nudged me. "You can't tell that I told you, and no, I don't know when. I just heard Mama and Papa talk about it." She didn't give me another moment before she glanced toward Mama and slipped away, leaving me with my questions and confusion. If I tried to sort out my feelings with her, it'd do nothing but cause her to regret telling me in the first place, but I considered sneaking into her room later to talk anyway. A slight tremor ran through my hand, and I pressed the rag into it to steady myself before peeking at Aiden. His eyes weren't on me, and I forced myself back into movement to hide my confusion.

As I worked, I constantly glanced up at Aiden, hoping for sudden clarity when I searched his face. He occasionally gave me a wink, completely unaware of the battle going on within my heart.

Anika was right. I needed time to process this before he asked for my hand.

I loved him. I knew that. But would I love him for the rest of my life?

A part of me, and I couldn't tell how big that part was though I knew it was there, wanted to marry Aiden. But along with that lived doubt, and that doubt cast a crippling fear into my thoughts. When I said yes, I wanted to be completely certain, and I couldn't say that I was there yet.

I wouldn't risk hurting Aiden's feelings by giving him an answer, then changing my mind later. That meant I had maybe a few weeks to become sure of a decision that would affect the rest of my life.

Chapter Two

"IS HE GOING TO fight in the war? Oh, his mama must be beside herself! She already lost one to the war!"

I shivered at the mention of war. What once instilled hope in us at renewed treaties and centuries of future peace now left a sour taste in everyone's tongue as it dragged on relentlessly.

I tried not to eavesdrop on Seamstress Kira as she spoke, but with the shop empty there was little else to listen to. She and her friend sipped dandelion tea as they chattered, sending a sweet smell through the air that made my stomach yearn.

"He leaves for training in a few days. Appears they are desperate for more men." Her friend had a thicker voice, while Seamstress Kira's was chipper.

Still, even Seamstress Kira's tone dropped as she sighed. "It seems to me they should just stop fighting and send all the boys back home."

Westfallen had been at war for what felt like ages. For nine long summers and even longer winters, our army fought against our neighbors, Osmelee and Tames, with the help of our allies in Vestalin. With each passing year the money grew tighter, and the tension grew stronger as families ached for relief and to have their sons back.

Everyone knew somebody who had gone to war, and most knew someone who had lost a loved one to the fight. I couldn't imagine their pain. I had no brothers to lose and Papa's bad leg kept him from putting on the uniform.

What had started as a border dispute turned into a renegotiation of treaties and trade rights, and gradually shifted into an all-out power struggle between the four countries that used to be sisters. It was said that a powerful, dark northern magic kept the war alive, but Papa said it was the pride of kings, not some magic.

"At least we have several ladies who are able-bodied to keep us going until the boys come home. Speaking of: you got a new apprentice, I see!"

I ducked my head just as I heard the rocking chair squeak as the friend leaned forward to peer in the back room. I hoped it wasn't obvious that I was eavesdropping. I hid in there, heckling the flax plants as I'd been shown. I'd envisioned myself sewing skirts or bell sleeves by now, but the first weeks of my apprenticeship had dragged by, and each day found me in the back room crouched near a barrel, heckling until my fingers were raw. It seemed I would be putting in the work so I could appreciate the end product, as Seamstress Kira had explained. That meant before sewing together pieces of fabric, I first had to make the cloth. I spent weeks hunching over a bucket, hackling flax plants across boards to prepare the fibers for spinning. The board in my hand had long needles sticking out of it, catching the flax and pulling the leftover plant and small fibers from the longer strands. It was a tedious task that I didn't much care for.

I chastised myself for being greedy for a simpler chore when was lucky to get this apprenticeship at all.

From where I was sitting, I could see the main room and front door. On one side of the room sat premade clothes, arranged near the windows so passersby could easily see them. The other wall held an array of fabric, each rolled up and stacked on top of each other so customers could pick their color. In the corner by the fabric, two rocking chairs swung back and forth. Wide feet would rock in and out of my view as Seamstress Kira chatted with a friend I couldn't identify. Their words floated into the room, preoccupying me as I ran my tool through the flax.

"Yes, she's quite good," Seamstress Kira generously said.

"Can't say I place her. What's her name?"

"Cosette, daughter of Mortan, who owns the Riverfront Tavern."

I waited to see if she would identify me. She clicked her tongue a few times before I heard a small gasp. "You don't mean...the girl with no..." There was a clear decrease in volume and the squeaking from the rhythmic rocking was halted short. I didn't need to hear the rest of her sentence to know she'd placed me.

"Yes, that girl, but it's not a problem."

"Can she work?" I didn't know if the friend sounded disgusted or intrigued, but her tone lowered.

"'Course she can, it doesn't affect her ability to do work," Seamstress Kira laughed, while my face flushed.

"I just mean, well, she's not like the rest of us."

I didn't know Seamstress Kira well, and she would have no reason to defend me. I stopped running the flax through the board to hear her response. It came gently. "I don't see why not. I don't use my Gift to work."

Another click of the tongue. "It's not natural. Someone that even magic won't touch? You must be careful about that one."

I had heard it all before, but each time I allowed the remarks to get into my head and pierce my heart. There had never been a child born in Westfallen in the past hundred years who didn't have a Gift. All the children before me and all the children since were marked with a Gift by the age of three.

I liked to say it didn't bother me, but the tears threatening to fill my eyes told a different story.

To spare me from future remarks from her friend, Seamstress Kira appeared with a golden apple to relieve me from my task. She admired my work, choosing a few pieces that needed to be heckled a few more times, but otherwise looked very pleased with what I'd accomplished. Once satisfied, I removed the smaller fibers from the needles and put them in their own pile to be used to stuff pillows or as kindling, whichever Seamstress Kira chose.

"Good, very good. Now you come back tomorrow, and I'll teach you how to spin this into thread. Sweep the floors before you go. I assume you don't need me showing you that?"

"No, ma'am. Thank you, ma'am," I said with a small curtsy. Seamstress Kira gave me a dimpled smile as she pointed toward the broom in the corner then took off her apron and hung it on a hook before returning to her friend.

"You know what really keeps that war going," the friend's heavy voice seeped back into the room, once again not caring if she was overheard. I turned my body so I could eavesdrop better as I swept. "It's that dreadful curse, that's what it is."

My ears perked up. A curse? This was news to me.

"Oh, you can't believe that."

"But I do! You should too, 'less you want trouble coming for you. That old king invited magic and mischief into his kingdom, and for a hundred years since it's brought nothing but trouble." Her voice was serious as she breathed the words and I could picture her shaking her finger.

The doubt persisted in Seamstress Kira's voice. "The war has only been going on nine years, not a hundred."

"It from that curse that the old king got! It's been sitting around almost a hundred years now! Not good to let it sit so long. The war is punishment. She must be satisfied."

Seamstress Kira clucked as she turned about to check on me. I had stopped to listen and stood there with the broom in my hand and eyes wide. She shook her head at me.

"Go on home now, Cosette. There's nothing but high tales here."

Quickly I put my broom back in the corner, ashamed to be caught eavesdropping on gossip. I grabbed my apple from my seat and thanked Seamstress Kira several times as I backed out of her home. Her friend was watching me with eyes that seemed to warn me to heed her story. I recognized the friend, but still couldn't pin her name.

I wondered if there was truth to her tale. Papa had warned us against strong magic, though I had never believed it to be true. Anika believed in the magic with her whole heart, but I prided myself on being more rational than her. I believed in the Gifts, of course, but those were different from strong, free-flowing magic. The Gifts held a bit of magic in their own way, but that was different. They couldn't cast curses that lasted a hundred years, and they couldn't create wars.

Like me, Seamstress Kira sounded like a rational woman and I figured we would get along well. She was a kind lady, a bit heavy with round eyes and even rounder cheeks. I enjoyed working with her, though I was not looking forward to seeing her daughter at the tavern. All the kindness that Seamstress Kira had didn't translate to Oria, who was a stuck-up hog if you asked me. Papa has asked me not to call people that, but even he said that he was glad I wasn't friends with that girl.

Aiden seemed to get along quite fine with Oria, and me working at the shop today meant that she'd be at the tavern tonight. She didn't seem to respect our courtship, though I guessed she would respect an engagement. There was one benefit to saying yes. *That's not a reason to get engaged,* I reminded myself. Clearly, I'd come no closer to a decision.

Thanks to the information from Anika, I'd been more intentional about my time with Aiden, constantly pretending that he was my husband to gauge how I felt about it. Sometimes it thrilled me and other times it scared me. Time and time again, the scenario of him asking for my hand ran through my mind, and each time I tested out saying yes.

I replayed the imaginary scene in my head as I walked home, wondering what it would feel like to be Aiden's forever.

Chapter Three

I'D BEEN STUDYING FOR only one month, and yet my family acted as if their problems were solved. "You shall make me pants, and I'll be rid of these horrid skirts." Anika bounce don the bed beside me, her bony knees bumping mine with every movement until I'd scooted to the edge.

"Anika," Mama said in a stern tone. She hovered in the doorway like a lithe shadow, but even her menacing stare couldn't bridle Anika's spirit. Three years younger than me, she had more energy than a horse on a first spring's ride.

"I mean it, Mama. I want to wear pants, and you're going to make them for me!" She pointed at me with her thick brows wriggling.

Father chuckled from behind Mama.

It was a strange but comforting sight to have them all in my room as if we were young again and about to hear one of Papa's tales before bed. I pressed my back against the wall and placed a pillow under my arm that had fallen away when Anika shook me.

"Well?" Mama asked. She kept a rag in her hands that she wound about her fingers. "Is it going well?"

They asked that every day. And every day the answer was the same. It is well. I'm still learning.

But it'd been a month now and they were hungry for a better answer. I'd yet to do more than heckling flax but the hopeful gleam in my father's eyes made it too difficult to confess I was a ways away from making clothes. He'd never ask anything of me, yet somehow letting him down felt like the worst crime there was.

"I'm getting better. As soon as I make clothes, your pants will be the first thing I stitch," I promised Anika. She settled back onto my bed triumphantly.

"You're welcome to wear a pair of mine, Anika dear. Just not in public, I beg you," Papa offered. Anika made a face and I could tell what she was thinking. Papa was tall, a trait which he passed onto me. But Anika was short, even more so than Mama, and any pair of his pants would need to be hoisted up to her chest to fit her.

Mama sighed. "I must admit, it would be nice to have someone who can make us clothes." Papa pulled his lips tight, but he nodded. It was the most he would say on it, but he couldn't deny the benefits. We didn't have money to spend on such things when we could barely afford the oil for our lamps. Mama had long ago planted an extensive garden to try to bring in extra income with the food, but it had little impact. The few meals and drinks we offered at the tavern were all we could afford to make, and the money we received for them was only enough to keep us afloat.

The first time I was aware of our financial shortcomings, I was ten. A man had gotten soused and broke two chairs in a squabble, and Papa was stressed for weeks. He didn't know if he should ban the man from the tavern, knowing he was likely to break things again and we hadn't the money to repair them, or let him continue to come because we depended on his tab. In the end he struck a deal with the drunk man's brother that he would come repair anything broken in return for one free drink, and Papa's shoulders had relaxed again.

The next year, Anika and I were sent to our cousins for a month because our parents couldn't afford to feed us. And I think that was the first time Anika realized how poor we were. She had cried and cried about how we were going to end up homeless like the Copper family, but I had shushed her.

Things never got that bad again, but I often skipped meals to help ration the food, and I knew that Papa did the same.

If I could make clothes for the family, maybe start my own business down the road, it would be a huge blessing to our family. For the first time in my life, I had something of value. I might not have a Gift, but I could finally do more than sweep the floors and wipe the counters.

"I'm so proud of you, Cozy." Papa came forward with his hands in his pockets and lightly kissed my forehead.

The praise felt premature. "We still don't know if I'm any good."

He shook his head at me as if I was being foolish. "Nonsense. I know my little girl. I have no doubt you could spin straw into gold."

The compliment, and his vivid imagination, made me smile. Gold wasn't reasonable, but as long as I could make a simple dress or some trousers, I'd be content. The hope that simmered in me dwelled in the eyes of my family, too. I saw it as I looked at them, each one looking at me in a way I'd never seen before, so foreign that it took me a moment to place it. Pride, I named it. For the first time, I could give them hope for a better life.

My next breath came slow, allowing me to enjoy the moment to its fullest.

Mama broke the silence first. "Customers will be here soon, so get started on prep." She wiped her eyes as she ushered Anika off my bed and out the door. Papa stood to follow them, but he stopped outside the doorframe.

"Are you happy, Cozy?"

My head tilted as I frowned. "Of course I am."

He nodded, but his hand raised to his mouth where he tapped his tooth for a moment. He rocked on his heels, his head almost grazing the top of the doorframe as he moved. "And Aiden, he makes you happy?"

My head dropped to look at the bed. That's what this was about. Papa had given me privacy on this topic, but he must have known Aiden's intentions, and now he wanted to know if I was in love.

"He's a really good man," I said, but I knew that wasn't enough. To cover my uncertainty, I asked Papa, "What do you think of him?"

Papa ran his hand back and forth on his head, messing with his dark grey hair. He took a long, deep sigh. "He's not what I pictured for you, but I agree. He is a good man."

We'd never talked about this, so it surprised me to hear he'd pictured someone for me. "What did you envision?" I held my breath as I waited for his answer, not realizing how much I craved his input on the subject.

Papa sucked his lip in before answering. "Someone simpler, I guess. Quieter maybe. But the decision is yours alone, and I support you wholeheartedly."

His answer did nothing to settle my nerves or confusion, and I'm certain my discomfort showed on my face, because he came back to the bed and sat down next to me with his arm over my shoulders. "From a young age, you would tell Mama and me all about the man that you were sure you would one day marry. I have no doubt that you know what you want and that you will make the right decision, and we will be happy to welcome Aiden into the family."

He said it as if Aiden would be my choice, but I wasn't so sure. "Did you know Mama was the one?"

He smiled at the memory. "I knew I wanted to marry your mama long before she even noticed me. She was all I thought of day and night, and I knew I couldn't live without her."

The beauty in those words quieted me. *I want that.*

Papa kissed my forehead before leaving me alone with my thoughts.

I had so many thoughts; I wasn't sure I'd ever sort them out.

There were no other prospects for me. If I turned Aiden down, I might not get another offer. More than that, Aiden was a good option. He was my best friend, and I considered myself happy with him.

Was that enough to base my life on?

Unexpectedly, tears began to stream down my cheeks.

I couldn't marry him. I couldn't say yes.

Over the past two months, I'd devoted countless hours and frustrating, endless nights, caught in my plight of indecision, trying to decide if I wanted to marry Aiden while I ignored the doubts brewing in my heart. If this was love, if this was true love, I wouldn't have these doubts. If this was love, my nights would be spent giddy with anticipation instead of feeling sick with fear.

Surely life could grant me something better than this, but even if it didn't, I couldn't live always wondering if I'd settled for less. Aiden didn't deserve that, and neither did I.

I'd thought this before, but something felt different this time. As I envisioned saying no, peace settled over me, and I clung to it.

With that peace in my mind, I resolved to settle the issue, though I dreaded the idea of hurting Aiden.

As if summoned by my thoughts, Aiden waited for me as I opened my door. He would be singing here tonight, but I didn't expect to see him right outside my room.

He paced with his hands behind his back, his nose rosy with the evidence of a day spent outside in winter. His coat was unbuttoned, and droplets of water hid in its fibers. He straightened himself at the sight of me.

"Your mama said I could come back here to find you," he stammered as he played with his hands, rubbing his palms together and flipping his hands over, then rubbing them again in a gesture I'd never seen him make before.

While he paced for a few steps, I waited, unsure if I needed to reply to his comment. My hands started shaking and I hid them behind my back so he wouldn't see. My words ran though my head, the confidence I'd felt the moments before now replaced by nerves at the difficult conversation at hand.

Aiden looked equally nervous as he bobbed his head up and down, turning back to the left to continue pacing. He only got a few steps in before he took a big one back to the doorway. His eyes danced up to mine, then skirting away again.

"I love you so much, Cosette," he started.

My chest fell. Though Anika had warned me, I'd hoped she'd been wrong about Aiden's intentions. It would be easier to break off our courtship if he didn't harbor such strong feelings for me, feelings that, without a proper explanation, I couldn't return. This was my best friend, and I had to hurt him in a way I'd never planned on doing.

"Aiden, I can't." My voice sounded hollow as it rang in my ears.

"What?"

"I can't marry you," I choked. His body froze and all expression fell from his face. I took a step back, not wanting to be so near to his pain. "I'm so sorry, I know that I love you, but there's something missing. I can't live my whole life with this uncertainty."

Aiden's face remained blank as I struggled to put my feelings into words. His tongue flicked across his lips before he replied, "People get married for a lot less than love. We have love."

I wished for tears to fall from my eyes to prove to him how much this hurt me, but none came. So, I placed my hands to my chest and took a shaky breath. "But it's not this powerful love; I don't feel consumed by it. I don't think about how much I love you every night or dream about you during the day. It's not the love that I read about as a girl."

He ran his hands through his hair frantically. "Cosette, those books aren't real. This, me," he grabbed my hand and clutched it to his chest. His heart pounded beneath my palm. "I'm real. This thing between us is real."

His breath found my face, bringing a momentary taste of warmth with them. That's what Aiden had always been to me, warmth. Now, I'd never felt so cold. I shivered beneath his touch and prayed my honesty wouldn't cut too deep.

"I need to give myself a chance at something more."

He sucked in his breath and pain flooded in his eyes, spilling out in slow tears that stabbed into my heart. The tears still refused to come from my own eyes, causing me to appear closed off from him. His eyes searched mine for a sign of emotion. When he spoke, his voice came out shaking. "I can't lose you. Can I change your mind?"

After what I'd just said, his resiliency surprised me. I raised my shoulders then let them drop. "I don't think you can."

He spoke with urgency now. "Let me try, please. My family has that trip in a few days, but we will be back in a month. Please wait for me. Let me try to win your heart."

One month. He needed one month to accept this change. It was hard to deny him when he asked for so little. Slowly, I nodded my head and his tension relaxed.

"Thank you," he breathed. He hugged me so tight I struggled to breathe. After a long moment, I pulled my head back to find the air.

"We should go. Mama's going to come by any moment to drag me out there."

He sniffed but let me go, still standing close enough that I could feel his breath as he spoke softly. "Alright. There's a story your papa is telling tonight that I want to hear, anyway. Said he's going to tell how you spin straw into gold."

Chapter Four

THE DIZZY FEELING REMAINED in my head through the night, and at a few points my stomach rolled like the fields outside our tavern. Aiden and I never continued that conversation, but the rest of the evening was ruined with the thought of it.

Aiden and I were the only ones not in a good mood that night while the rest of the tavern was alit and jolly with cheers that amplified my sorrow. As I worked, I kept my head down and my hands busy so not even Anika would sense my grief. It had been one of our busiest nights, filling the main and side rooms to the point where I was certain that if one more person showed up, they surely wouldn't be able to fit through the door.

Some soldiers came, or guards, from the looks of their uniforms. Whichever they were, Papa gave them free drinks to thank them for their work and invited them in for his stories. Besides those few drinks we gave away, we were sure to have made a decent profit from the night.

Mama proudly told any who would listen of how her daughter was training to be a seamstress. Anika rolled her eyes at me, but it was the one of the two moments of the night that brought me pleasure. The other came when Papa told his first story of me. He made me out to be a magician of sorts, spinning thread into gold. The gold I spun was enough to save the village from poverty. I came off as quite the heroine.

At the end of the story Aiden leaned over my shoulder. "That's my girl," he whispered. I smiled timidly but the title didn't feel acceptable anymore. Coldness settled in once more.

"Who's the girl?" folks asked as soon as the story was finished. They looked between Papa and each other with their half-empty drinks in their hands. "Who is this girl that you tell of?"

Papa looked right at me with pride on his face. "The tale is based on my sweet daughter, Cosette."

The people looked around, some uncertain of who I was. A few spotted me and whispered among themselves. Eventually, someone was brave enough to ask Papa, "Is it true? Can she spin straw into gold?" I spied the speaker as one of the soldiers who was leaning forward on his seat, eagerly awaiting the answer.

But Papa had no time to reply. Others started speaking up for themselves.

"Is that her Gift? I thought she was the girl who had no Gift?"

"Yes, yes that's right. She had no Gift. Maybe she's got one now?"

"Not finding your Gift until that age, I never heard of such a thing!"

I tried to hide behind the bar, uncomfortable with the sudden attention. Most still hadn't seen me, but the few who knew who I was had their eyes fixated on me as if I could create the gold out of thin air.

"Is it true, Mortan?" the people asked my Papa. "Can your daughter spin straw into gold?"

The murmurs of the room fell silent as they all looked to Papa. I knew Papa never liked to tell if a story was true or not, but he couldn't let them believe that I was capable of such a task. Had they not seen my dress? It was easily one of the simplest ones here, and this was the nicest dress that I owned. If I could spin straw into gold, wouldn't I be dressed in finer clothes?

I shook my head at Papa, and he gave me a knowing smile.

"My daughter is capable of wonderous things."

That's all he would say on the matter, as he transitioned into his next tale about a frog who wanted to be a swan. Surely the people didn't think that story was true.

The consensus on my abilities remained unsettled. Whispers continued and suspicious looks were cast my way. If anyone approached me for the truth, I would set them straight, but the rest of the night passed and only one nimble fellow did so.

I hoped he would spread the word, so folks didn't come by looking for gold.

The excitement of the night passed, bringing with it the gloomy chores of morning. I stood with Anika, taking stock of the mess.

This was always the worst part of festivities: the cleaning. Though, compared to how dreadful last night had turned out for me with Aiden, the mundane chores provided an appreciated distraction from my gloomy thoughts. But as I worked, I could think of nothing else than the mess with Aiden, and soon wished for the chores to be over so I could find a book instead.

The chores dragged on. Cleaning would be a splendid Gift to have, perhaps even better than spinning straw into gold. Who has the Gift of cleaning? Who could snap their fingers and have the house tidied? I'd never heard of such a thing, but there were many Gifts in Westfallen that I didn't know of.

Without anything to help me besides Anika, the cleaning would take the better part of the day, then we'd start prepping for tonight again. Most of the decorations that Papa and I had meticulously put up were now strewn across the floor in clumps. Dishes lay in looming piles on every flat space in the tavern, including the narrow mantle. Thick mud tracked through the entryway and across the floor, and none of the chairs or tables were where we had put them. Not a single one.

An unpleasant smell tinged the air, but I chose to ignore that.

"Think you can share some of your gold to pay someone to clean for us?" Anika joked. She had her hands on her hips and nose in the air as she examined the room.

"Very funny. I would give all my gold to have someone clean for us." I shuddered at the memory of all the eyes on me last night as they wondered if I could spin straw into gold.

We got to work taking the dishes into the kitchen. We could clean those later. Putting the dining area back in order seemed a less daunting task.

"So, you caused quite the commotion last night," Anika said as she pushed tables back to their places. Her dark hair was pulled back loosely, and her shirt was wrinkled as if it had been donned straight from the floor. "I wish I could spin gold."

She talked to herself as she continued straightening the room. Anika's Gift was the violin. Without ever having a lesson, her fingers could play the instrument perfectly. It was beautiful to listen to, though I had only heard it three times in my life. She had no care for music or pretty sounds and had discarded the trait as soon as it was discovered. When people asked about her Gift, she would tell them she could hit as hard as a boy. She had never been asked to prove it.

"I would have hoped you'd have this room cleaned by now." Mama came into the room with her arms crossed as she examined the remaining mess. A few strands of her hair hung loose around her face where they'd fallen from her braid last night.

"You should have seen it when we started," Anika grumbled.

"I did see it; I saw last night," Mama said. She let out a tired sigh as she joined us in cleaning.

Not a few minutes after Mama came, Papa appeared looking jolly. He kissed Mama on the forehead as he danced into the room. Anika rolled her eyes at him, but his joy brought a smile to my face despite my gloomy mood.

"Last night was splendid! I say no work for today! Leave this mess, we will tend to it tomorrow!" Papa ordered, waving his finger around the room.

Anika let out a whoop, but Mama shushed her. "We have customers coming tonight, and we can't serve them in a place like this."

Papa waved his hand. "Let the inn serve them."

Mama shook her rag at Papa. "The inn serves stale bread and spoiled wine. We will feed them here."

Anika and I both sighed as we went back to work. Papa picked up some decorations from the floor as he joined in the chores, though his smile never faltered. It was soothing, working in silence with my family. I rehashed the details of last night, specifically the complicated matter with Aiden, as I went through the motions of cleaning.

I needed something to distract me from Aiden. Papa came near me and I asked the first question that came to mind. "Have you ever heard of a curse from a hundred years ago? One that is causing the war?"

Papa straightened himself for a moment and shoved his hands in his pockets as he bobbed his head a few times in thought. "I've heard rumors, but nothing that I believe."

"What kind of rumors?" I asked hastily as I pushed two tables together.

Papa tilted his head at me. "Nothing of value. Just a story of a sad king who made a poor deal."

I thought to myself as I fixed the chairs around the tables. This tale was becoming more and more intriguing. Who was this sad king? What was the deal that he made? Who did he make the deal with? The questions whirled through my mind, begging for answers.

Papa set a chair down gently. "There's no truth to it Cozy, truly. This war is brought on by the greediness of men's hearts."

Maybe it was my love of books and interesting tales, but something in me didn't want to let the story go. I wanted to know more about the rumors, but Papa didn't look interested in sharing any more information.

"What about the stories you tell from your bar stool? Are they true?"

Father looked at me with a new light in his eyes. I think he enjoyed being asked this question. "A true storyteller never tells."

Ah. A new answer tonight. I raised my eyebrows in mock amusement.

"Do you know which tales you will spin tonight?"

Papa gave a small laugh as he brushed off his hands. "I never know until I sit on that stool. Perhaps I will tell another tale of how my daughter spins straw into gold! That seemed to be a popular story last night."

"People did seem to like it, though I still enjoy the one about the girl with fire the most." As I recalled, no one had asked Papa who that girl was. With the come of the morning and the lingering influence of mead, everyone's memories of my story would be muddled, all but forgotten.

We continued working in silence, each occupied by our own thoughts, until the tables were clean, floors spotless, and windows shinning once more.

Over the years, every inch of this tavern imprinted itself into my mind as a result of dusting the wood beams a thousand times and sweeping under every table a thousand times more. Fifteen tables and four booths fit in the tavern, and I knew every one of them by heart. The table closest to the door had a wobbly leg, and the one next to it had a deep gash in the side wide enough to fit a few coopers. The one closest to the west wall had my parent's initials carved into it from when they'd commemorated their first table purchased for the tavern.

Suddenly a knock came at the door before it creaked open, and we all turned with a start to see Farmer Renolds Bohnson in the doorway, folding his hat in his hand and looking uncomfortable.

"Renolds! Did you leave something here last night?" Papa asked, coming forward to offer his neighbor a hand. After shaking it weakly, Renolds brought his hand back to his crumpled hat.

"No, can't say that I did." He fell silent again, shifting from foot to foot and looking between us. His brown hair stuck out in different directions and curled out above his ear, and his wrinkled shirt was only half tucked into his trousers.

Anika leaned toward me, almost knocking me in the head with the end of her broom. "Hungover," she whispered as she rolled her eyes.

I shook my head, leaning back. "I don't think so." I had seen hungover men before and it didn't look like this. Besides, Renolds Bohnson wasn't the type to drink.

Our lands neighbored his, but we rarely saw him at this hour. He worked all day and we worked all evening, so our lives didn't cross much except for when he came in for an occasional meal.

Bohnson's Gift was predicting the weather. He knew the weather for each day of the week before it came. He had warned us all about the blizzard several years back and saved many of folks from starving. Anika took advantage of his Gift to plan which day she would have her birthday party each year. We couldn't afford much for a party, but the weather was always nice.

Even without his helpful Gift, he was a nice man to have as a neighbor, one who lived by himself and never gave us any trouble.

He licked his lips a few times. Then a pause. Another nervous lick. Papa cleared his throat. "What can I do for you today?"

"I have to ask, does your daughter spin gold? Because I could sure use some gold."

Mama's jaw fell open in unison with mine. Anika looked amused as she leaned back and waited for our answer. Papa chuckled.

"No, my good man. She's studying to be a seamstress, though. She's getting really good." It was a lie, I had barely sewed a skirt, but I was grateful to him for saying so.

Renolds Bohnson rocked back on his heels, looking unsatisfied. "You sure? Because I could work for it. It's been a hard year, you see."

Papa stepped forward and put his hands on the man's shoulders. "I promise you, she can't. We would share our wealth if we came by any."

Renolds Bohnson nodded slowly then ducked his head. "Alright. Well I'll be on my way then." We watched as he slowly exited, still fumbling with his hat.

It showed to his character that he asked us directly instead of participating in the spreading rumors, which I soon learned had spread overnight like the wildfire we had a few years back. Still, I questioned his sanity for believing the tale. Spinning gold would mean we had wealth, and this was not what wealth looked like. A rag in my hand, a broom in my sister's, patched up clothes that had been short on us three years ago.

This was not the look of a family who had money.

Still, Renolds Bohnson wasn't the only one to take Papa's story seriously. All week, I continued to get strange looks: the raise of an eyebrow, the squint of an eye, whispers behind hats and hands. Few approached me, but I could hear their whispers from afar.

"Doesn't seem right they don't share," some would say.

"Makes sense now, why theirs be the only tavern to blossom. All that gold," others would comment.

"Wonder where they hide it?" many asked.

"Always was a strange girl. Now we know why. She was hiding her secret," one said with a high raise in their brow, followed by a shifty glance. Other glances followed, and each wary eye studied my own with suspicion, their distrust brewing within like a dark cloud, casting a gloomy air over me wherever I went—one that I couldn't escape.

Along with the suspicion, there was something else. Admiration. As the curious eyes shifted over me, a distinct look of respect passed over them, one that I didn't deserve.

I should have corrected them, and if I had a bit more honor then perhaps I would have, but instead my vain heart held me back from setting the story straight.

It was nice, acting as if I had a secret. It was nice being thought of as Gifted. It was nice to have my name paired with words other than plain and poor.

My intentions were wrong, and the knowledge of this burned in the back of my mind each time I heard a whisper that I didn't correct. But it wasn't enough for me to approach them and clarify the situation. Instead, I walked on and allowed them to think that I held some sort of power.

This is what I had always wanted, and somehow, Papa's story had given me a Gift.

My pride faded a little each time a neighbor came to our door looking for us to share our wealth. Then we would tell them that I couldn't spin gold, and that I had no Gift, and I would watch their opinion of me turn back into one of pity, accompanied by disappointment. It was unpleasurable for us all. For good reason, I did not look forward to those knocks at the door in the middle of the day.

It was a few weeks later, in the few hours after my seamstress lessons and before the tavern got busy, that a new knock came at our door. A book rested in my hands and one of Lolly's biscuits by my side. I looked up, curious to see which neighbor had mustered up the courage to ask for gold this time. Aiden wasn't due home for another few days, but part of me feared he'd come back early.

Papa pulled open the door, and Mama gasped. With a squeak, the door swung wide to let not one, but several people in.

I blinked twice to be sure my eyes didn't deceive me, because in our doorframe stood soldiers with the Westfallen crest on their tunics, a blue and gold lion, and long swords hanging at their sides, and metal plates strapped to their legs and forearms. Five men stood within sight, but more waited outside along with horses. They wore an expression not many had when entering our tavern and none had when leaving it, calm and composed, scanning the tavern and its belongings.

What were they doing here? Were they on their way back from the war? Was the war over?

Without taking my eyes off the tall men, I folded my book away. A strange feeling crept over me, the sort I'd get when reading a book, and I knew something bad was about to happen, but I was powerless to stop it. I could do nothing but watch as the scene unfolded.

If fazed, Papa didn't show it. He extended his hand to the men. "Soldiers, can I interest you in a meal?"

The man who stood at the front of the group turned up his lip at the offer. "We are the King's guards," he said, his voice thick and deep. Mama fell into a deep curtsy upon his declaration, but in our trance, neither Anika nor I moved.

His narrowed eyes lingered on Anika then swept to me, while one of his hands rested on the hilt of his sword to remind us of his authority. Each of his men stood in a staggered line behind him, and I couldn't help but think they looked ready for battle. They'd brought a fight to our home, and we couldn't prevent it.

Seeing the King's guards surprised me but hearing what they had to say next sent me into shock.

His words would change my life forever. When at last he spoke, his voice sounded like a strong river, too powerful to resist.

"We are here for your daughter, Cosette. She is to report before the King."

Chapter Five

UPON ENTERING WESTNUT CASTLE, or rather, being dragged in while I stumbled about, I'd been forced into a small room where a bath was waiting for me, along with soap. It had been years since I had the luxury of bathing with soap.

All the questions that earlier screamed in my mind settled down in the calm of the bath. The water soaked my skin and the sweet aroma filled my lungs, and for a moment I enjoyed the unexpected hospitality of the King.

But this wasn't why I'd been summoned. Something waited for me after the wash, and I couldn't avoid it.

As the pleasure of the bath quickly wore off, I pulled myself from the tub and the worries rushed back before the first water droplets found the floor. My beating heart couldn't be quieted even when I pressed a hand to it, instead it drummed as loud as my footsteps while I moved to the large chair in the room with a dress draped over it. It was made of finer cloth than I'd ever touched, and more vivid blue than I'd ever seen, and my hands trembled to touch it while images of the dress falling apart at my touch pricked my mind. Surely the dress would know my hands aren't worthy of holding it.

It didn't fall apart as I touched it, and I savored the feeling of silk over my skin.

A pair of shoes lay next to the chair: soft slippers that warmed my toes. Unsure of what to do with my hair, as I had nothing to fasten it up with, I hoped they would find my simple braid acceptable.

I knew little of the King besides that he had no name, or that any name he might have once had was never used and long forgotten, like a memory of a dream that can't be recalled. Many claimed to know his true name, but they each spoke a different one, and few believed their tale. Now, he went simply by the King.

The opinions about him varied. He wasn't well liked by the people but wasn't particularly disliked either. Many assumed him to be greedy, driven to war with his envious desires, but he had set up food stations for poor villages and gave pensions for the elderly. When asked, people would shrug their shoulders and say, "He's the king, and that's all there is to it." People did have strong opinions about his son, however. Prince Conrad was adored. From what I'd heard, Prince Conrad was a virtuous man, compassionate, smart, and charming.

I'd never met him, nor knew anyone who had, so I wasn't sure where these opinions came from. Still, it was widely accepted that when Prince Conrad assumed the throne, our kingdom would flourish.

Perhaps I'd meet the prince today. The notion filled me with both excitement and fear.

The guards gave me no indication as to why I was being beckoned before the King, not even a hint as to if this was a good calling or a bad one, but I prayed that it would be the first.

Try as I might, I had not the slightest idea as to what the King would want with me. I had nothing to offer a monarch. I hardly had anything to offer our poor family.

Please, let this be a misunderstanding.

Something kept me in that room for longer than necessary, whether it was dread or awe, I couldn't say. The large bed tempted me to feel it's warmth, but if I crawl in, I might never leave its safety.

Village girls didn't belong before the King.

A loud knock told me I could delay no more, so I summoned any courage that lived within and opened the door.

A guard stood in the corridor, waiting to lead me to the King. The warmth of the room faded behind me while my heart started to pound in my ears and my blood rushed. My knees grew weak as I walked behind the guard, and I was unsure they would carry me all the way. My head spun with the confusion of it all, and my vision turned blurry.

I had come in through the west entrance, a smaller but still beautiful part of the castle, and traveled through open hallways to arrive at the guest wing. The castle itself was quite empty, with only a few people passing us even though our walk took several minutes. Earlier I'd caught a whiff of something tasty, but the scent vanished quickly. I searched for that same smell on the way to see the King, but whatever aroma had once been in the air was gone.

The first hallways we took were the same as those I saw on the way in, but after a few minutes we turned inward, heading toward the heart of the castle. A few more people filled these corridors, mostly guards, stationed throughout. They each gave us a look, and I searched their faces to find some clue as to why I was called here. No one's face spoke to me.

Other than the allusive guards, Westnut Castle was beautiful, but I had little time to enjoy it. I tried to remember details to recount to Anika later, but my mind kept pulling me back to why the King wanted me there, and I felt dizzy all over again.

I thought the guard who was leading me was with us earlier, but it was hard to remember. This all felt like it was happening too quickly. Just a few hours ago I was cleaning our tavern, and now I was dressed to appear before the King.

"I'm sorry, sir," my voice croaked as I spoke. "Do you have water? I'm feeling quite faint."

The guard glanced back at me but continued to walk. "I'm sorry, miss, but I do not. I have been instructed to take you directly to His Majesty." His voice, to his defense, sounded apologetic.

"Do you know why I am being summoned?" I asked meekly. My fingers played with the side of my dress as I worried. This time the guard didn't turn to answer my question. We'd come upon two large doors, where another guard stood.

"I bring the Lady Cosette to see the King," my guard said in an official voice. The second guard nodded at him and reached for the door.

A new feeling crept upon me, and I clutched my stomach. "I fear I'm going to be sick."

I didn't have time to compose myself. With a loud creak, the doors were pushed in and I found myself facing the King.

The room was larger than any I had ever seen. There was a long table set up along one side, while the other half remained open, and above a few balconies lined both sides, overlooking the splendor of the throne room.

It was stunning and would have taken my breath away if it wasn't already caught in my throat.

About twenty people stood in the room, not including the few guards along the walls to the left and right. One of the men had a crown on his head, and I assumed him to be the King. He was hard to see from a distance, but he looked impatient.

"Walk," the guard behind me said in a low voice, reminding my legs to move. I stumbled forward, keeping my eyes on the King. My mind was racing as I tried to memorize his face. This all still felt like a dream that I might wake up from at any moment.

The King turned and said something I could not hear to the man next to him, who nodded and left, taking a few people with him. The others stayed, clearing a path for me to walk to the King.

He made no move to meet me. Before I reached him, another man appeared at his side, one with soft skin, younger eyes, and a nice-looking face hiding under curly red hair. He was taller than the King, but not as broad. The quiet lad stood with his hands folded behind his back, looking at peace. I could see some similarities between them, and I knew that I was looking at Prince Conrad.

So, this is the famous, beloved prince.

My feet stopped before fully reaching the King. I was unsure of how close I could get before someone would stop me. Attempting my best curtsy, I poised myself with my head lowered, waiting for someone to speak.

"Are you the seamstress Cosette?" The King's voice was crackly, revealing his age.

The title felt strange to hear, as I was new to the trade, but I knew I needed to own it.

"I have only begun learning the trade, Your Majesty." I was surprised that my voice formed a full sentence while my mind went through any possibility as to why the King wished to see me.

My knees, thankfully, had yet to give out on me, and I kept them bent and my head up so that I could see the King as he spoke. His head remained fixed straight, so he looked down his rounded nose to me.

"And your father, is he the storyteller at the Riverfront Tavern?" The King's posture was stiff, so only his mouth moved with the words.

Ah yes. My marginally famous storytelling Papa. Perhaps he was why I was here. Did the King wish to hear one of his stories? If so, he called for the wrong person. I confirmed that I was the storyteller's daughter.

The King took his first step forward. He reached a hand up to stroke his chin. My legs felt weak from holding the curtsey and I hoped he would get to his point soon. All these eyes made me nervous.

"Then you are the girl who can turn straw into gold," he said slowly, his voice coarse like stone clashing against a sword. "And you will do it for me."

I found the strength to stand as the color drained from my face. "No m-my lord, I cannot do such a thing." I took a step backwards from the intense gaze of the King and his son. How had word reached the King that I could perform such a wonder? Papa told the story only a few weeks ago.

The King raised a curved eyebrow. "No? You cannot? My men heard your father confirm it at his tavern."

My heart beat fast in my chest and willed it to calm itself. "It was merely a story, Your Majesty. Nothing more. I can't spin straw into gold." My hands and forehead started to sweat.

His eyes narrowed, and he paced for a few seconds while his son stayed still. I searched Prince Conrad's eyes for a hint of the kindness I had heard of, but he stared blankly back at me. Disappointed, I dropped my eyes to the ground and watched the King's feet as he walked around me. When he formed a full circle, he stopped.

I shuddered as he reached out his cold hand and lifted my chin up. His voice was low as he hissed, "I don't believe you."

Shaking, I answered, "It's true, I have no Gift. You can search our home; you won't find gold anywhere." My voice vibrated with fear.

The King exchanged a look with his son that I couldn't decode. After a few moments, Prince Conrad nodded. The King brought his piercing green gaze back to me. "Either you are lying to us, hoarding your gold somewhere and refusing to share with us your Gift that could end the war, or your father lied to my men."

This day had taken a terrifying turn.

"My papa is a storyteller; he weaves tales. That does not make his stories true."

The King remained unaltered. "When asked if his tale was reliable, he said you were capable of wondrous things. You will show us these talents."

I wasn't sure how many ways I could say it. I tried to straighten myself and look confident. I wanted there to be no mistake in my words. "Your Majesty, I *cannot* spin straw into gold."

With my words, the King took another step toward me. A small whisper went through the room and I feared what would come next. "I hear what you are saying. Now listen closely to me. I believe you can spin straw into gold. You will share your Gift with me."

The King pulled away suddenly and waved his hand at my guard who came running forward. I protested, but he ignored my cries. Beside him, Prince Conrad studied me, and I shrugged my shoulders and shook my head at him, but he didn't move.

"Fill a room with straw, lock her in until the morning. She will spin it into gold for us."

My guard bowed and went to leave the room. I looked wildly around, begging for anyone to listen to me.

"I can't do it; I don't know how!"

"You are not doing this for me," the King said. "You are doing this for our soldiers, the men off fighting the war in Osmelee and Tames. Your gold will buy us the armies and weapons needed to end this war. You will be a hero."

I sank to my knees, unsure of what else to do. "Your Majesty, do not think me to be greedy in keeping such a thing from my country. I promise you, I cannot do what you ask."

The King was still giving orders to other guards, choosing not to listen to my words.

Anika would be ashamed if she saw me on my knees. I rose back to my feet and tried to summon the strength of my sister as I stood before the King and his court.

"What will you do," I asked, "when morning comes and there is no gold?"

The King turned to me and narrowed his eyes. "In the morning, I will either have gold or I will have your life."

The strength of Anika left me as I fainted.

Chapter Six

"THAT ROOM? *THAT'S* THE room that you filled with straw?"

I came back to my senses enough to know that I was being carried in the arms of a guard. My arm hung at my side and my head was tilted in an uncomfortable position. My mouth felt dry and my mind was thick with confusion.

"It's never used, and it only has one way to get in," a second guard spoke near to me, and I suspected he was the one who carried me.

"That's where *he* lives," the first guard said.

I tried to wake up fully, but I still felt only halfway there. Who were they talking about? Where were they taking me? The questions swirled through the fog in my mind.

"*He* is only a spirit."

"My mother claims to have seen him as a child. He's more than a spirit, that's for sure."

A third voice came, gruffer than the others. "I don't believe in him at all. It's all nonsense."

Finally, I pried my eyes open enough to see that they carried me down a thin corridor. The sun must have traveled across the sky, because there was a soft glow coming through the windows. There was a stale smell, and my hip felt bruised. I was still wearing the silk dress and slippers, though they didn't feel as luxurious as they once had. The memory of the day came rushing back to me, and fright took hold.

"Doesn't matter either way, I'm not moving all that straw again. Took us several wagons," my guard spoke again. He grunted as he shifted me in his arms.

"You dropped some." There was a sound of a foot kicking along the ground.

We slowed to a stop and I craned my head to see where we were. One of the guards fumbled with a key until he unlocked the small door in front of us. I twisted in the arms of my captor to free myself, but he held tight. *No, I must get free. I must escape.*

"Calm down, miss." He squeezed my arms harder than necessary. "Just make us some gold and you can be on your way."

My mouth opened in protest, but it was too dry to form comprehendible words. Instead, tight cries came out.

The door swung open and I was greeted with the crisp smell of straw. I twisted again, but the guard held on tight. He carried me effortlessly halfway into the room before dropping me.

I stumbled as I stood up, ready to bolt. Looking up, I saw five guards behind the first. They thought it would take six guards to lock me in a room. The thought of that made me smile a little.

One of the guards held a plate of food, while four others looked poised to stop me from running. The last guard was looking around the room as if something was going to jump out at him. That must be the guard who spoke of a spirit who lived here.

The guard with the food slowly put the plate on the ground with his eyes on me as if I were a hungry animal. I was aware that I hadn't eaten all day, but right now, food was the last thing on my mind.

Before the guard stood back up, I scrambled for the door. I didn't get more than a few steps before one of the guards caught me.

"No!" I yelled with all my strength as I ripped my arm from his grasp. I tried to kick at him, but he pushed me back to the floor where I banged my elbow on the unforgiving stone ground.

I slid my feet back under me and tried to run again, but the guards had exited the room with surprising speed. The last guard stood in the doorway for a second, looking around with wide eyes before studying me with an expression I couldn't place.

"Good luck, miss."

I suspected he wasn't talking about the straw.

He shut the door and locked it with a click, leaving me alone inside.

I was alone, and I was going to die.

Too much energy coursed through me to allow me to cry now. Instead, I whipped my head around, desperately searching for an escape.

The room was half as big as our tavern. The door was centered along the wall and had no windows on it. I ran to the door first, pulling on the handle with all my might. When that didn't work, I pushed it, then kicked.

The door didn't budge.

Perhaps I could beat the door in with something. The room had several carts full of straw dumped along one side, with a small rug next to them, and a spinning wheel on top of it, one nicer than the rotting one Seamstress Kira used. It might hold up if bashed against the door a few times, but it would break before the door would.

To the other side of the room was a small table set up with a chair on each side. The ceiling was lower there, making room for the balcony above. Wooden stairs rose up along the wall near the door, leading to a loft overhead. There were bookshelves up there, but it looked otherwise abandoned.

There were two windows, one on the wall opposite the door and a second up in the loft, both barred. My head might fit through, but my shoulders never would.

I ran to the window anyway. Maybe someone on the outside would see me and take pity.

A stream ran around Westnut Castle, and I could hear it before I even reached the window. Looking out, I saw that it wasn't more than a stone's throw away, though I didn't see how that would help me. Beyond the stream was an open field, leading to scattered trees, all layered with a hint of snow. There must have been a tree next to the window, because I could see the branches. I reached through and pulled one of them through the window, unsure of what to do with it next. Eventually I let it go, knowing it was useless to me.

I stuck out my arm and felt along the wall to see if there was a loose rock I could use to bash on the door. I clawed at the cold stone, but nothing came loose.

A growl escaped my chest, and I plunged my second arm out, feeling along the other side. Coming up empty, I banged on the bars, hurting my hand in the process, which only fueled my frustration.

With little else to do, I yelled for help. I yelled until my voice felt strained and my throat was dry. Somewhere along the way I started to cry, and I cried until my tears overtook my screams. Defeated, I turned my back to the window and slid down the wall, crying until my eyes were too dry to offer another tear.

With my tears emptied and my energy drained, I closed my eyes.

This would be my last night.

In the morning, the King would kill me because I couldn't spin straw into gold.

Did my family know? Surely they would tell them before I was killed. Papa could set the record straight, tell the King that the story was purely fiction, and he would save me.

But even that brought me little consolation. I was still trapped in a room in the castle with an impossible deadline hanging over my head.

I took a shaky breath as I tried to grasp what today had brought. I had one night to spin gold, or else the King would take my life. I couldn't spin gold, and Papa was too far away to come and rescue me with the truth. The room was locked with no apparent way out. Every option for survival seemed out of reach.

Unless.

Unless the dark magic that I had heard whispers of existed.

Unless there was a power here that was strong enough to save me.

I had no experience with magic, and I was bitterly aware that I was the only person in Westfallen who didn't have it in my soul. Would magic come to me, if I called? Would it hear the cries of a desperate heart and take pity? Would it turn my straw into gold, or change the King's heart, or set me free?

How did one call upon magic? I hadn't the slightest clue, but with nothing to lose, I lowered myself to the ground. This was twice in one day that I was begging from my knees. Anika would be so disappointed in me.

I wasn't sure how to start. I began to speak the words that were in my head, willing someone to answer. "Please, if there is a deep magic here, please save me. Please. I know that I am small and unworthy, but please spare my life. I don't want to die."

It sounded pathetic, but I kept uttering my pleas, hoping that someone could hear me. The words turned to frantic prayers mixed with tears falling on my cheeks. It seemed I had tears left after all.

"Please come to rescue me. Please give me some of your strong magic. Please help me live."

I cried out until my voice felt weak. I buried my head into my hands and sobbed until my eyes were dry and my stomach cramped.

It was only when I quieted that I heard the shuffling of feet on the floor. Small, hushed shifting in the dark of the evening.

My head yanked up and eyes darted around the room. Had I heard the noise inside, or was it the sounds of the night coming from the window behind me?

Now focused, I heard it again, but this time, I saw something too. In the darkness under the loft, a figure shifted. How had I not seen someone there before?

Was this the spirit that the guard spoke of? It had to have been. Either it was coming to save me or to hurt me. My breathing quickened and legs wobbled as I pulled myself to my feet, never taking my eyes off the shadows. Perhaps I didn't have to wait until tomorrow morning to die. Perhaps this figure would kill me tonight.

My back met the stone wall and my trembling hands pushed against it while my knees shivered with fear. I begged them not to fail me. Nothing around me could be used to attack or defend, and I doubted my hand could throw a stinging punch. Still, I'd fight if I had to.

Gracefully, the figure moved again, this time coming forward out of the darkness. I braced myself to see the face of a spirit.

Instead, I saw the face of a man.

"Dear one, why do you cry?"

Chapter Seven

HIS VOICE SOUNDED AS smooth as honey and as light as the wind. Golden curls circled his face and reached for his thin lips that turned downward as he examined my tears. His nose was long and sharp, his chin rounded, and he had two freckles on his face: one by his lips and the other above the arch of his left brow. He walked steadily toward me, and I moved backward, shifting myself along the wall to keep as far away from him as I could.

Not a spirit, but a man. I was no less afraid of the figure before me as I had been when I thought him to be a spirit.

As he examined me, his head tilted and his eyes squinted, not in aggression, but rather in confusion, pondering over the girl before him. In reply, I narrowed my own eyes at him, anything to make myself look fierce, but I trembled far too much to reflect fearlessness.

His gaze shifted to the straw and them the spinning wheel, where he arched his brow. I didn't dare take my eyes off him. After a pause, he turned his attention back to me. His face remained soft and eyes blank, so his thoughts were a mystery to me.

I knew what my thoughts were, however. *Run. Hide.* Neither of these options were available to me, and even if there was somewhere to run to, every part of me stood frozen in fear, waiting for him to do something

"Why are you sad?" he asked again in a gentle tone meant to calm me, but my growing worries would not be calmed by his soft disposition.

I gave him no answer as he studied me, not even when he came a few steps closer. The man was taller than me, but not by much, so I didn't have to tilt my chin more than an inch to look him in the eye. He wore a white tunic shirt with full sleeves and buttoned cuffs, an older style that not many wore anymore. His eyes looked dark, but in the dim light it was hard to be sure. He was older than me, by five years perhaps.

He didn't make another move, but kept those dark eyes focused on me, waiting patiently. My mouth opened, but what came out could hardly be called words. "You...who...who...?"

He smiled at this. "Ah yes. You wonder about the strange man who is locked in the room with you." His disposition changed suddenly and he grinned, pacing in front of me with his hands clasped together. "Well, my dear. I'm afraid you haven't answered my question yet. Give me an answer and I will do the same for you."

He paused in front of me, close enough to touch. I pushed myself further into the wall until the stone dug into my back. His voice came again, still soft. "Why are you crying?"

I licked my lips as I tried to form an answer. While encouraged by the fact that I wasn't dead yet, I still had my qualms about the stranger with the golden hair. I tried to find a simple answer to his question, and he waited for me patiently. "I ... I fear, come morning, they will kill me."

His eyes widened ever so slightly as he glanced at the locked door. "Have you done something worth killing you for?" The notion that I was a ruthless criminal trapped here for some horrible crime sounded ludicrous to me, he couldn't know any different, and while that was a possibility, he didn't sound scared.

I shook my head, keeping my back tight against the wall. My hands stopped shaking but my stomach still felt weak. I prayed this man revealed his intentions soon so my worries would be satisfied. "It's rather what I will not do."

He nodded his head as if he understood now, though I knew he couldn't.

"And why not?" he asked. His voice was still as gentle as a spring flower.

For the first time since he'd appeared, I took my eyes off him to glance at the spinning wheel sitting on the woven rug. It taunted me. "What they ask of me, it isn't possible."

The stranger tilted his head, keeping his eyes on me. "I know of nothing that is impossible."

I tightened my eyebrows. How could it be that he could not think of one impossible task? Hundreds of ideas came to mind, including the one given to me. His face kept the look of an innocent doe as he waited for me, so with a sigh, I spoke. "I can't spin straw into gold."

His eyes brightened as he looked back to the straw and the spinning wheel. "Ah. I see your problem."

He glided over to the spinning wheel, circling it, and his bare feet made soft padded noises as he turned about the room. He grew stranger by the second, but as peculiar as he seemed, he didn't appear dangerous. Relaxing slightly, I took a step away from the wall, keeping my eye on the stranger as he picked up some straw and pulled it through his fingers.

"Have you tried?" he asked over his shoulder.

His question shocked me. No, I hadn't tried. I hadn't seen a point to it. No one can spin straw into gold.

"The straw hasn't even been retted," I said from my corner. The stalks still had their hard shells, hiding the soft fibers underneath. They would need to be retted and hackled before I could spin them.

He laughed. "No, I suppose it hasn't."

He sat himself down at the spinning wheel, straw in his hands. I paused, curious what he would do next.

He put the straw through the spindle, binding it to some starter thread on the bobbin. His long fingers worked quickly as he brought the straw back down and placed his foot on the treadle.

Without a word, he pushed on the treadle, twisting the straw in his hand as it worked through the bobbin. With a creaking noise, the wheel started to spin. His hands worked effortlessly as he twisted the straw, then reached down to grab more and twisted it in with the first.

I was impressed he knew how to work the spinning wheel, though I couldn't fathom how he spun the straw without retting it first.

Quietly, I took a few steps closer to watch him work. It was thoughtful of him to try to help me, but thread would be no use to the King since it couldn't pay soldiers or settle agreements with other countries. Thread couldn't save my life.

As I got closer, a hint of moonlight angled off the spindle. My breath caught in my throat.

The spindle shone like the sun.

Gold.

He had spun gold.

I blinked, sure that I must have been seeing it wrong.

A few more steps closer helped my eyes see better. The man remained hunched over the wheel, feeding straw into the bobbin.

Where it entered as straw, it left as gold. The gold wrapped around the flyer, growing thicker as he continued to spin. My head spun along with the wheel.

I dared to bring my hand close as it kept spinning around. Could this be true? Was I saved?

He stopped spinning so I could touch the gold, which was woven into narrow strands like thread, but hard. I was unsure what gold thread felt like, but this was what I'd expected it would look like. I struggled to find my words as I held the gold in my hands.

"Is this real?" I breathed.

He grinned in triumph. "It is, my dear. And I will happily spin it all for you."

Questions flew through my head, but I chose them carefully, for fear that the wrong words may scare him away and I'd lose the gold. No doubt he'd expect payment for this service. What could I offer him? I had nothing; my family had nothing.

Perhaps he was a spirit after all, just as the guard had said. He certainly possessed unexplainable abilities. Whatever he was, I would be forever in debt to him for saving my life. It was funny that the King trapped me to spin straw into gold for him, when he had someone with the ability to do so living under his own roof the whole time.

"Who are you?"

He paused from his spinning, turned back at me, and offered a thin smile.

"Rumpelstiltskin is my name."

Chapter Eight

"SO," THE KING SAID, looking very pleased with himself, "you decided to share your Gift with us."

After the guards came in the morning to inspect my progress, the King had been called in. I waited for him while devouring the breakfast they brought. I hadn't found time to eat yesterday, and my stomach complained heavily.

The King walked, with his son in tow, around the room. He looked different than he had last night. There was no crown on his head, just whispers of hairs that were growing thin, and if it wasn't for his deep blue coat over his collared shirt with small gold buttons running down the side, he might have looked as any elderly man I might meet in the village.

Conrad dressed similarly, but he looked more regal than his father without the crown. I wondered what meeting I had walked in on yesterday that they were dressed so formally. Conrad's coat wasn't blue, but tan, matching his pants. The lack of color made the red in his hair stand out brilliantly, along with the mass of freckles across his face and under his chin. His jaw was wide and his nose thin, with thick eyebrows lying flat over light eyes.

The King wandered around the room. He stopped to touch every spindle of gold, turning each about in his hand. The guards stood along the wall, still blocking the exit from me. I didn't have a reason to run today. I had done my job; I should be free to go.

Rumpelstiltskin had worked well into the night. He had little to say, but he hummed an enchanting tune while he worked. I had watched him until I dozed off, not waking until morning came and he was already gone.

In his absence, he had left a room full of gold.

I knew now that he must be a spirit of sorts, for I searched the entire room and he was not there. The door remained locked, and unless he had a key there was no other way to leave the room except by magic.

That must have been how he made the gold. He had magic in his hands. Perhaps my pleas worked, and magic had sent me Rumpelstiltskin. I whispered my gratitude into the air as the King inspected the gold, hoping my words reached him, wherever he was.

Satisfied, I ate my meal as I waited for the King to finish his assessment. The warm bread melted on my lips with the taste of butter, and it took all my manners not to shove the food into my hungry mouth, but even slowing myself, it was devoured in a matter of minutes.

I was licking my fingers when the King was ready to face me.

"It seems you are not as selfish as you previously appeared to be," he said.

My heart twisted and I yearned to correct him, but I had no knowledge of the man who helped me and didn't want to spend any more time in this castle trying to explain it. I was ready to go home.

So I remained silent in the presence of the King.

He held two spindles, one in each hand, and looked at them with joy. "These will save our country and end the war."

I curtsied, happy that something good came of my time here. I would be so proud to go home and tell my family how I helped in the war. My family was probably worried about me. "May I go home, Your Majesty?" I asked.

The King looked surprised at my question, and dread came over me. "Go home?" He looked between me and the gold. "Home? You have just become our most valuable asset in the war. You can't leave now."

I motioned to the gold. "I already did my job."

The King laughed as if I was joking. "You have made only a little bit of gold. We will need much more to offer Tames and Osmelee in return for ending the war." He laughed again. "You'll remain here and assist us."

My stomach dropped and I felt sick. "I can't stay here. I want to go home." My voice sounded like a child's whine in comparison to the King's. Still, I was desperate. He couldn't keep me here. There was no telling how long these things took between countries. Even with all the gold, the war could still drag on for years.

And besides, I still wasn't the one who could spin straw into gold. Rumpelstiltskin was, but I had no idea how to find him again.

I felt like crying.

Prince Conrad came to my aid. "Surely, she can come out of the room, though, since she cooperated. She can be given food, and a proper bed to sleep in. If she's going to help us win the war, then she should be treated right."

Relief rushed over me that I wouldn't be spending endless months trapped in this room. I gave the prince a small smile to show my thanks and he grinned back, giving me my first look at his rumored kindness.

The King complied, and the orders were given. Most of the guards filtered out, but Conrad caught my hand before I followed them and leaned down to whisper. A red curl fell over his forehead, distracting my eye. "He's not as bad as he seems. The war has driven him mad."

I nodded but wasn't sure what to say back. I didn't have time to find an answer before one of the guards led me away, leaving behind a giddy king in a room full of gold.

I tried to enjoy the room and the endless food sent to me, but my mind kept reminding me that now I'd shown I could make gold, I would be expected to do it again. How many times would I need to complete the task before the King was satisfied? I had no way of guaranteeing that I could do it even one more time.

Worry followed me to my new room. There was a simple lock on the door with a key in it, which the guard took out and hung on the inside of the room. I was grateful that I would be staying on the other side of the lock. The room was wide, with a stone fireplace on one side and a bed on the other. In the middle was a deep window with dark blue curtains. Small flowers were stitched in the bottom of the curtains. I noticed a little door to the right of the bed, and guessed it led to a bathing room. A bath sounded luxurious, and my legs melted a bit at the thought of it.

There was a thick blue blanket on the bed, and pillows that would put all the ones at home to shame. A long vibrant rug lay at the foot of the bed with fibers so soft looking that I could fall asleep on them and be just as comfortable as I'd ever been back home. I turned to ask the guard if we were in the right room, because surely this belonged to some important guest, but he had left already. I wandered further into the room, hoping to get some pleasure out of it before they kicked me out.

Little did they know they were putting a poor girl with no Gift in such nice accommodations. I didn't deserve this.

I should leave now, return to the King and tell him the truth. He had gotten a room full of gold already; perhaps he would count that as a blessing and let me go. The longer I stayed, the harder it would be to convince them I couldn't spin gold.

I wasn't sure if it was fear or exhaustion that stayed me, but I decided I would never get another chance to enjoy a room like this and let my curiosity lead me to the back room behind the grand bed, where I found a deep tub by the wall. Vanilla-scented salts sat on the floor nearby, smelling as nice as a field in spring. There was no water in the tub, but I was determined to find a way to fill it so I could soak in the vanilla scents.

Behind me, a girl hovered in the doorway. "Are you the Lady Cosette?" Her short black hair looked as soft as the rug by my bed, and her smile as sweet as the vanilla.

"Just Cosette," I corrected her.

"I'm your maid, Anna." She bobbed into a curtsy, holding the edges of her light brown dress in her hands, revealing a large birthmark that covered most of her wrist. When she straightened, she clasped her hands in front of her waist, looking at me expectantly as if I had a list of chores for her to do.

My surprise couldn't have been more evident. What did they think I needed a maid for? I knew how to clothe myself. My mind was drawn back to the bath and I clicked my tongue.

"If you could tell me where to get water for the bath," I said. "I can go fetch some."

Anna laughed as if I'd told a joke. "We keep some heated water downstairs; give me a few minutes and I will fill the tub for you."

I shook my head, begging her to let me go with her, but she was adamant that I stay. "It's my job, and you wouldn't want to put me out of a job." I gave up at that. I didn't want to cause her any trouble.

With her smile still wide, Anna left to get water. She filled the bath after several trips and then gave me space while I enjoyed the warm water and salts. This bath was much more enjoyable than the last one, during which I fretted over what the King wanted. I wasn't without my worries this time, but at least I knew what I was up against.

After the bath, I found a dress waiting for me. "I hope it's your size, we have extras that I'll tailor to fit you."

I'd never had a dress tailored to me before.

Clean and dressed, I sat on the window seat gazing out over the gardens. Back home, we didn't have money for flower gardens, and only wildflowers grew. But here, they had an entire courtyard attached to what must be a magnificent garden in the summer months. For now, it was frosted soil with a few lingering bushes, barren of their leaves. For a second I was torn by my desire to leave the castle, and my desire to see the beauty of the flowers. Winter would leave us in a few weeks and then spring would bring blossoms. Westfallen wasn't as far north as other countries, which were plagued with thick, relentless snow. Winter touched us gently, bringing soft frosts and crisp winds that kept us inside, but didn't prevent us from doing our work.

Anna had started the fire while I was in the bath, and it crackled gently in the background as she perched herself on a large pillow near the fireplace to knit. I wondered if she would remain there all day. I had no tasks for her to do, and even if I did, I felt uncomfortable asking. Mama would have a fit if she knew I was using a maid instead of my own two hands.

The silence was periodically interrupted by Anna's questions. She was enthralled with my presumed Gift and had many questions for me about how I made the gold. I wished I had answers for her. Uncomfortable with lying, my shoulders shrugged, and I said the Gifts can't be explained. Luckily, she let it go. Anna was friendly and would be a delightful companion during my stay at the castle, however long that proved to be.

A knock came at the door, drawing my attention across the room. Anna must have heard the knock before I did, because she had already sprung up and dashed to answer the door for me. I slipped off the window seat as she pulled back the handle.

"Oh, Your Highness." Anna dropped into another curtsy far better than mine. Maybe I would have a task for her after all. She could teach me how to curtsy like that.

I waited for the King to come around the door, but it was Prince Conrad instead.

"Oh!" I started to curtsy, but he raised a hand.

"Please, it is me who should bow to you. You are saving my kingdom," he said. To prove his point, he gave me a deep bow. When he straightened, he brought something out from behind his back.

"I thought it might be nice to write a letter to your family, let them know you are alright." He came forward with the paper, quill, and ink. Embarrassed, I took it, not wanting to tell him that I couldn't write.

He rocked on his heels for a moment, and I was unsure what to do, keenly aware of my inexperience with speaking to nobility, especially the likes of a handsome prince, but in the same moment that I started to panic, his eyes softened and shoulders relaxed as he looked at me in a way that comforted my nerves. There was a distinct difference in how he looked at me compared to the King—Conrad didn't regard me as someone he commanded, but rather with the gentleness of a friend offering a gift.

I placed the writing equipment down on the wide desk near the bed as I thanked Conrad. When I turned around, he was still standing in the same place, looking uncomfortable.

"I'm sorry, I'm not used to being in a lady's room," he said as he looked between me and Anna. Now it was my turn to feel uncomfortable. "You will let me know if you need anything else?" he asked as he took a few steps back toward the open door.

"Of course, Your Highness," I said.

He put a hand up. "The girl who is saving my kingdom may call me Conrad."

Behind him, I saw Anna raise her eyebrows. I ignored her and thanked the prince again. Before he left, a question came to my mind.

"Your Highness?" I called out quickly, forgetting that he had just asked me to use his name, but he didn't seem bothered.

I wasn't sure how exactly to ask my question and wished I had thought it through a bit before blurting it out. "I've heard stories. Stories of a spirit who wanders the castle?"

Conrad's face was difficult to read at first, but after a pause his chest rose. "Yes. There are tales of an old king from long ago who made a bad deal with a sorceress. As a result, he was left to wander the castle until his curse ended."

My interest grew. These rumors were related to the ones Seamstress Kira had spoken of.

Seeing the look on my face, Conrad quickly spoke again. "They are only stories. Don't worry, the only magic in this castle is from the Gifts. Your Gift is the most magical of all."

My Gift. Right.

I stayed still as Conrad left. Spirit or not, I had met someone last night. Someone who could spin straw into gold.

As soon as Conrad closed the door, Anna started babbling about the Gifts again. "I wish my Gift was elaborate like yours, but I just make flowers grow. They are very pretty flowers, but they can't help the King! They pleased the late queen, but she's gone now, and the King has little use for them."

I nodded politely, but my mind was on what Conrad had said. An old king who made a bad deal with a sorceress. Was I meeting some old king who was forced to wander the halls? It was possible, but not likely. Rumpelstiltskin was no more than a few years older than me. Twice now, the king in the story had been referred to as old.

Other options, besides him being a spirit, was that he had a key to the room. He could have slipped in while I was crying or yelling and back out when I was asleep.

Another option was that there were two ways in and out of that room. A secret door behind the bookshelves in the loft, or an exit under the rug.

Under the rug. How had I not checked there before? I would be sure to look there first that night. If Rumpelstiltskin showed, and for the sake of my life I hoped that he did, I wanted to see how he was getting in.

Anna's voice snapped me back to the present. "I've heard those tales too, from my papa and his papa before him. They swear them to be true. Said the king made a deal to bring magic to the land. But something happened and he got cursed. Until his curse is broken, he can't be free."

"What happened? How did he get cursed?" I asked with more intensity than I meant to show, but she smiled at my eagerness.

"Don't know, but I do know that he's not to be trifled with. He has a lot of dangerous magic to him. And a man who wanders for a hundred years? He's likely more animal than man now."

Chapter Nine

"RUMPEL!" I CALLED OUT to the empty room. "Rumpelstiltskin!"

I had checked under the rug, and there was nothing but stone floor. I tried to check behind the bookshelves, but they were too heavy to push aside, and I decided I would hear them being moved if that was how he was getting in the room.

I waited for a few minutes until I started to fear that he would not come. The King had filled the room with even more straw than last night, and once again the door had been locked behind me. I tried not to worry, but time after time I called Rumpelstiltskin's name and he did not appear.

I wondered if it was because I was watching the room like a hawk. Perhaps he wanted to keep his point of entry a secret. I weighed my desires in my mind—the desire to know how he was getting in verses my desire to live in the morning, and decided I preferred my life.

Keeping my ears sharp, I turned back to the window and began to count silently.

A noise frightened me, though I shouldn't have been startled. I was waiting for him, after all. When I turned, I found him already sitting at the spinning wheel, feeding straw through the bobbin.

"You came!" I said, relieved. I hadn't made up my mind if I trusted him, but he was my best chance at survival. I was grateful he had showed.

"Of course I came. You'd die if I didn't," he said matter-of-factly. "Plus, I like having the company."

I approached him with much less fear than I had last night. If he had intended to harm me, I believed he would have by then. So far there was nothing but gentleness in his eyes, and he never made a move to touch me. I needed to know more about this strange man. I needed to know how he made gold. "Can you tell me who you are?"

He kept his eyes on the spinning wheel. "I already told you. My name is Rumpelstiltskin, though you seem to like calling me Rumpel."

"Ah. Yes, well. Rumpelstiltskin is far too long," I said. Slowly, I lowered myself to the ground next to him, keeping my eyes focused on him. He continued to spin without giving me a glance. I felt guilty that I wasn't helping, but I didn't see any way around that. Instead, I tried to rephrase my question. "I mean, who are you? Where did you come from?"

He tilted his head to the side. "Those are two separate questions, I think. But I shall answer them in return for two questions of my own."

"As you are saving my life, that seems like a fair trade." I remained sitting stiffly, waiting for him to answer my questions. He took longer than I anticipated, but I had nowhere to go, so I was content to wait.

His gentle voice was no more than a whisper, so I had to lean in closer to hear him speak. "I'm not human like you are. Not anymore, that is. My shape takes form when I want it to, otherwise I am like the wind, drifting wherever I desire to go."

I squinted as I tried to process how that could be. Giving in to the temptation, I swiftly reached my hand out to touch his arm, and he smiled at my curiosity.

"Yes. You can touch me. But I'm not bound to this room as you are."

"I see," I said, though I didn't. I couldn't understand. Was he verifying that he was the old king from the tale? Was he the one who made a deal with a sorceress?

"I can promise you," Rumpelstiltskin said as he continued spinning gold. "That my intentions in helping are pure. I know you have nothing to give me, and I won't ask you for any payment. I'm helping you simply to save your life."

"Why?" I blurted the question out.

"Because I'm a nice person. You can never be sure of that anymore. Not around here, that is. Far too many evil-hearted people." His voice trailed off as he spoke, so I wasn't sure if that last part was directed at me or himself.

He finished a spindle and took it off, resetting the wheel with a new one. Then he sat himself back down and got to work again. His hands worked effortlessly, as if this was a familiar task to him.

I still had many questions to ask him, but I didn't want to be so greedy for answers that I scared him off. So, I sat and watched in silence. While I stared at him, he didn't glance at me more than twice.

My mind went through several possibilities as he worked. I thought about him trying to gain my trust, then all the ways he could hurt me. My feet inched away from him at that point. I had no reason to trust this man before me. It was safe to say that my mind had still not settled from arriving here yesterday. It all still felt like an elaborate dream that I would wake from and my mind was still trying to work through everything that was happening.

But while the situation was difficult to process, I understood why the King wanted me here. I understood his desire for gold and why he thought I could provide it; that was easy to wrap my mind around. But Rumpel? I didn't understand him at all. He had given me nothing about himself to try to understand. He was a mystery to me.

I didn't know Rumpel, but I wasn't afraid of him. Knowing that helped settle my nerves. It could have been wrong, but something about him relaxed me. Studying him, I leaned back on my elbows and listened to him work.

It was several hours before he finished, and while my eyes were sagging with tiredness, I had managed to stay awake.

"I believe you owe me two answers now."

"That's right." I sat up straighter and rubbed my eyes. He spun around on the seat so that he was facing me and leaned forward on his knees.

"One: why would the King think that you can spin straw into gold?"

"Ah. Good question. My dear papa, who had the best intentions, mind you, told a story of me spinning straw into gold. So as to not ruin the fun, he gave a sly answer when asked if the story was true, and the King's guard mistook his sneakiness for honesty."

Rumpelstiltskin nodded, looking interested. "So, then the greedy king drags you here and demands you spin him gold, or else he'll kill you?"

I affirmed that yes, that's how the story finished. "I thought he would only want the gold from last night, but it seems he wants me to continue supplying it as a means to finish the war."

At the mention of the war, Rumpelstiltskin's eyes went dark. The look passed so quickly, though, that I couldn't be sure it had been there at all.

"Second question. Are you close with your family?"

I wasn't sure what I was expecting the next question to be, but that one threw me off. "Very much so, why?"

"Then why did you not write them a letter when Conrad offered you the means to do so?"

I gasped at him. He had been there for that conversation! I hadn't realized he could do that. "You eavesdropper! Did you spy on me all day?"

He held up his hands. "I am a gentleman, so I gave you your privacy when needed!"

"That doesn't make it okay! You have to ask before you do something like that!" I said, pointing my finger at him. He looked confused, but also amused.

"Alright. I will ask the next time. Though if you must know, I was watching Conrad first, and he led me to you."

That did make it a little better, though now I wanted to know why he was following Conrad. I still couldn't be sure I fully understood what he was capable of.

It dawned on me that if he was there to see Conrad give me the paper, he must have heard me ask the prince about the spirit that wandered the castle. I waited to see if he would acknowledge that, but he didn't.

"So," Rumpelstiltskin said. "Why did you not write to your family?"

I was embarrassed to answer his question. I lowered my head to my hands, so my voice was muffled. "I can't write."

He goggled at me. "Can't write, can't make gold, what can you do?"

"I can read!" I said proudly. "And do a few sums."

"Count. You can read and you can count. Is that all you know? How have you not been eaten by now?"

I choked. "Because we don't live in a savage world!"

He shook his head at me like I was a child. "In my day, women were taught better than that." I wanted to ask him what he meant by *his day*, but he was already standing up and sprinting toward the stairs. He ran up them, disappearing behind some bookshelves. There was some shuffling as he rummaged through things. A few moments later he skipped back down the stairs with a book and quill in hand.

He sat down beside me and opened the book. The pages were plain. He lifted the quill and looked at me readily. "It seems I am doing everything for you tonight. What is it you'd like me to write to your family?"

Unexpectedly, my eyes filled with tears of gratitude. It had only been a day but so much had happened since I saw my family that the thought of reaching out to them gave me immense joy. First spinning straw into gold, twice, and now writing to my family. I doubted I would ever be able to thank Rumpel enough for what he was doing for me.

I thought before I began. He wrote as I spoke, in a handwriting more beautiful than any I had seen before. When he finished, he folded it gently.

"Don't be afraid to ask them for something in return," Rumpelstiltskin said as he handed me the letter. I held it tenderly in my hands. "You're giving them gold; they should be giving you something too."

Chapter Ten

"I ASK FOR BOOKS."

The King walked around the room, impressed once again. Rumpel must be here too, watching us, but I resisted the urge to look around for a hint of him.

At my request, the King looked up. "Books?"

"Yes," I said with a nod. "Books. I can get quite bored and I would like books to pass the time."

"Ah. I see." The King walked slowly to me. "We have a library, and you may borrow any books you please." He gave me a smile as he patted me on the back. I stiffened at his touch. He was being friendlier to me, but I knew it was only because I was supplying him with so much gold. I had not forgotten how he threatened to kill me.

Pleased that he agreed so easily, I moved on to my second request. "And I would like something for my family as well."

"Oh?"

"It's only fair, seeing as how you took me away from them, that they get something in return," I said.

The King thought for a moment. "And what would I give them?"

I bowed my head. In truth, I hadn't any idea. The first thing that came to mind was a spindle of the gold, but he assumed I had spun them plenty of gold when I lived there, so I felt odd asking for that. "Whatever Your Majesty thinks is fair."

I didn't like my answer, but it was the best I could come up with. He stroked his chin with one hand, resting the other on his belly. "I suppose it's only right. If you continue to make gold for Westfallen, then I will give you and your family a title."

My mouth fell open. I hadn't expected that offer.

"With the end of the war coming, I will be acquiring land. There are also a few lords who have fallen in battle and had no heir to take over their manors. Your family is welcome to one of those. I will send a guard with the invitation along with your letter." The King patted his pocket, where my letter was kept.

I didn't know if my family would want to leave the tavern, but I felt honored that I could provide them with the opportunity. A title came with wealth. I could help bring them out of poverty.

In gratitude, I bowed my head again. The King bobbed back before leaving the room with his guard trailing behind him. I was grateful they were no longer ordering me around.

"I asked," I whispered to the empty room. "Are you proud of me?" I was sure Rumpelstiltskin had watched the whole encounter.

After leaving the small room, I longed for some air and an escape from the high castle walls, so I convinced Anna to show me a place I could relax outside with little chance of seeing anybody. She led me through a maze of dark hallways and past the raised eyebrows of other maids until we reached a thin door. Upon opening it, she revealed the perfect hideaway place. The door sat on the outside wall of the castle, overlooking the back field touching the forest. She said that, unless there was a hunting trip planned for the day, there was little chance of anyone coming back here. The castle wall turned outward sharply to the left, forming a blockade from the rest of the field, and to the right ran the expanse of the side castle, heading toward the town further away. If I walked past the wall to my left and looked up, I was sure to see the barred window where Rumpel spun gold at night.

I thanked Anna, confident that she could be an ally of sorts here, and she left with a curtsy. I wasn't sure I could get back to my room later without her help, but I would worry about that when it came time. For now, I strolled away from the door toward the village, settling in where the ground looked dry.

Outside the chaos of the castle, my mind quieted and my breathing slowed. If any place could help me make sense of my thoughts, it was here. I spent part of the time thinking through my dilemma with the King and debated telling him the truth, and another part thinking of home, my family, and Aiden.

Part of the time I thought of nothing at all, but instead leaned my head against the hard stone and closed my eyes, listening to the birds tell their songs. It was almost enough to make me think that everything would be okay, and I started to drift into sleep.

A voice jolted me awake, and I scrambled to my feet. The voice came again, calling out my name.

It couldn't be.

I turned to the right and peered at the figure coming my way, certain that my mind was playing tricks on me, or that I was still dreaming.

He called again, running toward me at full speed as I stood there, dumbfounded.

"Aiden?" I breathed in wonder. He ran into me, crushing me in his embrace and sweeping me off my feet. In my confusion I clung to him, wondering when I would wake up. This couldn't be real.

"How did you get here?" I asked as he spun me around. He set me back on the ground and hugged me again.

"I asked around and someone told me where you were," he said.

My eyebrows drew in as he released me from the hug. "No one knows I'm here. What did they look like?"

"Does it matter?" Aiden asked. It mattered to me, because unless the person was Anna, which I doubted, it meant my new safe spot wasn't as safe as I'd hoped. Aiden's face was bright with his smile. "It's been so long, I've missed you."

At that, all questions of who led him here, which I guessed then must have been Rumpel, vanished as I recalled our last conversation. What should you say to someone you told you didn't want to marry? I heard my voice say that I missed him too, which was the polite answer.

"Your family told me you'd been taken; I had to come make sure you were okay." Aiden soaked me in, as if checking to see if I had been hurt in any way, but I felt uncomfortable with his eyes on me so intently.

"It's been an adventure, but aren't there other things we need to talk about?"

He settled on the ground, patting the place beside him. "That can wait, I want to hear about your adventure."

I sighed, but I told him everything, hoping he could make sense of it better than I could. At the end, he stayed quiet for several moments. Finally, he said, "I don't trust him."

"Who?"

"Rumpel."

"Ah. He's one of the few that I do trust. It's the King and Conrad that I can't be certain of."

Aiden rested his elbows on his knees as we sat together. Small flickers of touch ran between us as he swayed closer to me. "I don't want anything to happen to you, and I don't understand why he would help you freely. He'll ask for something soon."

"I think he's just lonely."

Aiden barked a laugh. "I don't like the sound of that either. Lonely men can find some other companion besides you."

I promised to be careful, and while I wanted to talk to Aiden about us, it felt so nice having him there that I didn't want to ruin it. We stayed for a while, talking about the castle and the gold and the food until the sun started to drift back down to the land.

"You won't make it home in time."

"I stayed in an inn last night, and I'll stay there tonight as well. You don't need to worry about me." Aiden took a few deep breaths before looking into my eyes. "Have you changed your mind about us?"

Treading lightly, I replied, "I'm really sorry."

Aiden didn't look bothered. "I'll get you to change it. I know you love me."

"I don't doubt that I love you," I said. "I just doubt that I love you to that extent."

His face remained calm as he repeated my words back to me. "You just want more." I shrugged, unsure of how else to say it. He leaned his head against the wall. "Don't close your heart to me yet. Wait until you come back home to make a decision."

"Aiden, I know it's hard, but I've already made my decision," I reminded him gently.

He shook his head, not accepting the words. "Just promise me we will talk when you get home."

It seemed like an innocent thing to ask, so I agreed. I could give him that. Before he left for the inn, Aiden kissed my hand, his lips lingering on my fingers. "I love you," he breathed the words into my skin, leaving his warmth behind. Content with that, he left, and I made my way back into the castle that felt more like a prison.

My evening passed with Rumpel, still quiet and mysterious as ever. I didn't try to break the walls down tonight since I had enough on my mind with thoughts of Aiden. The only time Rumpel spoke was to tell me he hoped my friend found me alright, confirming that he had led Aiden to me.

"You didn't stay to listen?"

"You asked for privacy," he said. I nodded, impressed that he'd honored my wishes, though aware that I wouldn't know if he was lying or not. He returned to silence as he spun.

Before I could leave the room the next morning, Conrad strode in. He looked well, his red hair tamed and his clothes casual, and he beamed when he saw me.

"Good morning." He gave me a small bow. A prince shouldn't bow to a village girl, but making gold gave me privileges I didn't deserve.

"I was wondering if you would accompany me to dinner tonight?"

Flustered, I pinched the side of my dress between my fingers. Go to dinner with the prince?

Seeing my hesitation, Conrad quickly spoke again. "It's not a formal thing, just my father and I and a few council members. Completely casual. No music, no dancing, no crowds. Just a few people and some good food. I can leave you to eat alone in your room, if you'd rather."

Knowing it wouldn't be just me and Conrad made me even more nervous. With my lack of etiquette, I shouldn't be allowed to eat with the King.

Still, I knew better than to turn down the crown prince; Mama would have a fit if she knew that I even thought about it. "I'd be honored." I dropped into what might have been my best curtsy yet, but Conrad held up his hand.

"You have to stop doing that," he said, waving his hand at me with a big smile. "It's embarrassing."

I couldn't tell if he meant embarrassing for him or for me, but either way I'd be relieved to stop.

"I'll come fetch you tonight." His smile looked like it could swallow his ears as he darted out.

I didn't have time to fret over my dinner with the royals. I needed a nap.

I dragged myself to my room and collapsed onto the bed. Anna sat on the sofa with her needlework in hand, but I kindly waved her off, relieving her for the morning. I didn't bother removing my shoes as I climbed under the covers and pulled them over my head as I settled in, letting sleep take me.

Content, I slept most of the day away, only waking when Anna opened the door. I grumbled, but knew I needed to get myself ready before dinner tonight. My stomach was complaining of hunger already.

Anna gave me a small smile as I threw my feet over the side of the bed, flinging my shoes off. I pulled myself out of my haven and dragged myself to the window, opening it. The cool air greeted me and helped wake me up. I breathed in while my mind recapped the unbelievable events that were occurring. *Still trapped in the castle, still faking a Gift, still accepting help from a curious man.*

"This came for you while you were sleeping; found it under the door." Anna's timid voice pulled me away from the window. *That's right, and still being waited on by a maid.*

Anna pulled a note out from her pocket and handed it to me. She'd likely read it already, but I didn't mind. Curious, I unfolded the paper and immediately recognized the beautiful handwriting. It was from Rumpel.

Cosette,

Be wary while you are with Conrad tonight. A friendship with him is not in your best interest.

-R

I turned it over, but there was nothing else. I read the cryptic note again.

Be wary of Conrad?

My first impulse was to be upset. Who did Rumpelstiltskin think he was that he could tell me who I should form a friendship with? If the prince wants to be my friend, then let him. His father seemed eager to kill me if I didn't appease his desire for gold, but a friendship with his son could be the means to saving my life. Conrad was my best chance at survival if it was discovered that I couldn't in fact spin gold. I'd need to build a friendship with him to protect me from his father's wrath when the truth came out. Hopefully I could form a strong enough bond with Conrad that he wouldn't be upset when he learned that I had no magic in my hands.

To be fair, I didn't lie to them. I couldn't spin gold. But we were past that, and all I could do was get my things in order for when the truth was revealed. So, if Rumpelstiltskin didn't want me to be friends with the prince, I needed him to explain why. The thought that Conrad could be dangerous sent shudders down my spine.

"Is it from Prince Conrad?" Anna asked as I folded the note away. Apparently, she hadn't read it after all. When I didn't answer, Anna went on. "I think he fancies you."

I raised an eyebrow at her. "Oh?"

She shrugged as she moved to grab a hairbrush. "You're not a princess, but you're pretty enough." Her tone dropped at the last word, and I couldn't tell how high of a compliment that was.

She ushered me into the chair by the desk and ran her fingers through my thin hair. It felt strange letting someone do my hair for me, but Anna had insisted that my skills were no match to her own and I wanted to look my best tonight before the King, Conrad, and the advisors. Besides, she had added, she enjoyed her job.

"There aren't that many princesses Conrad's age. There are the twins from Beiyonbor, but they are both betrothed already. There's the Osmelee girl, but the King would never let his son marry one of them. Then there's the slew of daughters from Tilburr, but that's all the princesses his age that I know about." She rambled on as she worked. I wasn't sure if Anna was talking to me or herself at this point. I tried to enjoy the impromptu history lesson, but I found myself distracted by Rumpel's note in my fumbling hands. "We all thought he was sweet on Lady Marianne, but she stopped coming by a few years ago. No one's got any idea why. I suspected the King had something to do with that; she didn't come from a rich family."

"I don't come from a rich family," I pointed out.

Anna stopped brushing long enough to give me an incredulous look. She shook her head as she started back up again. "With your Gift, you don't need to be a princess. You're more valuable than that."

Her words brought mixed emotions.

I had lived my entire life being the girl without a Gift. A nobody.

Now, the King referred to me as one of the most valuable people in the country. I would be appreciated and honored. It wasn't something that I was used to, but I had always wished for this.

I wanted to belong.

Now I did. Even though it was a lie, I had a place. I had caught the eye of the King, and perhaps his son. But the thought of that brought fear along with joy. There was something about the King that made me cringe, and I didn't like the idea of being tied to him for the rest of my life. I loved being needed, but I didn't want to become so valued that I was irreplaceable and he never let me go.

Especially because I couldn't actually spin straw into gold, and there was no telling how long Rumpelstiltskin's generosity would last me. My hands shook with nerves, and I folded them in my lap to hide from Anna. I wanted more than anything to go home.

"I'm only here until the end of the war," I mumbled, but Anna wasn't listening. She was busy pinning up my hair and saying how lucky I was. I studied my reflection in the mirror as each pin and brush of powder took me further from a person I recognized.

Chapter Eleven

EITHER CONRAD AND I had drastically different ideas of casual, or he had been greatly mistaken, because the image before me was one straight from a book, one that I didn't belong in.

From one side of the room to the other stood people of all shapes and sizes, conversing around the tables. Two-thirds of the room's occupants were men, but the women could easily be spotted standing out from the dark suits with their brightly colored dresses. I had thought that the dress Anna picked for me was too much, so I convinced her to find me a simpler style. Now I see that the first dress would have still been more understated than most of the ladies' attire here. Some dresses included feathers, making them look like birds flocked around the room.

The dining room, located adjacent to the throne room, was smaller but no less grand. It didn't include the wide balconies, but it did have marble floors and two large chandeliers set up on each side so that only the farthest corners remained in darkness. A row of columns split the edges of the room, forming a slender hallway that one could walk through.

Between the columns, five large tables were set up: three in a row and the other two situated sideways at either end. Large windows spread along the back wall, showing a courtyard outside, and there was still enough light to see the empty trees and the stone paths. Elaborate curtains hung to the sides of the windows, and I longed to go hide behind them.

In the midst of all this beauty and nobility, I stood out as an imposter.

I was certain as soon as we walked in, all eyes would turn to me, silently questioning why I was there, but only a few people turned our way, and their gazes didn't linger long. There was one that watched us longer than the others. The King stood near the side columns with a full glass of wine in his hand, distant from everyone else. I turned away from him, but curiosity made me peek back a few moments later to see his eyes still following us.

Conrad seemed oblivious to his father's watchful stance. He led me, my hand in his arm, toward the tables.

Each had candles spaced atop them, along with bowls of fruit. The King's spot was easy to identify at the center of the head table with the finely carved chair decorated in jewels, an identical, slightly smaller one sitting beside it. A shudder ran down my spine at the thought of sitting beside Conrad at that table with everyone looking at us.

Conrad's hand twitched on my back, and he gently pushed it to the side, steering me away from the head table. "We can sit here on the side where we'll be less noticed."

The prince would never go unnoticed, but it was a kind gesture, and I let him lead me to the side seats where people ventured our way to say hello and meet the girl who could spin straw into gold.

It seemed I was wrong. Conrad was not the one who drew eyes tonight, but me. The village girl with the unique Gift.

Under my smile, I willed myself not to do anything foolish. I would be lucky if I was able to carry on any sort of conversation, or even remember their names.

"I'm sorry," Conrad leaned over and whispered to me. "I meant this to be informal, but I mentioned to Father that you were joining us tonight and it seems he turned it into a spectacle."

I smiled tentatively back. We didn't have another second before another cluster of finely dressed men were upon us, introducing themselves and reaching to shake my hand.

"Hello," I managed to squeak out. There were four men, each middle aged and wearing thick suits with gold buttons, who tipped their heads and looked at me expectantly, but I was unsure if I needed to say more. A few glanced to my hands, then back to me like some spectacle or show that would soon start. I moved my hands to my lap.

"How's your wife, is she still sick?" Conrad saved me by turning to one of the men.

The man looked pleased that the prince remembered. "No, she improved a few days ago. She's still resting, but color has returned to her face."

Conrad nodded. He still had a big smile on his face, and I wondered if he ever dropped it. But then I recalled when I met him. He hadn't smiled once. I much preferred his face with the smile.

"Good, and the baby? All still well?"

The man shrugged. "Far as the midwife says. I'm hoping for another strong son."

"We shall see! And are your cousins still visiting?" Conrad turned to the next. He made a disturbed face.

"Unfortunately. I've been hinting at them to leave for a week now." The men all laughed.

It went on this way, Conrad asking each a personal question or two, and each man seeming pleased that he'd remembered something about them. With every person that came to greet us, Conrad knew their name and their kids' names and all the little details of their lives. He even spoke to some in their native tongues.

I was beyond impressed. No wonder he was so well liked, he seemed to really care about the people.

Partway through the caravan of well-wishers, Conrad reached over and put his hand over mine. My whole body froze. I let his hand stay, but for the remainder of the night I could feel his hand on mine, even long after he withdrew it.

Anna's words flickered through my mind—she'd mentioned the King might be looking for a match between me and his son. By the way Conrad had so fearlessly taken my hand, it made me think the match could be on his mind as well. He was a kind man, from what I had seen: smart and relatable. Handsome too. But I was just a tavern owner's daughter. How had I suddenly become important to the prince?

I would be honored if he sought a relationship with me, but if asked, I wouldn't say yes.

I didn't belong here. It would only be a matter of time before they found out that I couldn't spin straw into gold, perhaps by then they would be grateful enough for what wealth they had received to not hold my deceit over me. At that point I could return home.

Back to where Aiden waited. The thought of that sent a tremor to my hand.

I peeked over to Conrad. He didn't look anything like Aiden, but they held themselves the same. Both confident, both with wide smiles and chins tilted up. They both could make anyone laugh. But one was a poor villager, and one was a prince. I had no doubt that if Aiden had been born a prince, he would be exactly like Conrad.

A flicker of gold caught my eye, interrupting my thoughts, and I almost gasped out loud.

Standing at the edge of the room was Rumpelstiltskin.

I blinked. He was still there.

He stood along the wall opposite of us, standing out among the crowd of well-dressed folks with his plain tunic shirt and trousers. His arms crossed over his chest as he looked at me with a frown on his face. People walked by him, and I watched for their reactions, but they didn't seem to notice him. Was I the only one who could see him?

Slowly, he shook his head at me disapprovingly. Confused, I pushed my eyebrows together.

"Are you alright?" Conrad asked. He looked at me with worried eyes, then twisted his head to stare in the same direction I was.

I looked back to the wall, fearful that Conrad would spot Rumpelstiltskin, but he was gone.

My eyes sifted through the shadows to see if I could spot him somewhere, but if he was still in the room, he kept himself hidden from my sight.

I put my hand to my head. "Yes, just overwhelmed."

Conrad leaned closer to me. "Don't worry, I'll send everyone else away tonight. We can just enjoy our food and each other's company." His voice was calming, and it was nice that he was so considerate. Servers had just brought us our food, and my eyes grew wide at it. I had more food on my plate then I had ever eaten in one meal. My surprise grew when another plate was brought out with bread and fruits. I held the bread in my hand. Was it normally this soft?

Conrad did most of the talking as I ate as politely as I could. He asked me about the village I was from, and what I thought of Westnut Castle so far. I said I liked it, and asked how they got the name, launching Conrad into a story about a man and a squirrel.

I never fully relaxed, keenly aware of all the eyes on us, but being with Conrad made it a delightful evening. When the evening ended, I excused myself. Conrad offered to walk me back, but I told him I could manage on my own.

I wanted to get my thoughts together and change out of this stuffy dress before I saw Rumpel. He owed me an explanation.

Chapter Twelve

"WHAT IS THIS?" I shook Rumpel's note at him.

"A note. You told me you could read," he answered calmly. He sat at the spinning wheel and began to thread the bobbin. He had a thin jacket on over his plain shirt, protecting him from the last month of winter's chill. It was the same outfit that I had seen him in at the dinner earlier that night.

I put myself in front of him as I waved the note again for effect. "I know what it says. I'm asking what it means."

"It was a caution, which I see you did not care to follow." Rumpel started spinning, ignoring me with his eyebrows set low.

I scoffed. "You don't get to send cryptic messages, then be upset when I don't heed them."

"I'm not upset," Rumpel corrected me. "If you want to make a mistake, then that is on you."

I threw up my hands. "What are you talking about? I'll have you know that Conrad was nothing but pleasant all night! The perfect gentleman."

Rumpel finally stopped spinning and stood up. He was a few inches taller than me, but if I stepped back, I didn't have to tilt my chin up to look at him. "And now, after one night, you know everything about him? You know him well enough to be confident in his character?" He raised his eyebrows at me.

"I don't know everything about him. But I'm a pretty good judge of character."

He laughed, and I detected a hint of mockery in his tone. "Everyone says that. I've never met anyone who didn't think they were a good judge of character. You're wrong, though. You're wrong about him."

"Is there something I need to know?" I folded his note back up and put it in my pocket before crossing my arms and looking at Rumpel with the best arched brow that I could manage.

Rumpel took a step closer and a strand of his golden hair fell across his face as he bent down like he was about to tell me a secret. His voice, usually lyrical and soft, was thick as he spoke. "I have wandered this castle since Conrad was a baby. I know him more than you ever could, and I don't trust his motivations."

Swiftly, he turned back around and reassumed his position at the spinning wheel. I watched silently for a few minutes, unsure of what to say next.

Now calm again, I settled myself on the floor next to him to feed him straw as he worked. The process would go faster if I could help.

"What are *your* motivations?" I asked flatly.

He paused for a second to look down at me. He opened his mouth then shut it again, turning back to his spindle. "I have none. If I don't spin for you, you will die."

I continued to watch him work, biding my time before I pressed further. The straw flowed effortlessly through his hands as he continued to feed it through the bobbin, turning it into gold as it wrapped around the spindle. I was right; it was going faster with me handing up the straw for him. I should have helped the last two evenings.

"I still don't understand why you're helping me," I said. "What's it to you if I die?"

Rumpel paused again, looking down at me with amusement in his eye. "Would you like me to stop? If that makes more sense to you, I can do that."

I shook my head quickly. "Of course not. I just want to understand you."

"And I would like to understand you," Rumpel said. He pushed back one of his sleeves and continued to work.

I jerked my head up. "What do you mean?"

He stopped working again and twisted himself around to face me. "You asked me my motivation. I want to know yours." He folded his hands on his lap and tilted his head as he waited for my answer.

"I don't want to die," I said plainly.

He laughed for a second before his face turned blank again. "No. That's not all. You could argue with the King. Tell him you've given him his gold and now he has to let you go home. He can't keep you here. But you didn't. He didn't have to push too hard to get you to stay here until the end of the war. You really think he will let you go then? He won't. And you won't fight him. You don't want to go home."

I threw down the straw and stood up. Why did he feel like he knew me? "You're wrong!" My voice was louder than I intended, and I lowered it slightly. "You're wrong, I want to go home more than anything, but I'm just a girl from Autumn Leaf Village, who can't argue with the King. He can kill me if he wants."

Rumpel stood too. "You like the appreciation. You like being wanted by the King, wanted by Conrad. It feels good to be needed, doesn't it? You aren't ready to go home, back to your old, undervalued life. For the first time, you matter, and you care too much about others' opinions of you to give it up."

My face flushed with anger as I balled my hands into fists. "If you think so little of me, why are you helping me?"

Rumpel laughed again, though I saw no humor in the moment. "If I don't help you, you will die. Then it won't matter what anyone thinks of you. You'll be gone."

He was avoiding my question, whether intentionally or not, I couldn't tell, but I was too hurt by his comment to say anything more. So, I sat back down, keeping my head angled downward while he calmly picked up the straw and continued spinning.

It hurt to hear his words, but it hurt more knowing that he was right. I did care what others thought of me. I wanted to be more than the girl with no Gift. At dinner, all those people had looked at me like I was their savior, and while it had made me uncomfortable, it also filled me with pride. Infuriatingly, Rumpel saw right through me, when I saw so little of him.

How could I learn more? History books in the King's library might speak of Rumpel, if he really was an ancient, cursed king.

"I'm sorry, Cosette," Rumpel said, stopping to look down at me.

I shook my head, still upset. "We need to hurry, at this rate we will never finish." The King had filled the room with more straw than ever before. Rumpel nodded, and we spent the rest of the night in strained silence.

Before leaving, Rumpel tried to make amends. "I didn't mean to hurt you. I think highly of you. You have a good heart."

I paused, my arms folded across my stomach as I breathed. Holding a grudge against him, one of my few allies in this strange new world, would do me no good, so I pushed down my hurt with a sigh. "Thank you. I really am forever in your debt."

Rumpel got a funny look on his face. "No. It's important to me that I do this for free. You don't owe me anything."

"Why?" I asked. Why was he so adamant that he got nothing in return?

"I can't explain. But I need to hear you say it. Tell me that you don't owe me anything."

Exhausted from the night, I gave in. "Alright. I owe you nothing."

"Thank you. I'll leave you to the rest of your night."

He bowed deeply, but his image started to shimmer. Before he stood back up, he had floated off like the wind. The air around him was void and empty.

He turned straw into gold before my own eyes every evening but vanishing into the night left me staring at the space where he once stood, a clear reminder that this was not the world I thought I knew.

A stubborn king, a charming prince, and a magical man who spins straw into gold. What had I gotten myself into?

Chapter Thirteen

I WOKE UP ANGRY at Rumpel, his words coming back to stab me all over again the next morning. I scowled as I rolled out of bed and slid my feet into the slippers that I was becoming so attached to.

Suddenly, those slippers felt like another way in which I was forgetting the village girl that I was, and I kicked them off in disgust. I was sure Rumpel would say something like I cared more about the comfort and fine things than being true to myself. His assessment had a bigger impact on me than I thought it would.

"There, are you happy?" I shouted to the air, where Rumpel might be listening. "I'm not wearing the nice shoes!"

Barefoot and still grumpy, I trudged over to the mirror to pull myself together. Rumpel's words replayed in my ears as I yanked the brush though my hair.

Was he right? Did I care more about people liking me and fitting in than I cared that the King was using me?

Part of it was true. I liked to please people, and I liked to be accepted. I had always known that about myself. But wasn't that only natural? Didn't we all want to be loved? What was so wrong with that?

Still bitter, I put my brush down. Since Rumpel seemed to know so much about me, I figured it was time that I found some things out about him. The library seemed like a good place to start.

I changed quickly, putting on the plainest dress I could find and leaving the slippers on the floor. I was surprised that Anna wasn't in yet this morning, but I usually slept later so I figured she would stop by in a few minutes. I wasn't in the mood to talk to anyone, though, and hurried to leave before she could find me.

It only took a few minutes to regret that decision. Anna could have pointed me in the direction of the library, but on my own I was lost. Bored guards were stationed around the castle, and I thought about asking one of them, but I was determined to not need help. I wound about on the stairs, trudged through hallways, and peeked into more rooms than I could count. I found the kitchens, where I was offered some biscuits, but no library.

Munching on my biscuit, I tried another hallway. A guard stood along the wall, and I was fairly certain I had seen him three times already.

"Can I help you, miss? You seem lost," he said generously, stepping forward.

"The library?" I asked hopefully.

He nodded. "Right this way."

He led me to the books, and I was glad he did because I was nowhere close. I thanked him numerous times before he left with a bow.

I still wasn't used to the bowing and doubted I ever would be. I didn't deserve a bow. Rumpel would have something to say about it, I'm sure.

Reinvigorated with my goal in mind, I ventured in among the shelves to find some answers. What I found caused me to stop and hold my breath. There were more books here than I had ever seen.

Back home, the bookkeeper had four wide bookshelves, and I had thought that was a lot. But this room, which was twice as large as our tavern back home, put them to shame. Tall shelves lined the walls, each one brimming with books. There were also rows of shelves in the middle of the room, holding more books than I thought there were in the world. Even Anika, who I knew disliked reading and had little eye for beauty, would find this room magnificent.

Plump chairs formed a circle in one corner, while three others sat by the tall windows. The rest of the chairs were dotted throughout the remainder of the room. Each chair was a different size or color or shape, and they each caught the light in a different way.

The bleak, cold, stone walls were covered with bright tapestries, each depicting a different scene with colorful threads. One was a dragon, one was a maiden in a field of flowers, and a third was a cozy cottage littered with trinkets and illuminated by an active fireplace. I wondered if books correlating to those beautiful pictures were hidden somewhere in the library. The chairs and tapestries, combined with the tall windows and colorful books, made quite the picture. I could look at them all day.

Getting over my initial wonder, I started trekking through the shelves, searching for anything on Westfallen history. It took all my strength to pass by other books that looked interesting. I would come back for them.

On the sixth shelf that I checked, I found a cluster of books that looked promising. *The History of Westfallen*, *Westfallen Kings and Queens*, *History*, and *Westfallen Past*. I pulled out each book and hauled them over to a chair.

The first one didn't go back far enough to talk about Rumpel, assuming he was the old king that I had heard whispers about. The second one looked more helpful, and I flipped through its pages until a picture near the back made me stop. It was the present King, only several years younger. He stood with two older people behind him; his parents, I assumed. He looked happy here, even though he was in a serious pose. When did that light leave his eyes? I scanned the top of the page. King Henry, Queen Germaine, and Prince Bellifusa.

Bellifusa? No wonder he went by simply 'the King.' I'd have shed that name too.

With a small smile on my face, I turned back to the beginning of the book and flipped until I found what I came for.

Rumpelstiltskin

There was a small picture of him that I had to squint at to see. It looked like him, but all dressed up. The Rumpel that I knew never wore more than a plain shirt, but this one was dressed in so many jewels that I doubted he could do more than sit for that portrait.

The other parts were still him, though, like the long curls and the thin lips. It was Rumpel, alright. He looked very solemn there, but handsome. I hadn't realized before how handsome he was.

I stared at that picture for longer than I intended to. Blushing, I moved on to the words.

Family:

Prince Rumpelstiltskin was born to King Herold and Queen Helenette, the third monarchs of Westfallen. He was followed by his sister, Princess Elite. Rumpelstiltskin was raised under Governess Maude.

That's all it said about his family. I wanted a picture of his parents and sister, but I couldn't find one. Disappointed by the lack of information so far, I turned the page.

Reign:

Rumpelstiltskin ascended to the throne after his father's early death due to sickness. In accordance with an arranged marriage, he wed Princess Clarissa three days before his coronation. One year after their wedding, Clarissa gave birth to a daughter, Posey.

I stopped to read that again. Rumpel had a wife and a daughter? I found a picture of them and stared at it hard. Unlike the earlier picture, Rumpel looked happy in this one. He had his arm around a girl with dark hair and dark eyes, and his body was turned toward her. She was beaming so wide that I could see all of her teeth. In her arms was a small bundle. I couldn't see Posey's face, but if she looked anything like her mother, then she was beautiful.

Rumpel looked the same age as he was now. Eagerly, I kept reading.

It went on to talk about some of his achievements as king: treaties made, and small disputes settled. Some kind of rock was discovered while he was king, and it brought new wealth to the kingdom.

The next chapter took a dramatic turn.

Queen Clarissa died at the young age of twenty-six. After her passing, Rumpelstiltskin handed the throne over to his cousin, Rupert.

That was the end of Rumpel's section. The next page went on to talk about Rupert, and while I read that one too, it said nothing more of Rumpelstiltskin.

I felt tears filling my eyes. Rumpel had a wife, who he looked like he loved, but she died. It made me see him a little differently. I wondered what became of the daughter.

I picked up the next book, searching for more answers. This one was thicker, so I hoped it had more thorough information. My back was sore, and I needed to stretch before I dug in to find out the secrets beneath the pages.

I thumbed through until I found Rumpelstiltskin's section. It had the same picture of him as before, with the same family history, but I could tell from the first glance that this page had more writing than the other book had. Eager, I read on.

Sure enough, this one mentioned a few things that the other one didn't.

For example, instead of simply saying that Queen Clarissa got sick, it elaborated, saying that during an epidemic, she got the Black Sickness. The name of it didn't strike fear in me, for it hadn't come around for as long as I'd been alive. I'd heard stories from the elder ladies of how devastating it could be, though. From the few pictures included, it looked upsetting. To save his wife from the Black Sickness, Rumpel brought magic to the land. With his magic, he had the power to heal her. But she still died. I tried to find out why, but the book didn't say. At the end, as a result of using magic, Rumpel was cursed. Unless he could somehow make things right again, he would remain cursed for one hundred years, at which point he would fade away into the spirit of magic.

I had to read that part three times, and yet I still didn't understand. If Rumpel was able to bring magic to the land, why was he then cursed for using it? And what did it mean when it said he had to make things right?

I heard a noise and slammed the book shut. I craned my neck to see around the oak bookshelf, though I still couldn't see the main doors. After a quiet moment, Conrad's voice echoed through the room.

"Cosette, are you in here?"

I shoved the books away and stood up quickly. "Yes, I'm coming." I didn't want him to see the books on Rumpel. I wasn't sure what he was taught in history class, but I didn't think he knew that Rumpel still lived in his kingdom.

What would he do if he knew? I doubted he could do anything. I knew that Rumpel didn't like the prince, but I wondered what Conrad's thoughts on Rumpel would be.

I came around a bookshelf and almost ran into Conrad.

"Oh!" I laughed nervously and he held out his arms to me.

"You alright?"

"Yes, just clumsy I'm afraid." It took me a second to remember that I was standing before the prince, and I started to curtsy, but he held out his hands to stop me.

"Remember, you really don't have to do that," he said with a big smile as I stood up straight.

"Are you enjoying the library?" He looked around as if it was a new place to him.

I breathed out, slowly conquering my nerves. "It's so beautiful."

"Just like you." Conrad winked at me. The nerves came rushing back.

He held out his arm to me, his blue sleeves fluttering as he did. "I came to see if you would like to take an afternoon walk with me in the gardens?"

I looked outside. Was it afternoon already? That meant only a few hours until dinner, then my evening with Rumpel spinning straw. Should I ask him about his family? Or would that be too painful for him?

Conrad's hand waited, and I knew better than to turn down the prince. "I would be honored."

"Great, perhaps you would like to stop by your room first for shoes?"

I blushed, looking down at my bare feet. I had forgotten about that. I felt foolish for how upset I had been when I kicked off my shoes this morning. Conrad had his eyebrows raised at me. I tried to tuck my toes under my dress.

"Yes, that would be lovely."

I peeked back at my books, resolving to come back later and finish solving the mystery of Rumpelstiltskin.

Chapter Fourteen

I WATCHED RUMPEL SPIN gold silently. I couldn't get that picture out of my head, the one of him holding his wife and baby. How much heartache had he endured in his past? I felt sorry for him now, cursed to stay alive in a world where his wife was dead.

"Are you still mad at me?" Rumpel asked quietly, causing me to perk up.

"No."

He nodded. "Just quiet then?"

"I'm thinking, I guess."

"Ah, about our charming Prince Conrad?"

I acknowledged his joke with a grin. "Not at all. About you, actually."

"Oh?" He turned his face down to look at me but kept spinning. "What about me?"

Unsure how to bring up what I had found, but wanting to know more about it, I thought through my words. Rumpel's life was turning into quite the mystery, and I wanted to solve the puzzle. Finally, I came up with a question that could lead to some answers.

"Have you ever been in love?"

His hands froze. His chest rose with his next breath, but the rest of his body remained still. He didn't turn to look at me, but kept his eyes fixated on the spinning wheel. I wondered if I had crossed a line by asking. We didn't know each other, and that was a personal question. I was about to take it back when he spoke. "Yes."

I waited, hoping he would say more. His hands resumed spinning and I leaned back, dissatisfied but accepting that I may never get him to open up.

Rumpel's steady breathing kept time with his spinning. I focused on the rhythmic sound as I watched him attentively. I was seeing him differently now that I knew what he had been through.

I sensed he knew that I was watching him so intently. Did he know that I had researched him in the library? Was he there watching me? I continued to study him as I pondered. What had become of his daughter? How had his wife died? Why was he cursed?

Knowing that my curiosity would best me in the end, I gave in and picked another question to ask. I had already started asking about his wife, so I figured I could build off that. "How did she die? The woman you loved?"

His hands didn't freeze this time, and I suspected he had been expecting another question. When he didn't answer after a minute, I figured he had discarded my question. With nothing to do, I waited, hoping he would give me some clarity.

There hadn't been as much straw tonight, and he finished spinning before saying anything else. I held my breath when Rumpel faced me, looking thoughtful. Slowly, he spoke. "She was killed."

After a few seconds I raised my eyebrows. I had waited so long for three words? That still wasn't a complete answer. I didn't know more than I had before.

Rumpel sighed as he crossed his legs. "Alright. I'll tell you my story."

The excitement must have been evident on my face, because Rumpel gave a small laugh as he moved to the ground next to me to tell his tale.

"I can't promise to tell it with as much eloquence as your father would," he warned me. I was touched that he remembered my father's Gift. But I wiggled on the floor, excited to hear his story, and he smiled again at my eagerness.

"More than a hundred years ago, I became king of Westfallen. I'm still known as the youngest king Westfallen has ever had. In my youth, I was advised to marry quickly to make our country appear more stable. My parents had arranged a marriage for me since birth, and we moved ahead with the wedding. Her name was Clarissa. She was the cousin of the Tames' queen."

His eyes grew soft when he said her name and I felt a pang of jealousy. I'd never been loved like that before. Nearing twenty, my experience with love was limited to my time with Aiden.

"We had a daughter, sweet Posey. Oh, she was so beautiful. She looked just like her mother. Clarissa and Posey were the pride of my life." His eyebrows lowered and his smile turned to a frown. "But then the Black Sickness came. It took so many lives. We tried to keep our family isolated from the sickness, but soon Clarissa showed symptoms. She got worse with time, no matter what we tried. I grew desperate. I didn't want to lose her."

He paused. "Do you know how magic works?"

I shook my head.

"It must be invited into the kingdom, and at this time, Westfallen was without magic. But I'd heard tales of a woman in the North, someone who wielded magic. More than that, she was, she *is*, the heart of magic. I knew she had the power to save my wife, so I left Clarissa and Posey and I set out alone to find her."

I leaned forward, engrossed in his story. The history books didn't say anything about this.

"I found her, or rather she found me, and I pleaded with her to save my wife. Though I had nothing to offer her, she took pity on me and brought magic to our country. She taught me how to use it and how to save my wife."

Rumpel breathed deeply.

"Did you save her?" I asked with anticipation. I could hardly believe that I was getting Rumpel to talk so much. This was more than he had spoken in the last three nights combined.

"I did. My wife was one of the last inflicted before the Black Sickness left our land, and my daughter never caught it. For a while, we were happy again. I used my magic to help rebuild Westfallen and keep my family safe. But others didn't see it in a positive way. They worried there would be a price to pay. A life for a life. There were rebels who felt the queen should have died and that it wasn't fair of me to have saved her. Everyone lost someone they loved to the Black Sickness, and they worried I had upset fate by keeping Clarissa alive, that fate would take revenge on Westfallen."

A small tear fell down Rumpel's cheek and I sucked in my breath. His voice cracked as he continued. "The rebels broke into the castle one night and killed Clarissa. I couldn't save her from that."

He was quiet for a while as a few more tears fell. Unsure what to do, I remained still and gave him his space. He sniffed, rubbing his eye with his sleeve.

"Unhappy with the way things had gone, the sorceress from the North came to Westfallen. For not using my magic well, she cursed me. I would have one hundred years to make things right, or else I would become a part of magic. Unsure of what to do, I took Posey and we retired to the countryside. I raised her there until she was old enough to marry, and then I returned to Westfallen to try to break the curse."

I pursed my lips together. "What does that mean, 'make things right?'"

Rumpel looked lost as he raised his hands then let them fall again. "I have no idea. She said that she won't take back the magic from me, but I had to learn to control it before it took me over. I had to make things right. That's all she said. I've tried everything I can think of, but I can't find the way to break the curse."

Confused, I squinted my eyes. "Why would she not tell you how to break the curse?"

"I think me figuring it out is part of breaking it. I spent years finding potions, spells and enchantments. I've done good deeds, danced with frogs and butterflies, spun by a river, tossed stones, but nothing has worked. The sorceress is too powerful to cast a simple curse."

I wished that I had something that could help him, but I didn't know anything about curses. And of course, I seemed to be the only one in the land without a bit of magic in me. "It doesn't seem fair for her to curse you. You didn't do anything wrong. Clarissa would have died either way. The sorceress just came, cursed you, and left?"

Rumpel was still a moment before he coughed. "Basically. She pulled the magic from the land and put it back in everyone in the form of Gifts. That's why Westfallen has Gifts."

"Why don't I?" I asked him. I shifted on the ground, so my feet were crossed to my side. My back was getting stiff from spending so long on the stone floor.

Rumpel pulled his hair back, then let it fall again. "I have no clue. I've been trying to figure that out since you told me. I thought it could be connected to my curse."

I was intrigued by the thought. With all that Rumpel had done for me, it would be nice to do something for him. While Rumpel confused me, and I wasn't sure he particularly enjoyed my presence, I didn't want him to be cursed forever. I vowed that I would do everything in my power to help break his curse.

A new thought came to mind. By the way he told his story, it didn't sound like he had much time. I asked, hoping he had a few years left. If I was going to try to help him, I could use all the time I could get.

He sighed, and for the first time since I met him, he looked small and helpless. "Six months. After that, the curse can never be broken."

Chapter Fifteen

THE LIBRARY WAS QUICKLY becoming a dear place to me, and it amazed me that it was empty every time I visited. Once, I noticed some books had been moved around and chairs pushed back, so I knew someone had come, but I had yet to see anyone else there but Conrad and Rumpel. If I grew up in a place like this, the charm of the library might soon wear off for me too, but for the time being, I was still blown away by its beauty every time I visited.

The air smelled like cinnamon this morning, and I could hear birds chirping through one of the open windows. Some leftover tartlets from breakfast sat by my side and I swore they tasted better with a book in my hands.

Anna had gotten used to me coming here, so she picked out comfy dresses for me and pulled my hair back so that I could be cozy as I read. I appreciated her thoughtfulness, as well as her ability to do my hair. She was quite the magician. I'd never looked as beautiful as I had these past few weeks. My beauty might rival Anika's. *She would be shocked if she saw me now.*

I wished I knew how my family fared. While I was treated well in Westnut Castle, it was made clear to me that I was still working for the King, and as such, I had to stay in the castle. Rumpel had offered to write another letter for my family, but I had said no, not wanting to look like I couldn't handle things on my own.

Rumpel had somberly allowed me to try to break his curse, though he warned me that it was nearly impossible. He'd given up. I'd pretended to be offended that he didn't think I could do it, but if I was being honest, I didn't have much faith in me, either. Still, I relentlessly studied as much information on magic as I could, hoping to find something he had missed.

I brought my books to the back-corner couch, near the window, and settled in next to my crumpets. I had two volumes with me, both on folklore magic. They seemed to be composed of small tales from people who used magic, compilations of their stories. I hoped to find someone with a curse like Rumpel's to see how they broke it.

I read for hours. My eyes felt dry as I blinked, and my mouth swelled with thirst as I thought that I should have brought tea with me. I folded the book open next to me and stretched my arms. I needed a break before continuing. I had found nothing of value yet.

I looked up, startled to see Rumpel standing with his back against a bookcase, watching me. He had his arms crossed and looked amused.

"What are you doing here?" My heart had skipped five beats in sudden fright, and I worked to regain my breath.

He pushed off from the bookshelf and strode over to me. "Looking to see if you found anything. I've read all these, by the way." He plopped himself down on the couch and picked up my book, flipping through the pages. I sighed in frustration.

"I want to help, I just don't know how," I said.

He calmly folded the book, stacked it on top of the other, and put them both on the floor. "It's okay, Cosette. You really don't have to help me. This isn't your mess."

I picked the books up and put them on the small table next to me. "You've been so helpful to me that I want to try. Frankly, I don't think it's fair that you were cursed in the first place."

A strange look crossed Rumpel's face, but I didn't know him well enough to place it. Just like had happened before, it was gone before I could be sure that I had seen it. He sat up straighter. "I appreciate you trying. But it's too late for me, I'm afraid."

A new idea came to mind, and I smiled at the brilliance of it. "Have you sought the sorceress out? The one who cast the curse?"

"Yes," Rumpel admitted. "But I couldn't find her. I couldn't find anyone who could explain the curse to me." He folded his legs up on the couch.

"I feel like someone has to have an idea," I thought as I picked up my last tartlet. I bit into it as Rumpel watched. Suddenly I felt selfish. "I'm sorry, do you want some?" I extended it to him, but he backed up from it.

"No, I don't eat anymore."

My jaw dropped open, revealing a mouth full of food. "You don't eat? Ever?"

Rumpel laughed at me. "I don't need to anymore. I'm not human enough to need it."

I lowered my eyebrows as I thought about that. "But you could, right? Just because food tastes good? You could eat, if you wanted?"

Rumpel thought for a second. "Yes, I could, I guess. But there's no point to it."

I shook my head at him, shoving the last of the apple tartlet into my mouth. "I don't think you've had this cook's food. He's amazing. It's his Gift, and it's a good one." I pretended to melt with the taste of my last bite, just for the extra effect, though it really was good. I never had food like this at home.

"You like living here, I can tell," Rumpel said with a sly smile, pointing to my stomach. "You're getting plump."

I patted my belly, pleased with the observation. "Plump and happy."

It'd hardly been three weeks, so I knew I hadn't filled out yet, but it was coming if I kept eating like this. I wouldn't mind. The other night the cook had made some bread with a cinnamon sauce, and I had practically melted on the spot.

"They're treating you like a princess already."

I stuck out my finger at him, warning him. I spoke in a stern voice. "There is nothing wrong with that. I'm giving them gold, well, *you* are, so they have every reason to treat me well. And I have every right to enjoy it." My logic sounded straight to me, but Rumpel didn't look so convinced.

Rumpel shrugged, tilting his head. He had on a deep blue shirt today, making his hair shine brighter in contrast. "You can enjoy it, but don't forget who you are."

I crossed my arms, upset that the last bite of tartlet was ruined by his reminder. How could I forget who I was? What was wrong with enjoying privileges when they were given to me?

"So, since I was born a poor girl in the village, I'm not allowed to enjoy nice things? Do you want me to dress in rags all day?"

Rumpel was shaking his head before I had finished. "I'm not saying that–"

"You are," I cut him off. "You are saying that since I wasn't born into money, I have to live my whole life that way. You think

I'm a horrible person for enjoying the food and fine clothes and big bed while my family still has little."

"No," Rumpel stood up. "I'm saying that you're letting this get to your head. You care so much about what others think, you'd be willing to do whatever the King asks in order to maintain their opinions of you. Including marry his son."

I drew my chin in and clenched my fist. "And you've given up on yourself. Even though you have all this power, you're too weak to fight for yourself. You'll wait the last six months out and be cursed forever."

Rumpel raised his eyebrows. "You don't know how hard I've fought! I spent years and years trying to find the answer. I've given up everything to be free."

"You've given up nothing!"

He stood closer, so he was looking down at me. "I gave up a life with my daughter to be rid of this curse. She grew old and died without me there."

That should have quieted me, but my temper had few boundaries. "That doesn't mean your life is over. You still have a chance if you break the curse. You don't seem to care enough about yourself to try."

He ran his hands through his hair and turned in a circle. My arms were crossed as I watched him. Shaky breaths came from his lungs as he turned back to face me.

"Is this what you think of me?" His voice was low and flat. "That I'm weak? That I don't care to live?" His body was still as he looked me over.

"I don't see you fighting very hard."

He crossed his arms. "I don't see you fighting the King. At all."

I laughed humorlessly. "Because I value my life! And for the record, I wouldn't marry Conrad if he asked."

My breathing had slowed back down as my anger subsided. Rumpel still looked unnerved as his eyes narrowed.

"You'll miss the castle when you're gone. You won't want to go back to your old life after this."

He turned around again and placed a hand over his chest. I could hear him taking deep breaths. I waited to see what he would do next, suddenly feeling guilty for getting so angry. I didn't mean to provoke him.

He turned back around, and while there was still anger in his eyes, his shoulders had relaxed. He let his arms hang by his sides. "In six months, when my curse is final, I don't know how much of me will be left to help you. I'll try to keep spinning gold for you, but I don't know if I'll be able to." He took a step back. "But if you keep angering me, I'm not going to save you from the King. I'll leave you on your own."

This was my chance to apologize. What did I know about being cursed? What did I know about Rumpel and how hard he'd fought to be free? I couldn't claim to know him, and I shouldn't be mad at him for seeing through me. My pride kept my mouth shut for longer than I was proud of. Just when I was ready to apologize, Rumpel cocked his head to the side.

"Ah," he whispered. He turned his nose up. "Your prince is coming."

Before I could say anything, his image shimmered. Just like that, Rumpel was gone, leaving me facing an empty couch and an empty feeling in my heart.

Chapter Sixteen

"IS SOMETHING WRONG? IS the tea not right?"

Conrad and I were walking in the gardens together. The rain from last night left a fresh smell in the air and small puddles on the ground, but nothing that couldn't be avoided if we watched our step.

Conrad was telling me all about growing up as the crown prince, including a funny story from a diplomat's visit. My ears were open, but my mind was not. I tried to stay focused, but I was distracted by my argument with Rumpel. Poor Conrad had mistaken my distraction for displeasure, so I plastered a smile to my face and ordered myself to forget Rumpel. I had a perfectly nice man by my side who wanted to make pleasant conversation, and I was being a poor companion.

"The tea is perfect, thank you." I raised the cup toward him before taking a sip. We had stopped by the kitchens before heading to the garden for our walk, which was becoming a biweekly thing for us. Conrad had made me the tea himself, while I stood and watched in wonder, trying to wrap my head around the fact that the prince had rolled up his sleeves to make tea for me, a common girl.

"I want to know more about your family," Conrad said. The question almost stopped me in my place, but I forced my feet to keep going.

"My family?" What could I say about my family to amuse the prince? "Well, I have a sister. She's younger, but she's more outspoken than I am. She has no filter, truly. But everyone loves her anyway. It's hard not to."

Conrad smiled as he bobbed his head. "I wish I had a brother or sister. It's like a built-in playmate."

He walked closely next to me, listening intently as if I was telling a story as riveting as one of my father's. "We aren't anything alike, but I guess we are close in our own way."

"And your parents?"

"My mama is hardworking. She hardly ever takes a break. She expects everyone to be as motivated as her, which leads to me disappointing her constantly."

Conrad laughed, as if that was funny. "How could you disappoint her? You spin gold!"

I got a strange feeling in my stomach. Guilt. Though filled with good intentions, I was lying to Conrad while he was being so nice to me. My fingers couldn't spin gold; they could hardly spin cloth.

I tried to move past the pit in my stomach. "Gold can't clean the counters or sweep the floors."

"True," Conrad said, laughing again. It was easy to get a laugh out of him. I'd assumed that being in his shoes would be stressful, but either it wasn't as trying as I had thought to be a prince, or he handled it very well. He had such a bubbly personality and lively laugh. I was jealous. I had no doubt been dealt much less pressure in my life then he had, and I didn't exhibit half the joy that he did.

It was contagious, and I found Rumpel shrinking from my mind.

"That just leaves Papa."

"Yes, the great storyteller!" Conrad raised his cup as if toasting.

I smiled. "Yes, his stories are incredible. They come alive when he tells them. Besides that, he's kind and, I don't know the right word for it. Soft, I guess. He's easy to be around, relaxed. He evens Mama out in that way."

Conrad smiled bigger. "They sound great. I bet you miss them."

He couldn't know how true his words were. My heart ached at the thought of them. The adventures of the castle were enough to distract my mind, but I wasn't able to shake the feeling of loneliness that came with being separated from them for so long.

"I've missed them so much since your father practically dragged me away from them and won't let me leave."

My muscles stiffened. I hadn't expected it to sound so harsh, especially while speaking to the prince. There must have been some leftover anger from my argument with Rumpel, and I'd let it bleed into my words. I cringed as I waited for Conrad's reaction.

The prince had stopped walking and looked at me with his eyebrows raised.

My hands flew to my face. "I'm sorry, I didn't mean that to sound so ungrateful."

"No, I understand your frustration," he said. He played with his empty cup in his hands. He had finished his tea in four big gulps while I was still nursing mine. "I wish I could change Father's mind, but I'm afraid he doesn't listen to me."

A thin man came around the bushes with garden clippers in his hands. He smiled when he saw us and waved a dirty hand. Conrad called out to him, by name, greeting him warmly. I smiled timidly and waited for him to pass us by. When he was gone, I leaned in toward Conrad.

"I have to admit, I'm not a fan of your father."

Conrad smiled at me and leaned in as well. "Neither am I." He looked both ways, his eyes lingering on the gardener. After a pause, he gestured me over to a bench. I set my cup down next as I faced Conrad. He had a sparkle in his eye as he stayed close to me. "Do you want to hear a secret?"

I was intrigued. What secrets did the prince of Westfallen hold?

I nodded eagerly, and Conrad leaned in even closer so that a few pieces of his wild, red curls brushed my forehead. I turned my head so he could whisper in my ear.

"I'm forming a coup against my father."

My eyes grew wide and I gasped. I turned my head quickly to look at him, almost banging my forehead against his.

"Are you serious?" I whispered loudly.

He motioned for me to settle down as he nodded. "He used to be a great king, but when my mother died she took all his softness with her, leaving behind a bitter old man. He doesn't have a bright vision for the future like I do. I'm supposed to take over in six years, but I'm ready now. And most of the advisors agree with me."

I soaked up the royal drama. "How does a coup even work?"

Conrad settled back on the bench as he explained it to me. "A peaceful one? All the advisors come together, and we explain to the King that we no longer support him, and strongly encourage him to resign early. No public spectacle made, and he resigns with dignity. That's our hope. It can get violent if he pushes back, or if not all of the diplomats are on board."

I was surprised. "You'd get violent with your own father?" I didn't care for the King, but I supposed that if he were my father, I would have some compassion toward him.

Conrad shook his head. "It won't come to that." He didn't say no, though. In fact, he looked elated as he put his cup down and started talking with his hands. "I have so many ideas for Westfallen. I'm going to make this country the best in the world. The people will be happier, our army will be stronger, our land will be richer. Oh, Cosette, I have so many plans for my reign!"

He looked giddy, squirming in his seat as his hands waved around wildly. I laughed at his excitement. Pleased, he reached down and grabbed my hands. "It's going to be the best years of Westfallen. With all the tools I possess, I'm going to lead this country to greatness."

My hands tingled in his. Were they another tool that he spoke of? Uncomfortable, I slid them away. He was too delighted with his aspirations to notice.

Rumpel's warning flashed back through my mind. Conrad is not to be trusted.

Why?

Was there something that I was missing? What did Rumpel see that I couldn't? The man before me was committed to his role as ruler, eager to take charge, and driven to provide a better life for the people. I didn't see selfish motivations or a lazy attitude.

I had heard nothing but great things from the people in the village, and even coming in with high expectations, I had been blown away. He knew the gardener by name. That was not the mark of a distant prince. He wasn't removed from the people or drunk on power. He was a kind, educated man.

A kind, educated, *handsome* man.

Conrad sighed, looking up at the sky then back at me. "We should get going to dinner. Will you accompany me?"

With some hesitation, I put my arm in his. I could feel the muscle underneath his suit. Confident, Conrad led me out of the gardens and back into the castle, where I prayed Rumpel wasn't lurking to spy on us.

Conrad led me to my room so I could change into something more presentable for dinner. Before he left me, he asked, "Would you stand with me? In the coup?"

Confused, I pulled my lips into a thin line. My opinion held no importance in the matter. "Why would you need me?"

Conrad smiled gently. "It would just mean a lot to have you on my side."

Anna opened the door behind us, looking surprised to see the prince. She curtsied quickly, stepping back to give us space.

I turned back to Conrad, who was waiting for my answer. Not seeing the harm, I nodded.

He looked relieved. "Thank you, Cosette. And thank you for the lovely evening. I look forward to seeing you tonight."

In front of Anna, he shamelessly lifted my hand and kissed it. I watched the way his curls bounced as he raised his head again. He gave me one last deep smile before heading back down the hall, leaving my hand floating in the air in his wake.

In a daze, I turned to Anna, who had an amused look on her face.

"I really do think he fancies you," she said as she ushered me in.

"Yes," I whispered. "I'm beginning to fear so."

Chapter Seventeen

ANNA DRESSED ME EXTRA well tonight. My dress was flowing, with bell sleeves and lace trim. Wearing it made me feel angelic. Anna braided a ribbon into my hair, blue to match my eyes, and put a silver necklace around my neck.

I hardly recognized my own reflection.

Rumpel had been right, my face looked fuller now. Not much, but I could tell the difference. My cheeks had rounded out a little, making my face look less skeletal. No one from here would notice, but I was sure my family would be able to tell the difference when I saw them next.

Whenever that would be.

After dinner, I changed from the nice dress into a plain one before going to the straw room. My hands started to let my hair down, but I decided to leave it in the braid. I wanted to feel pretty for a bit longer.

Rumpel was, once again, hard at work when I arrived. The guards had long ago stopped walking me to the room, so there was little danger of him getting caught. I wondered what would happen if he was caught. Would he vanish on sight, or would he stay to explain? Tell the guards that I had been telling the truth my first night, and that I couldn't spin straw into gold? That I couldn't do anything, in fact.

I hoped we would never get caught, but if we were, I hoped Rumpel would stick around to help me out. I wasn't sure I deserved it, though, after how I had yelled at him earlier.

Expecting the air between us to be tense, I entered the room nervously. Surprisingly, Rumpel looked up from his wheel and smiled at me. Smiles from Rumpel were rare, I'd found, so to get one then confused me.

Timidly, I offered one in return, and a moment later he turned back to the wheel as his hands spun on. There was something different about the room. The table and chairs, which were never used, had been pushed closer to the window, leaving more room under the low loft roof near the staircase. In their place, someone had brought in a small bed. It wasn't much, but it had a blanket and a pillow, and that's all I was used to back home anyway.

Every night I came to the straw room after dinner, helped spin the gold, then was often too tired to go back to my room. Instead, I'd curl up on one of the chairs with a pillow and blanket. The castle was dark at night, with foreign shadows and eerie sounds, so it wasn't uncommon for Rumpel and I to finish so late that I had to spend my nights here, not heading back to my own bed until the morning brought its first light. It wasn't bad, but it had taken its toll on my back, which was another reason why I spent the days in the comfort of the library couches.

"Did you do this?" I asked, gesturing to the bed.

Rumpel nodded, and I was touched. Even when we were fighting, he had looked out for me. I didn't deserve his friendship, or his help. My desire to break his curse was reaffirmed. He deserved it.

I approached him slowly, prepared to apologize for my temper. "I wasn't sure you'd be here tonight. Thought you might give up on me."

Something between a laugh and a grunt came out of Rumpel's mouth. "Honestly? I debated it. But I promised myself I'd protect you. So that means I stay."

His need to help me still baffled me, but I was grateful nonetheless.

"There's something I wanted to ask you," Rumpel said. "When my time comes, I'm not sure how much of me will be left. I don't know if I'll be able to spin for you, but I don't want to take the risk of leaving you helpless. So, on my last day, I'd like to take you away from here, to Vernes or Tilburr, if you'd like. Anywhere that you'll be safe from the King's reach."

I couldn't even consider it. "I can't leave my family like that."

Rumpel looked at me with soft eyes, and I knew he understood the pain of being separated from family. "If I leave you here, even with your family, they will find you and drag you back. It'll be significantly harder to convince them that you can't spin gold after all this time."

He had a point. They wouldn't believe me now. And they knew where I lived. There'd be nothing stopping them from coming through the tavern, day after day, until they found me and pulled me back before the King. My heart felt heavy as I considered his offer. It was crazy, dropping me off in a random kingdom to start over, but it was likely the best option that I had.

"Let's just worry about breaking your curse. Then none of that will matter."

Rumpel nodded, not saying any more. He was near finished with the straw, but I lowered myself on the floor beside him to help him finish. We had settled into a nice routine together. I knew when he wanted more straw, exactly how much he liked at a time, and how to place the straw so he could use it best. I had memorized his hand motions so thoroughly that I could mimic him perfectly, though no gold would come out for me, had I tried.

When we worked, we worked as a team.

For some reason, my mind flew to Clarissa, and I wondered how much like her I was. Did Rumpel see any of her in me?

"So," Rumpel glanced up from his work. "How was your day with Conrad?"

I rolled my eyes at him. "It was perfectly lovely, thank you."

Rumpel looked like he didn't believe me, but he turned back to his work without saying anything more. His attitude fascinated me. As far as I knew, Conrad was the only one who made Rumpel scrunch his nose like that. I had to find out why.

"I want to know why you don't like him. What did he do to earn you as an enemy?" I asked as I twisted the straw in my palm to give him.

Rumpel took the straw as he knitted his eyebrows together. "I'm not sure how much I should tell you."

That didn't seem fair. "You seem to think that I'm planning to align myself with the prince, so I feel any information you have should be shared."

Rumpel smiled at this. He had a little dimple in his cheek when he smiled. "Alright, I'll tell you. You know how the war has dragged on for years? Well, Westfallen aligned with Vestalin early on. It seemed like a good union; we had money and they had numbers. But then they came into money through their mines, and suddenly we weren't as valuable to them."

I listened intently; I didn't know any of this.

"In fear of losing our allies, we needed to gain more soldiers. Problem was, very few men could leave their families."

It was true, I didn't know many people who could spare a husband or a son. Everyone was needed to keep food on the table.

"So, Conrad came up with his own solution. He stole the soldiers."

I furrowed my brow. I didn't understand what that meant.

Seeing my confusion, Rumpel explained. "He travels to towns to recruit. He gets them excited about the idea of war and brotherhood formed through it. Not many can say no to a prince." He gave me a look at that. "But if some of them decide not to enlist, he forces them to. Threatens them, drags them here, whatever it takes to get his army. Without giving them a choice, he enlists these boys to a life of hunger and pain. In return, he leaves little more than a note to their families as if from the son, saying they chose to go fight."

My jaw dropped. That didn't sound anything like the Conrad that I knew; Conrad was kind and considerate. He knew the gardener's name, and the health of his cook's family. That man wouldn't rip apart families to send their sons to war. He had just greeted everyone at dinner by name, asking about their families, their children, their hobbies. He couldn't be the same person.

"That can't be true."

Rumpel sighed. "I've seen him do it repeatedly. It worked. We kept our alliance with Vestalin and are in a position to win the war, especially with the money from this gold to pay the soldiers."

I thought back to earlier, when Conrad spoke of his plans for the country. He wanted to heal the country, restore its beauty. Someone wasn't being honest with me, but neither Rumpel nor Conrad had given me any reason to doubt them or their intentions. Could Rumpel be mistaken?

"You're telling me," I said, trying to process his words against the man that I knew. "That Conrad is kidnapping boys to force them to fight in his army?"

Rumpel nodded. "He brings the boys to the army, convinces them that it's their duty to fight and they would be cowards to run back home. Standing among soldiers tired from war and a powerful prince, it's hard for young boys to argue."

I felt tears spring to my eyes as I thought about kids being ripped away from their families to fight in a cruel war.

"He just today told me his plans to make Westfallen a strong country," I said quietly, unsure it I was talking to Rumpel or to myself. My mind felt upside down and my thoughts were spinning.

Rumpel snorted. "I'm sure he did! He's determined to be the greatest king of Westfallen, he's okay with whatever path gets him there."

If this was true, it was no wonder that Rumpel didn't like Conrad. "Why didn't you tell me this sooner?"

"I didn't realize how close you'd be getting to the prince."

The way he said that sounded condemnatory. I quickly defended myself. "We aren't that close. But it's nice to have a friend who doesn't hide when someone else comes around the corner." I looked at him accusingly.

He tilted his head with a quick smile. "It's an adventure, being my friend." His smile faltered. "Still, you should choose your companions more carefully."

My head shook, still unsure if I could believe this. Rumpel did have the means to follow Conrad and get proof. And the prince would never have known that Rumpel was nearby, watching his every move. Rumpel had the means to do just about whatever he wanted, including save those boys. He was powerful enough, he could have stepped in and done something. I pointed that out to Rumpel, who stopped spinning and twisted his body to regard me with wide eyes.

"Have I done something to offend you? Are you set on hating me for some reason or other? Why is it that when I tell you of this awful thing that Conrad does, you ask why *I* let it happen?"

My cheeks filled with color. "I didn't mean it like that. I have nothing against you, truly. I actually like you."

Rumpel raised an eyebrow. "You sure yell at me a lot for someone who likes me."

"I didn't yell this time," I pointed out.

"Cosette, you just yelled at me this morning."

I buried my face in my hands. "I promise I'm not usually so temperamental." Once again, Rumpel didn't look like he believed me, but he let it pass.

He was still for a while, save for his hands as he worked. He kept his back straight and head angled down. The spinning wheel creaked, but other than that, there was no noise.

After several minutes, Rumpel sighed and turned toward me. I was surprised to see tears in his eyes. "I did try to help a boy once. A young lad Conrad stole away whose spirit reminded me of Clarissa's." He shuddered as a tear spilled down his cheek. "I returned him home to his family. Somehow Conrad found out, and he personally went to the boy's home to fetch him back. Afraid that the boy would expose his secret, Conrad killed him." Another tear fell. "Because of me, that boy died. That's the last time I helped anyone, until you."

Chapter Eighteen

WE MADE A SILENT rule to avoid talking about Conrad after that night. Over the next couple of months, we talked about everything until I felt he knew me better than I knew myself, but we didn't speak of the prince. Rumpel would hang out with me most mornings until Conrad came by to fetch me after his morning meetings, narrowing his eyes or pursing his lips before disappearing just as Conrad arrived. I would see Rumpel later that evening and he would act as if nothing was wrong.

But something was wrong. If what Rumpel told me was true, then something was very, very wrong.

I hadn't found a way to ask Conrad yet about Rumpel's accusations. Hello Conrad, I know we don't know each other well, but I was just wondering if you kidnapped boys for the war in your free time?

I knew he wouldn't willingly offer that information to me, even if I asked. Despite the prince's kind exterior, I believed Rumpel's story. While I wasn't sure how, I was determined to do something about it.

My focus was split between that and Rumpel's curse. After weeks in the library reading books and brainstorming, we were no closer to breaking it than the day I'd started looking into it.

Rumpel was sitting stiffly in a chair next to me, looking bored as he flipped through pages. I had tea next to an empty plate, three books sitting on my lap with a fourth open on top of them. Spells and enchantments filled the pages, but nothing like the curse that Rumpel had described. I had already looked through this book, but I was getting so desperate for an answer that I was rereading them all.

Rumpel closed his book and threw it across the room. He ran his hands through his hair, lips pulled tight.

He was getting more on edge every day. He only had four months left until his curse was finalized. While he had appeared at peace with the fact two months ago, I think the seriousness of it was dawning on him as the end loomed in sight.

In four months, Rumpel would be gone. All that would be left was his spirit, as an essence of magic.

He took a deep breath, throwing himself back in the chair and covering his face with his hands. I gave him his space as I brought my teacup to my lips.

"So, have you ever been in love?"

The sudden question almost made me choke on my tea. "What?"

"I need a distraction. You asked me the same question before. Now I want to know."

I held my cup with both hands as Rumpel peered at me, waiting for my answer.

"If you must know, I've been in love recently."

Rumpel perked up. "Yeah? Is it with some devilishly handsome man, with blonde curls?" He shook his hair for effect, and I laughed at him.

"Not you." I mocked him with a disgusted face. He pretended to pout before growing serious again.

"Please tell me it's not Conrad."

I shook my head. "A boy from back home. Aiden." His name felt odd on my lips, as if I was saying a stranger's name. I had been so distracted, I hadn't had time to think of Aiden.

Rumpel urged me to tell him more. I sighed at his enthusiasm, but I was grateful for the distraction too. My books were getting me nowhere. Leaning back, I recalled our story for Rumpel. "His family moved to our village when I was twelve. That first spring, their roof leaked. Knowing that they had no friends yet, Papa insisted we go help. I was over there every day for months, helping fix little things, or playing while our parents talked. We didn't see each other for a while, until that summer when we were low on food. His parents somehow knew, and they came over often with meals. They brought Aiden with them.

"Aiden saw Papa's stool for storytelling, and he sat there and sang a song for us. I was enchanted. That's his Gift, singing. It's beautiful. Mama thought so too, and hired him on the spot, though we couldn't pay much. He came over constantly after that. I guess life put us together? Our friendship was easy, but it took almost ten years for it to develop further."

Rumpel's jaw dropped. "Ten years? It took you ten years to decide you liked the bloke?"

I blushed. "We were so young at first, a friendship was the only option! After that, it felt like a big deal to make it into something more."

Rumpel crossed his feet and arms. He squinted his eyes at me. "And how long was it more than a friendship?"

I shrugged. "Half a year before I was brought here to the castle. We'd just ended it."

Rumpel's eyes narrowed. "Have you cried since?"

I laughed. "I've cried plenty, but not about that. I've had other things on my mind."

Rumpel threw up his hands. "You weren't in love!"

I drew my chin back and stuck my hands on my hips. "Of course I was! How would you know?"

Rumpel moved over to the couch and sat down next to me. "When you're in love, you think about that person constantly. You can't help it. Nothing could keep you from them, and you couldn't imagine your life without them. When you're in love, it consumes you, and when it ends, even if you're the one to end it, it kills you. That's love. I've spent every day with you for months and this is the first I'm hearing about *Aiden*. That's not love. You might have liked him, but you weren't in love."

My lower lip jutted out. "We had other things to talk about besides who I love. That's why I didn't bring him up."

Rumpel snickered. "Cosette, I know your favorite kind of tree for each season. I know you refuse to eat soup unless you are sick. I know that when you're in trouble, your papa calls you Cosette Victoria, and despite the fact that it should incite fear in you, Victoria is the name of the main character of a book you would write, if you knew how to write. I know more about you then I know about anyone else alive. There have been plenty of times you could have brought him up, but you didn't."

He was right. I could have brought Aiden up if I wanted to. Honestly, Aiden didn't feel like he had a place here. He was part of my old life, my life of working hard for enough to feed us, wearing old dresses and shoes with holes. He was a part of my life at the tavern, scrubbing counters and stealing moments to read in the corner.

Here, Anna did my hair and picked out my clothes each morning. I had a fresh bath drawn whenever I liked, and more food than I could eat in a lifetime. I walked in soft shoes down tall hallways with painted glass and stained tapestries. I took strolls with princes in the afternoon, dined with the king and his counsel, and watched a magic man spin gold at night.

Where did Aiden fit into that?

Although it had only been a few months, it felt like ages ago that Aiden and I had talked. I wondered how often he still thought of me. Had I begun to slip his mind, like he had mine? My thoughts flickered to our last conversation, where he begged me to wait for him and let him change my mind. I wondered if he still held me to that promise.

"Tell me your love story, if it's any better than mine," I urged. I was curious to hear more of his life before the curse, and eager to move away from the topic of Aiden.

Rumpel lit up. "Ah. That is a good story. We were engaged at birth, but neither of us knew it. Our parents wanted us to fall in love on our own. When I was little, I remember when she'd come to visit with her father. She was shy, so was I, so we didn't interact much. I thought she was pretty, but that was all there was to it."

He sighed as he tilted his head back. "I didn't see her for several years. Then, she came. She came without her parents to speak to our council. She had changed. She was taller, her hair was thicker, and her smile was sweeter. She was beautiful. She stood in front of that council as a woman and spoke with confidence. I was blown away. She didn't notice me, but I fell in love with her that day. I pursued her after that, sending her flowers and letters and sweets and gifts. I held nothing back. She was all that I could think about during the day, and she haunted my dreams at night. It took her a few months, but after relentless letters she agreed to meet with me. I guess I got lucky, because she fell for me too. Then our parents told us we were engaged, and everything fit into place."

A pang of jealousy shot through me. I had never been pursued or loved as Rumpel loved Clarissa. I didn't know if I ever would be.

My silence must have given away my thoughts.

Rumpel reached for my hands. "I'm sorry, I should have been more considerate. I didn't mean that your story wasn't beautiful."

I looked at his hands wrapped around mine. "No, I know that it isn't the same."

"You'll find it someday."

"Maybe," I said as I nodded, but my heart ached. As I looked at Rumpel's hands on my own I felt a strange pull at my heart, something other than jealousy. It was a feeling so small that I couldn't be certain of what it was at first, but I recognized it from when I was with Aiden.

Fear gripped me, and I worried my jealousy was more than wanting *someone* to love me the way Rumpel loved Clarissa.

Did I want *Rumpel* to love me, as he had Clarissa? Is that why my mind hadn't been on Aiden? I pulled my hands away from his, hoping the sudden feeling would dwindle as soon as our hands no longer touched, but it stayed like a candle in my heart. Uneasy, I excused myself. Rumpel watched, baffled, as I stood up to leave without an explanation.

I wouldn't let myself fall for him. There was nothing there for me. In a few months, when his curse was set, Rumpel would be gone.

I would not allow him to take my heart with him.

Chapter Nineteen

I HAD DECIDED THAT my sudden feelings for Rumpel were no more than projections from his love story with Clarissa. What girl wouldn't be infatuated with a man who told her how relentlessly he charmed his sweetheart? How deeply he loved her? Who wouldn't be smitten looking at those bright eyes and soft curls, hearing all about how big his heart was?

In addition to all of that, Rumpel was saving my life by selflessly spinning gold for the King every night. That fact had to have added to my misplaced feelings.

Upon realizing this, my mind cleared and the feelings started to drift away. Rationality came back to me and I was determined to keep it.

I had no commitments to Aiden, and no promises had been made. My heart was still open to love, and there was nothing saying that I wouldn't find it someday. Maybe I would find it here at the palace. Maybe some guard standing along the hallways held the key to my heart. Or maybe I would fall in love with the charming, considerate Conrad.

That was assuming that he didn't kidnap boys to fight in his army. That would be a deal-breaker for me.

The point was, I was a young, somewhat attractive, slightly educated woman. If you could see past my flat hair and big feet, I was a decent choice in a mate. I could find love like I'd read about in my books.

I was thinking about these things when Conrad found me. He burst through my door after a small knock. I dropped my hairbrush and looked up from my seat.

"Sorry, I should have waited for your answer," he said, hurrying to my side with a big smile across his face. "I'm just so excited to tell you."

"Tell me what?" I stood up, curious as to what had made him so eager.

He grabbed my hands, just as Rumpel had yesterday. "I've been thinking about how you miss your family, and I convinced my father to let us visit them."

My mouth fell open and something between a gasp and a choking sound came out. I searched his eyes to see if he was joking. "Are you serious? Please tell me you mean it."

Conrad laughed and he shook my hands. "I'm serious! We can go see them today! You don't have to spin gold tonight. We can spend all day there and the next, then come back here the day after."

I feel dizzy with happiness. I hadn't seen my family in months. I had never cried out of happiness before, but tears were forming in my eyes. I threw my arms around Conrad and thanked him profusely. He quickly wrapped his arms around my waist and squeezed. "I'm glad you're pleased. We can leave as soon as you're ready."

"Now," I spoke immediately. Pulling back, I looked him in the eye. I was barely holding back from jumping up and down. "I'm ready now."

Conrad laughed again. "Then let's go see your family."

We were out the doors in minutes. Conrad and I rode on horses, followed by four guards. I tried to tell them that nothing would happen to us, but they insisted on coming along. I was too excited to argue. I wanted to gallop there as fast as I could, but my riding skills were nonexistent, causing us to move slowly.

I told Conrad everything about my family on that ride. It took a fair part of the day to reach home, so the light was starting to leave the sky when my village peeked through the trees. By the time we saw the smoke rising from the chimney, I felt like Conrad knew everything there was to know about my family.

Besides the fact that we were not rich. That was something that I could not explain.

Yes, I spin gold for you. But my family has never held gold in their hands. I was sure that Conrad would think me greedy, or heartless, for not sharing the Gift he thought me to possess, so I simply stated that it was a newly found Gift and left it at that.

He seemed eager to meet my family. I wasn't entirely sure why he insisted on coming for this reunion, but he assured me that he had business in the town, and I was doing him a favor by accompanying him. Of course, my mind went to the boys living there and I wondered if he was here to take them to the war. I hoped that my supply of gold was enough to end that bad habit of his, if Rumpel's story was true.

We could hear noise coming from the tavern as we tied our horses outside. The thought of walking in with Conrad made me nervous, and I found myself hesitating. Would he be recognized here? By the looks of it, it was a busy night. Through the windows I could see familiar faces sitting around tables, laughing amongst each other. I thought I caught a glimpse of Anika, but the figure passed too quickly for me to be sure.

"Are you ready? I'm sure they are excited to see you," Conrad said. He stayed by my side, staring at the tavern. I wondered what he made of my humble home. The Riverfront Tavern sat at the end of a path made by feet over the years. It was down a small hill off the main road, so it didn't take much for travelers to find. If we looked to the right, we would see a small stream that ran south toward Renolds Bohnson's farm. Behind us, on the other side of the hill, was a cluster of homes that supplied us with frequent customers.

The tavern itself was a small but noble place with thick wooden beams and narrow windows. Two long posts ran along the outside for horses to be tied upon, and three stairs led up to the front door. I had swept those stairs so many times that I lost count. It felt strange seeing them again, so familiar and yet so foreign at the same time.

It looked nothing like the castle we'd come from.

Excitement curled within my chest, along with nerves. So much had happened over the past few months, and it had changed me. It wasn't a drastic change, but I knew I was different. I thought I could hear Aiden's voice inside, singing one of his songs. What would he think when he saw me?

Conrad gently placed his hand behind my back, reminding my feet to walk. I led him up to the door. Pushing it open, I scanned the room for my family. They found me first.

"Cosette!" My mama's voice tore through the room as she shrieked. The room fell quiet as my family exploded, surrounding me quickly. Papa was by his stool, which he abandoned as he flew toward me with his arms open wide. Mama was crying already, petting my hair and squeezing my hands. Even Anika looked relieved to see me and gave me a rare hug.

Conrad laughed, drawing attention to himself. Papa turned to him to shake his hand. I saw him peek at the guards who stood behind us, unable to come through the doorway since we'd inadvertently blocked it.

The room was half full, with most of the people sitting at the booths lining the two walls. Only one of the fires was lit, and those who did sit at tables chose one closest to the fire. I was welcomed by the familiar smell of Lolly's cooking drifting out from the kitchen.

There were stark differences between the tavern and the castle that stood out to me. The castle was filled with colors, from the walls to the clothes to the floors. Everything was bright and illuminated by sunshine through tall windows. But here, I struggled to find much color at all. I should have thought of that before coming dressed as bright as a flower. Even Conrad, with his dark suit, had more color than most of the villagers. He had ditched his riding coat with the horses, so he looked more casual then I was used to seeing him, but he still stood out among others in the room. It was obvious that we didn't belong here.

Looking perfectly comfortable, Conrad introduced himself to my parents. His name sent ripples of hushed conversation through the room. Papa's mouth fell open as he bowed.

"Sire, I did not expect to see you. I didn't expect to see either of you."

Conrad laughed as he shook off their attempt at bowing and curtsying. "The honor is mine. Cosette has told me so much about all of you, I feel as if I know you already."

Mama looked beyond pleased to see the prince standing in her tavern, but Anika gave me a questioning look. I wasn't surprised that she wasn't impressed by royalty.

My family had a stream of questions, which I let Conrad answer as I peered across the room. Where was he?

There he was. Aiden stood next to the bar with his arms hanging by his side as he stared at me. He was wearing his dark shirt, the one I had told him was my favorite. I mouthed a hello to him, and he gave me a timid smile back. Uncertain, he looked between Conrad and me. I shifted away from Conrad instinctively. Aiden's eyes moved with me.

Anna had picked out a simple dress for me to wear today, but it was still nicer than any I owned back home. The fabric was yellow as the sun and had flowers stitched into the hem. My hair was twisted half up, and my skin was smooth thanks to the soap they used in the castle. I was getting dangerously addicted to the nice baths with soap.

No doubt, I looked different from the girl that Aiden used to know.

Mama kept my hands in hers as she shook me, bringing my attention back to her.

"We don't have room for all of the men, but we can make room if Your Highness would like to stay here tonight. There is an inn down the road, if your men would like," Papa offered.

Conrad's smile hadn't faltered, though I was sure the thought of sleeping in a place like this sent chills down his spine. He accepted Papa's offer with polite eagerness before turning to inform his men. They didn't look pleased, but they nodded at him.

"Sire, I must insist that I stay with you." One of the men stepped forward. His hand was on his sword and he was looking about the room as if one of the jolly fellows here was going to lunge at him. Most of the eyes were still settled on us, and I was sure this would be the talk of the town tomorrow.

Conrad stepped in closer to his guards. "Thank you for your concern and your loyalty, Dwayne, but I will be fine with Cosette tonight."

Clearly concerned, Dwayne nodded. His eyes shifted over me, no doubt assessing how well I'd hold up in a fight if it came to that. There was unmistakable doubt in his expression, and I didn't disagree with him. I'd be the last person they'd want protecting the crown prince.

Obediently, Dwayne beckoned his men to retreat. Papa gave them directions to the inn while Conrad turned back to us, rolling up his sleeves and making himself at home. It felt strange, seeing him here in my tavern. Not at all the palace walls he was usually surrounded by.

Mama ushered us to a booth where Conrad and I sat on one side while she, Papa, and Anika squeezed into the other. They leaned forward eagerly.

I knew they wanted to hear my tale, but the information I could share was limited with Conrad by my side, so they shared what they already knew. It seems they had been told nothing until a few days after I was taken, when a messenger came to deliver my letter and offer thanks from the King. They had been told that I was serving the King with my talents and helping end the war. A few days later they had been contacted again with a small payment as thanks.

I remembered asking the King for something for my family. I had been so afraid of him back then. Truth be told, I still wasn't fond of him, but my fear had eased.

I also recalled how he had offered to give my family a title and wondered if he had been true to his word. I'd ask my family later, when Conrad wasn't nearby.

I continued to glance at Aiden as my family prodded me with questions, which came in no particular order.

"No, I'm not a soldier. Yes, I have my own room. No, only one maid. Yes, the palace is beautiful."

I tried to appease their curiosity as I watched Aiden move about the room. He was helping the customers in my family's place. His eyes shifted to me as often as mine did to his. I wished I could speak with him, but my family surrounded me.

Conrad stepped in and tried to answer some questions himself. It was his second sentence that pulled my full attention back to the table. "She's spinning straw into gold to pay for our soldiers and to offer the other countries to end the war." He kept on, saying how great of a job I was doing and how everyone in the castle loved me. Meanwhile, the color drained from Papa's face as Mama's mouth fell wide open. Anika's eyebrows shot way up. I shook my head slightly at them, silently begging them not to question the prince. My lips pursed together as I shook my head again, harder.

They looked beyond confused, but at my silent beckoning, no one gave me away. Eager to move past the topic, I geared up my own questions to ask my family as soon as Conrad stopped talking.

Anika beat me to the punch.

"So. She's spinning gold for you." Anika said plainly as soon as the last syllable had left Conrad's mouth. There was amusement hiding in her eyes. I sucked in my breath. I should have known that Anika would push this.

Conrad smiled at me. "She does indeed! Your sister has the greatest Gift of anyone that I know." I blushed at his compliment, still feeling uncomfortable.

Anika kept her eyebrow raised. "And what is your Gift?"

I realized that I had never asked him that, and suddenly felt selfish for it. Conrad turned his head to me, as if I had asked the question. He knew that I didn't know. "I was born with the ability to speak every language."

I gawked while Anika grunted. "That's helpful for a prince."

Conrad erupted into a laugh. "It certainly is."

Mama and Papa laughed along uncertainly, but they still had their eyebrows scrunched in and lips pinched. I needed to find a way to explain this to them, and that meant getting Conrad away.

"Do you want to meet some people?" I laced my arm around Conrad's, urging him out of the booth. He looked between my parents and me but didn't argue as he slid out. I knew he wouldn't; he was too polite.

He did lean his head down to me and whisper, "What was that about?"

"I'm just overwhelmed, I guess." I halted in front of the bar where Lolly had come out from the kitchen. I asked her for a few glasses of water, which she served quickly.

"Fancy seeing you back here again! And with such a handsome man too!"

I blushed, certain that Aiden, who was standing nearby looking busy, had overheard.

Conrad laughed and introduced himself by his informal name. Lolly took his hand in both of hers as she shook it wholeheartedly. "Pleased to meet you. Thanks for taking care of our Cosette."

"She's no trouble at all. She's taking care of us, more than anything." Conrad winked at me.

I let Lolly think of that what she would. Some brave folks had approached Conrad and were introducing themselves. I was grateful for their gusto, as it gave me a moment to slip away. I whispered to Conrad that I would be back in a moment before making to retreat to my family.

I turned right into Aiden.

Boldly, he grabbed my arm and pulled me away. I staggered as I hurried to keep up with him. He led me behind the bar and into the hallway.

Aiden stood close as he looked me over, breathing quickly. I sucked my lip into my mouth, waiting for what he would say. He took another deep breath, then embraced me tightly.

I wriggled my arm free and wrapped it around him, squeezing back. After a long moment, he pulled away and sighed.

"The prince?" There was sadness in his voice, as well as accusation. I shook my head.

"It's not like that."

He peeked over my shoulder, though I didn't think he could see Conrad from here. "It could be, if you wanted it. You did tell me you wanted more."

My brow furrowed and my feet stepped back to look him over. Aiden's looks hadn't changed in the few months since I had seen him; he was still Aiden. Meanwhile I was an entirely different person than who I'd been when I left, and no doubt he could see a change in me.

Perhaps I did see a change in him, after all. I couldn't read his eyes anymore.

"Are you mad?"

He ran his hand through his hair. "Over the past few months, I've been so many things. I've been sad, I've been confused, I've been frustrated. Since I came to the castle, I've thought a lot about us and about what you want. I thought you would have been home by now."

"I'm sorry, the King wants enough gold to negotiate an end to this war."

"And Rumpel is still spinning for you?" he asked, and I confirmed. Aiden looked away. "Still don't trust him."

"He's a good guy, he's—" My voice cut out as I realized I was about to say, "my best friend," but that title used to belong to Aiden, and saying so would only hurt him.

"Tell me about this prince." There was bitterness in his voice.

"It's hard to explain. I owe you answers; I just can't give them right now." Back in the main room, my family waited for me, waited for answers that I owed them.

Aiden's shoulders dropped and his mouth turned down. I'd hurt him again and would leave him without an explanation.

"I'm sorry," I said meekly. "I will give you answers, just not now. But we should talk soon. About us." Aiden nodded and stayed back to watch me go. Guilt filled me upon leaving him so quickly, but I'd tried, twice now, to end things with him, and he insisted on keeping something between us. By the end of this trip, I would need to set things straight. Even though he was doing this to himself, it wasn't fair for him to hold onto the idea of us.

My family hadn't moved from the booth where I had left them. A decent crowd had formed around Conrad, who had pulled out a stool to sit on as he talked with everyone, so I had a fair amount of time to fill in my family.

I hurried back to the booth and collapsed in it, breathing out heavily. Papa took Mama's hand as he looked me over.

"Cosette, what is going on?"

Chapter Twenty

MY HEAD DROPPED TO the table in exhaustion. Mama reached out to me and I gladly took her hand.

"The guards that came for me brought me before the King. Apparently, your story about how I could spin straw into gold had reached his ears." I nodded at my Papa, whose eyes grew wide. But I didn't want Papa to blame himself. "It's not your fault that he believed such a story. But no matter what I said I couldn't convince him of my inability to do such a thing. He thought me greedy, keeping such wealth to myself."

"Should have just come to the tavern, seen our lack of money himself," Anika scoffed.

I nodded quickly, waving my hands. "I tried to tell him that, but he wouldn't listen! He demanded that I spin straw for him, or else he'd kill me."

Mama gasped, causing Anika to roll her eyes. "Mama, obviously he didn't do it." She motioned toward me. Anika's calm was soothing to me; it felt familiar, and it was good to know that some things never changed.

"So, what happened?" Papa asked earnestly. I glanced over to Conrad, who was talking with Mr. Nelson; that would take a while.

I leaned closer to my family, though everyone in the tavern had migrated close to Conrad and we had little chance of being overheard.

"Someone helped me," I tried to explain. "The guards locked me in a room full of straw and gave me until morning to create gold or I'd lose my life. I was sure I was going to die. But someone came. He had magic in his hands! He spun the gold for me and has been doing so ever since. He's saving my life and expects nothing in return."

My family didn't look relieved by the news. "He asks for nothing? Who is he?"

I wasn't sure how to explain who Rumpel was. "He's a good man. Truly. He means me no harm."

Anika squinted her eyes as she rested her head in her hands. "No one does anything for free."

I shrugged. "I doubted it at first too. I suppose if I'd died and he knew that he could save me, he would have to live with that. Likely, he didn't want that burden."

"But how long will he need to help you? When can you come home?" Mama asked.

I twisted my mouth, wishing I could give them a better answer. "I think I'm stuck until the war is over."

Mama looked about ready to cry. Papa wrapped his arm around her as he sniffed. "I'm so sorry, sweetheart. I didn't mean to put you through this."

I shook my head quickly, realizing I had painted a bleak picture of my time there. "Don't be, it's been good for me. I'm enjoying my time there."

"With the prince?" Anika wriggled her eyebrows at me.

"Is something going on between you and the prince?" Mama perked up. Funny how fast her mood changed. Hope danced in her eyes and I was sorry to disappoint her.

"Not that I'm aware of. He's just grateful for the gold he thinks I'm spinning."

Papa hadn't looked eager at the thought of me and Conrad together. If anything, he looked disappointed. I wasn't sure why, but it made me love him more.

Conrad was slowly making his way back to our table. He had worked his way out of that group faster than I thought he could. I quickly told my parents to not say a word about Rumpel, and while they looked confused, they nodded. I smiled politely at

Conrad and slid over so he could join us. Now that my parents had gotten some answers, the conversation flowed easier. My mind was still trying to make sense of this picture, huddled into a booth with my family and the crown prince, while Aiden shot us looks from across the room. It was strange to see, and I had seen some crazy things recently.

I found myself wanting to tell Rumpel all about it. I wanted to tell him how all the people were staring, and it didn't make me as uncomfortable as it once did. I wanted to tell him how odd it felt having Conrad there with my family. More than anything, I wanted to recount every detail of my conversation with Aiden and get Rumpel's thoughts on it.

I told myself that it was the constant time spent together that made me suddenly miss him. I hadn't spent an evening away from him in months. Half a year ago, I didn't even know who Rumpel was, yet somehow, he'd become one of my closest friends.

I tried to pull my mind away from Rumpel and back to the present, but conversation was limited with groups of people gravitating toward us. Most wanted to be near Conrad, but a few just wanted to know where their food was.

Papa sighed as he stood up and began to push through the group of people. "We should get back to work; there will be more time to catch up in the morning." He waved everyone off and back toward their seats.

"I'll go make up a bed for you. Anika, you are relieved from the rest of your chores tonight; I can manage with Lolly and Oria."

Mama stood up as well. "Cosette, do you mind sleeping with your sister tonight?"

The idea of Conrad sleeping in my old bed didn't sit well with me, just as I knew Anika wasn't thrilled for me to sleep in hers, but there was no way around it. We said our farewells as we headed for the bedrooms, eager to be rid of the mass of neighbors. I passed by Aiden before leaving and his hand brushed mine, stopping me for a moment.

"Tomorrow?" he whispered. I nodded. Tomorrow, we would talk. He didn't meet my eyes as he pulled away, leaving his still familiar smell behind.

With a sigh, I left the main rooms and turned toward the bedrooms, where Conrad waited for me outside my old room with his back leaned against the doorframe with the top collar of his shirt loosened and his shoes in hand. I smiled meekly as I approached him. Now away from my family, exhaustion hit me hard and I was eager to escape to Anika's room, but it felt rude to tell him so after he had so graciously brought me home for a long-awaited visit.

I leaned against the wall next to him as I breathed out heavily. Conrad tilted his head to look at me and grinned. "Quite the day, huh?"

Something between a choke and a laugh came out of my mouth. "You can say that. It's so strange being home. I never noticed how low the roof is."

Conrad looked up. "The ceilings of the palace are unnecessarily high." He was quiet for a second as he studied the ceiling before rolling his neck to face me again. "I feel I haven't properly thanked you for everything you are doing for us. Your gold, it's saving my kingdom. I can't tell you how much that means to me."

Guilt stabbed me as my lie burned my tongue. Was it fair that I was deceiving him? Would he care if he knew about Rumpel? Selfishly, I knew that his interest in me would fade if he knew that my hands didn't hold magic. Was that why I wasn't telling him the truth, because I liked the attention? Or was I protecting Rumpel?

Unable to speak, I nodded timidly. Conrad didn't seem to mind my silence.

"I know it can't be easy for you, leaving your home to spin gold for a cold king. But just know, I'm glad you came. You bring warmth to the palace."

I wasn't sure what to say to that. With his side still against the wall, Conrad tilted toward me until his face was closer than it ever had been. I gulped. The sound of his breathing was close to my ear, and my heart jumped.

He was about to kiss me.

I coughed as I stepped back, pulling my face away from his. Conrad didn't look embarrassed as he turned in time with me.

"It's been a long day, I should rest," I said, folding my hands and ducking my head.

My feet started to leave but Conrad reached out and grabbed my hand. "Tomorrow will you come with me into the village? I want to meet more people and show you some of the work I'm doing."

Images of him stealing boys for the army flashed through my mind, and I prayed he couldn't see my face. My lips pursed together as I nodded, and he smiled wide. "Great. I'll see you in the morning then." He let go of my hand and retreated into my room.

"Wait!" I held up my hands. He stopped and looked back with eyebrows raised. "I need some clothes; these feel too extravagant."

He graciously waited in the hall while I changed into one of my old nightgowns. It felt rough to my fingers and scratched as I put it on. I thought perhaps I should remain in my palace clothes, then immediately chastised myself for it. These were the sort of clothes I used to wear every day. I had done nothing to think that I was too good for them. I yanked it over my head and grabbed an outfit for the next day.

This was the most at home I had felt all day, standing in my old room in my old clothes with the familiar trees out the window and smells in the air. If I tried, I could almost forget about the prince waiting outside my door as I pretended this was just another evening at home. My shoes were the only things I didn't change; I couldn't bring myself to take off my soft slippers.

Ready to go to bed, I opened the door and let Conrad take in my appearance. After a pause, he bowed. "Still as beautiful as any princess," he said. I could imagine Anika rolling her eyes.

I bid him goodnight as I trudged toward Anika's room. She would be upset with me for taking so long and wasting some of her candle that she would have kept burning for me.

Unsure if I was allowed to walk in freely, I knocked on her door. Anika answered a moment later with her hair down and lips drawn back. "I know I took a while, I'm sorry," I began. She shook her head.

"You have a visitor."

She pushed the door wide to show where Rumpel stood beside her bed.

Chapter Twenty-One

MY MOUTH DROPPED OPEN as all desires for sleep flew from my mind. Rumpel stood in a grey tunic with his hands by his side, clearly pleased by my confusion. His hair was straighter than usual, and he was wearing shoes. I could count the times I had seen him in shoes on one hand.

My eyes darted to Anika to see her expression. She squeezed in behind me and pushed me into the room.

"You have one minute, then I'm coming back to go to bed," she ordered. She pulled the door between us, leaving me alone in the room with Rumpel.

I'd lost the ability to form words.

"Your sister has spirit. I thought she was going to kill me when she found me in here," Rumpel said with a laugh.

I could picture Anika threatening him. It spoke to our differences. The first time I met Rumpel, I had been unable to move. She had tried to beat him. I wished I knew where she got her strength from.

"What are you doing here?" I asked. The shock washed out of me as I dropped the clothes I carried to the floor.

"I wanted to keep an eye on Conrad," Rumpel said innocently.

I wagged my finger at him. "You were spying again. We talked about this!"

Rumpel shook his head and held up his hands defensively. "I promise, it's Conrad I'm spying on."

"It's still spying, even if it's for a good cause." I paused. "Do you think he'd try to take some of the boys from the village?"

Rumpel shrugged. "Honestly? No. Your gold is helping bring an end to the fighting. It's amazing the problems that a heap of money can fix. But I wouldn't put it past him."

I shuddered as I thought of all the youth that he could take. Lonely Bonnie's son, or the Van Derson boys. I shook the images from my head. "I'll be with him all day. He won't have the chance."

"Can't say I like that, you being with him all day."

I raised my eyebrow. "Can't say I like him taking any of the boys from the village, so unless you're going to guard him all day—"

"No, I don't want him to see me. I can't stand that man."

"He's quite charming, if you can get past the kidnapping."

"So you believe me about that?" Rumpel looked hopeful.

I bit my lip. "I trust you more than I trust him. But I'd like proof before making my final decision."

Rumpel nodded slowly. "Just be careful."

How many times had I heard him say that to me? I folded my arms. "I don't need you to watch out for me. I can handle myself."

"And I don't need you to help break my curse, but you insist on being a part of that."

I gawked. "Because without help you'd fade to nothing!"

"Without my help, you'd be dead right now!"

I didn't feel fierce, yelling at Rumpel in my old nightgown, so I put my fists on my waist for extra effect. He didn't look threatened. I needed Anika's fire, she always scared people. As if summoned, the door opened behind me opened and Anika slipped in, no doubt drawn in by the yelling.

"His Highness is trying to get beauty sleep in the next room, and I really don't want to have to explain another angry man in my bedroom to my parents," Anika said.

Another?

Rumpel put up his hands. "I'm sorry. Your sister can be frustrating sometimes."

"Funny, she's always acquiescent with us."

"I find that hard to imagine. She yelled at me within a week of knowing her," Rumpel told her. He cleared his throat and stood up straighter. "I'll leave you ladies to the rest of your night."

He bowed to Anika then walked toward the door. Before passing me, he bent his head down to whisper, "Aiden would be a fool to let you go so easily."

Unexpectedly, tears sprang to my eyes. I wanted to be mad that he had spied on such an intimate conversation, but his comment was kind enough to ease my anger.

"Thank you," I breathed.

He smiled gently before leaving the room, closing the door behind him. I knew he would vanish into the air as soon as he was out of Anika's sight.

Anika. I turned to see her expression. She was already climbing into bed, unfazed.

"So, he's the one who's helping you," she guessed. "He's handsome."

I laughed as I slid into the bed next to her. "He's almost a hundred years older than you."

She didn't look bothered. "Wise and handsome then."

I laughed again. "And stubborn."

Anika lay on her pillow with her arm propped under her head, looking at me. "Do you like him?"

I sighed as I lay next to her on the tiny bed. Anika and I had never talked about this stuff before. I knew several of her friends were interested in guys, and I had always guessed that she might be too, but it was never something we discussed. I guess I figured she wasn't the type to be serious about it, and before Aiden, I had never had anything to talk about.

I pretended to think about it, but there was nothing to mull over. Rumpel was cursed, and in a few months, he would be gone. Being interested in him wasn't an option.

"I'm grateful to him, for everything he's doing for me. And he's easy to talk to."

"And yell at," Anika added.

I giggled. "Yes. That, too. But I don't think I have feelings for him."

"Because of lingering feelings for Aiden?" Anika asked, surprising me. I hadn't told anyone that Aiden and I were through, and I had assumed that since he planned to win me back, he hadn't announced our end to anyone. Anika saw more than I realized she did. At the thought of Aiden, I sighed again. He was a complicated topic. I didn't know where we stood, or where I wanted us to stand.

"Aiden was always the practical path. There's just so much that I don't know now."

"And Conrad, is that really nothing?"

I flopped down in the pillow and buried my face inside. "When did I get so many options?"

Anika laughed. "When you became the King's most important tool in the war, as Conrad so generously put it."

I came up for air with a grunt. "Things certainly have taken an interesting turn, haven't they?"

"Very. Did you know that we were offered a title? Nothing grand, but Lord and Lady."

I perked up. It seemed the King had made good on his word. "But doesn't that come with land and a stipend?"

Anika nodded eagerly. "It does! Mama and Papa don't want it, partly because it lies so close to the Vernes border, but also because they didn't want to give up their tavern here. They gave the rights to me, and I can take charge of it in a few years."

"I don't understand how all of that works," I confessed.

She took a deep breath. "Well, I don't fully understand either, but the land and the manor would be ours. I'll figure out the rest as I go. I'd need help at first, until I learned how to manage a house. It's not a large manor but compared to this it's massive."

"You're leaving the tavern, then?"

Anika looked giddy. "Not right now. But in a few years, when I'm older, I'm going to take charge of the manor and the land. Papa has already agreed to it. It's in the hand of a steward now, waiting for me. You can come too, it's equally yours."

I remembered Rumpel's offer to take me away when his months were up. I had been debating his offer more and more as time went on and I saw little escape from the King. I doubted I would be welcome at the castle without my ability to create gold. Would I come back home, take up my old life?

A life with Anika running a manor didn't sound bad, and I was tempted to take her up on it. In the end I settled with "we'll see," and let her go on telling me all she knew about the home. It was refreshing, to see her so happy about something. She had always worried me, acting distant and uninterested in our life here at the tavern. While I knew it would break my parents' hearts to have her so far away, it would be good for her heart to be free.

Would my heart break when it was time to leave? Or would it be chained here forever? Right now, I was still so focused on navigating the palace and keeping away from the King that I hadn't had time to figure out what I would do when Rumpel's curse timed out, and though it may have been as foolish as it was futile, I still hoped I could save him somehow.

My childhood worries felt so trivial to me now when compared to the stress of the past few months.

I went to sleep with Anika curled up by my side and dreamed of curses and manors and magic that couldn't be tamed. Several hours before usual, I woke up. I wanted to stay in bed, but I pulled myself out and got dressed. Today, I was going to find some answers.

Chapter Twenty-Two

THE BOOKSTORE'S DOOR WAS unlocked as always, and the air smelled like dandelion tea. A new rug sat beneath the bookshelves. The fire was going, helping light the room as much as the morning sun.

Old Mr. Walters sat in his chair with a pipe, rocking back and forth gently. He had a teapot and cup sitting on the small table next to his chair, and his feet were propped up to soak in heat from the fire. At the sight of me, he almost dropped his pipe.

I intended to come out before the town woke up, and before the stories of me returning with the prince could circulate. I knew that Old Mr. Walters would be awake, though; he always woke before the sun. *Only a lazy man lets a thing as slow as the sun beat him to the day*, he always told me.

What was left of his hair had been cut recently, and his jacket seemed to have new buttons. His late wife had always stitched his clothes before, and I wondered who was taking care of him.

He started to rise and greet me, but I motioned for him to stay seated. I carried myself to his chair and sat on the floor beside him.

"I'm looking for a book on old magic, particularly curses."

"Got yourself in a bit of trouble, eh?" he asked. I grinned. Old Mr. Walters was a bit of a strange man, and not many folks stopped by to talk to him. He had always been a dear friend to me, however, as we shared a similar spirit. He owned the largest collection of books in the town and was always quick to share them with me.

I slid a few coins out of my pocket, grateful that I remembered to grab them that morning. "Any information you can find. It's important."

He got up slowly. "Are you looking to cast a curse, or break a curse? Because those are two very different books."

I laughed at the glint in his eyes. "Break one. A very old one."

He nodded as if he knew just what I was talking about. He moved around me and toward his books. "The old king from that castle of yours?"

My head whipped around to him as my mouth dropped open. "How did you know?"

Now it was his turn to laugh. "Many from my time spoke about his curse. When I was a lad, the young king was going crazy trying to break his curse. I never knew what became of him, but I figured he settled down in the castle to wait out his punishment."

I had so many questions for him, but the most important one came out first. "Do you know how to break it?"

He moved away from his books and disappeared into his room without another word. Confused, I waited for a few moments as I heard his shuffle around. A while later he reappeared with a book in his shaky hands. "I know how to break some curses, but I'm not sure about his. That was strong magic that caught him. Still, you might try a few tricks in here. True love's kiss might work."

I tilted my head and wondered if Rumpel tried that. His wife was already dead before he was cursed, and I doubted he had fallen in love since then. I shook my head as I reached out to help him back to his seat. "I don't think that will work on him."

Old Mr. Walters nodded. "Closed off his heart, has he? Well, there's not much that can be done for him then. My guess is he needs to find a way to make his sins right again."

I furrowed my brow as I took the book in my hands. The sun was higher now and shed more light on the cover. It was a beautiful book, deep green with painted ivy running down both sides. There was a ring in the middle of the page, with sparks flying from it as if it was on fire. I tucked it under my arm as I looked over Old Mr. Walters.

"What sins are you talking about?"

He clicked his tongue and his back cracked as he leaned forward off his chair. "You're making me move a lot this morning," he complained with a smile. He shifted his feet over to the bookshelf where he spent a few minutes looking through his supply. Finally, he clicked his tongue again and pulled a short book out.

He held it up for me to see. "This book will tell you the things he didn't."

Confusion washed over me as I reached to help him back again to his seat. He patted the book lovingly. "This was one of my favorite bedtime reads when I was a younger man. It'll give you some answers."

My curiosity was itching but I held myself in check until he was ready to pass up the book. Even then, I tried not to appear too hasty as I clutched both books to my chest.

"Knowing that sorceress, breaking the curse is going to involve more creativity than strength."

My head snapped up and the books that I clung to and I almost fell to the floor. "You know the sorceress?"

He grinned at my surprise, rocking his frail body back and forth in the chair with delight. "Oh yes. Yes, yes, yes. I know her. Knew her quite well, once upon a time." A wink. My eyebrow raised. "But it's been many years. So many years."

"Mr. Walters?" I crouched down next to him, balancing the books on my knees and cupping his hand in mine. "Do you really know the sorceress?"

I couldn't trust his frail mind, but something in the way he nodded at me convinced me that he did. My next question was the most important. "Can you contact her?"

Another nod.

"Would you be willing to send her a note for me?"

One more nod. I dropped my books and wildly searched for a pen and paper. I brought them to him and told him what to write. It took him a while to pen the words with his shaky hand, so I kept it short. When he was finished, I folded it up. I bent my head bent low again and adopted a serious tone. "Please get this to her. Please."

I patted his hands and he nodded back as if that was clear. I studied him for a few moments more, trying to find the truth in his soft eyes. I wasn't sure if he was crazy, or if I was crazy for believing him, but I released my grip on his hand and stepped back, thanking him repeatedly.

I stayed for a cup of tea until the sun reached a point where I needed to go home. I'd left Conrad alone with my family for long enough. Hopefully, my trip would prove a success. Even if he didn't know the sorceress, perhaps a clue hid in these books.

Wishing I brought a bag to hide my books, I hurried back home and counted down the moments until I could slip away and read the secrets hidden in their pages.

Conrad was sitting with his ankles crossed on my papa's favorite barstool, his head thrown back in laughter. Beside him was Anika, her smile matching his own. I froze for a second, hardly believing my eyes. Very few people could make Anika laugh.

My shadow lingered at the window. Conrad's wild red curls were out of control and he wore what looked to be one of Papa's shirts, with his dress pants rolled up. If I hadn't known he was the prince, I would have mistaken him for any common village boy.

If the people didn't know he came into town last night, they would think he was a visiting cousin. Surely the news had reached the curious ears of the village gossips by now and would be spreading quickly to the barn boys and kitchen girls. The chatter would grow, and it would take a few months to fade away. Around the time that Rumpel's curse was finalized, the people would lose interest in the prince's visit.

As far as I knew, Conrad had never visited our village before. Perhaps that was for the best, if he truly did lure boys into the army. But the boy I saw now didn't look like the kind who would hurt a soul. If it weren't for Rumpel, I would have trusted Conrad with my life.

I clutched my books to my side, hiding their covers. My hand pushed the door open and I feigned surprise at seeing my family up.

"Went to visit some friends this morning, sorry I took so long getting back!" I closed the door behind me and smiled widely at Conrad and Anika. Mama came around from the kitchen with two plates in her hands.

"I didn't know you were close to anyone, honey," Mama said as she put the food before Conrad and Anika.

Anika chuckled. "Just anyone over seventy."

Conrad hopped up to get another stool and brought it next to his own. "Not a problem, I was just getting to know your family a little better," he said graciously.

Apologizing again, I promised to be right out. I practically ran back to Anika's room and stashed the books under the bed before returning to regulate the conversation. Despite my indifference to Conrad's potential feelings, I didn't need Anika telling embarrassing stories about me.

We gobbled up breakfast before taking off to the village square. We would be out in the heat of the day, but I doubted it would hold the people back in their homes. Everyone would want to come outside to see their beloved prince.

No one would be coming to see me. Most people still didn't know who I was. For those who did know me, it was as the girl with no Gift. That was about to change. Suddenly, I would be the girl with the prince. The girl from the castle. The girl who spins straw into gold.

I had been uncomfortable meeting the King, and that feeling never fully went away. But this was different. This was my home.

These were my neighbors. These were folks who I would come back home to live with, and who would continue to have an opinion about me for the rest of my life.

For me, this was bigger than meeting the King.

Unaware of the butterflies in my stomach, Conrad held out his hand to me and walked with me to the village square, to all the eyes that waited.

Chapter Twenty-Three

GUARDS STOOD AT STRATEGIC spots around the square. One was in front of the shoemaker, one the toymaker, and another by the baker. Lolly was standing there talking sweetly to the guard.

I had been right; the heat of the day didn't stop anyone from coming out. If they hadn't heard the news last night, they knew soon enough. I spotted boys running by on my way home from Old Mr. Walter's, shouting out that Prince Conrad was in town. They would have reached the outer farms by now. Never before had the whole town gathered for such an occasion.

I recognized half of the people, even if I couldn't put names to them. Most folks stopped by our tavern from time to time, so we had a way about knowing everyone. What I didn't recognize were their clothes. It seemed everyone donned their finest for the occasion. There was no need to wear fancy clothes to the tavern, so I'd never seen the village like this before.

My feet faltered as I took it all in.

Hair was braided, collars turned, and shoes polished, all to impress their prince. As soon as we got close enough to be spotted, a cheer started, and it lasted until we reached the center. A few guards came quickly to escort the prince. Uncertain, Anika and I stepped back and watched as they walked forward into the mass of people.

"Is it always this bad?" Anika asked. She crossed her arms and turned up her nose as she inspected the scene. People reached forward, crowding Conrad and the frantic guards. The prince simply laughed and picked up a child.

I wasn't used to seeing the people like this, but I also wasn't used to seeing this side of Conrad.

Back at Westnut Castle, Conrad was respected but known. We were used to seeing him every day, and he went out of his way to greet everyone, even the gardener and cooks. They knew him, they loved him, but they didn't scream his name when he walked by.

I searched for the word. *Adored.* I had never seen Conrad so adored.

"Aiden's coming," Anika warned me. My eyes darted to where she nodded. Aiden was perhaps the only one not fawning over

Conrad. He turned his shoulders and weaved through the crowd to reach me. Anika slipped away before I could thank her.

I took a deep breath as I prepared for this conversation. I had given too much thought to Rumpel's curse this morning and not enough to what I would say to Aiden.

He stopped several paces away. "Are you ready to talk now?"

Jumping right in, I see.

I nodded, and Aiden motioned his head around the bend. I followed him behind the shoemaker's shop to a quieter, shaded place. Aiden leaned against the shop in the shade of the tree and sighed, looking at me with gentle eyes. I'd missed those eyes.

"I've missed you," he said.

"I've missed you too," I told him, though I was sure we meant it in different ways. Aiden pushed off the building and wrapped his arms around me as I breathed in the comfort of his touch.

It had always been easy, with his arms around me, to ignore the rest of the world. I blocked out the cheers of the people as I stood in his warmth. My arms tightened around him and he did the same. It was a security I hadn't felt in months. But I pulled back from his embrace, not wanting to give him the wrong impression.

"Marry me," he breathed.

I gulped. It was too late. "Aiden, I can't." My feet shuffled back and my chest tightened.

He moved forward to close the space between us again. "We love each other, that's all there is to it."

My head dropped into my hands. "I can't keep breaking your heart."

"Then don't!" His hands flew to the side of his head before he ran them through his hair. "I've been playing your words through my head since I proposed, how you told me you wanted more, and I was mad—*so mad.* I was angry with you for wasting my time when you didn't want me, and for choosing the night I was going to ask for your hand to tell me you didn't want to marry me. I was mad at you for not loving me as much as I loved you. But seeing you yesterday, I don't feel mad anymore, because I realized none of that matters. That's all part of our story, and it's going to make us stronger. The only thing that matters is that we love each other." Aiden's eyes were searching mine, looking for a glimmer of hope.

For so long I'd struggled with this concept of love, and how I could love Aiden but not want to marry him. Now, the answer seemed clear. The love I had for him was reserved for a best friend, or a brother. It wasn't the love of a husband and wife.

"Don't you want more? Don't you want someone who loves you with all the breath in their chest? Someone who puts you first above all else, who would do anything for you, who would give up everything to be with you? We would be happy together, but we would never have that passion."

As I spoke of love, a name came to my mind, tugging on my heart and causing me to stutter for a moment. Overwhelmed by the sudden feeling, I pushed the name down as I focused on the glint in Aiden's eye.

"That's the way I love you." His words were soft and etched in pain. I closed my eyes to shield myself from the hurt I caused. When Aiden spoke again, his voice was choked. "It's all those books you read that paint an unreasonable expectation for love. Nothing you find is going to live up to that. I can't promise to be waiting around when you change your mind."

The cheers of the villagers sounded like mockery to my ears, and I tried to block out the noise. Aiden shifted back against the building with his lips turned down.

I took a shaky breath. "I don't want you to wait for me."

His eyes narrowed as he cocked his head toward the main square. "Is it him?"

Unsure of what he meant as first, I looked toward the people. "Conrad?" I thrust a finger around the shop. "You think this is about him?"

"C'mon Cosette, why else would he come back here with you? I don't understand why he'd pick a village girl, but I know I can't compete with a rich prince."

Suddenly my heart hurt from a new angle, and I took a step back. "A simple village girl? There's nothing I'd have to offer a prince?"

Aiden raised his eyebrows at me. "Really, Cosette? What could you offer the heir to Westfallen?"

My mouth gaped open. True or not, it wasn't a polite thing to say. "I have plenty to offer. And besides that, do you think that I'm shallow enough to want him simply because he's a prince?"

"I never said that."

"You did! You said you couldn't compete with a *rich* prince, as if that's the only thing that matters to me."

"If it's not him, then there's someone else. You'd have no other reason to say no to your only marriage prospect."

His words felt like a knife cutting into me. I didn't need his help remembering that I had no other options. "I won't be guilted into a marriage."

"No, but it looks like you can be bought into one. Whatever the prince is offering you, he only wants you for your gold, which isn't real anyway. No one will ever love you again the way that I loved you."

I held back tears, turning my head so they wouldn't be spotted. "I want you to leave."

"Cosette," Aiden said as he reached for me. "Please think about this."

I couldn't raise my head to look at him, the boy who used to be my best friend and my safe place in this village. Aiden was everything to me, and I never imagined his words could hurt me in such a way; but now rejected, his frustration lashed out and stung my heart, leaving me short for breath. Confusion swirled within me, along with anger, and desperation for something that made sense. In a way, it was only fair. I left him with difficult words when we last spoke, and now it was his turn to hurt me.

"Please. I need a minute by myself." My voice came out as a whimper, and I willed myself to be stronger. Aiden waited a moment before giving up and leaving me alone.

Still keeping my tears at bay, I jogged further away, under the cover of trees so I wouldn't be bothered. A few slipped from my eyes and rolled down my cheeks, and I sniffed as I hugged my chest. Out of sight at last, I pressed my back to a tree. Something like a snort came out of my mouth and I couldn't hold the tears back anymore, so I let out a pitiful sob.

Once started, the tears flowed freely, releasing the emotions that built up inside.

Though I tried to forget them, Aiden's words pushed themselves into my mind and coursed through my thoughts. No one will ever love you like I loved you. You're making a mistake. The prince could never want someone like you.

I knew these things weren't necessarily true, but that didn't lessen the sharp pain that gripped my heart. An added disappointment came when I realized that the conversation likely took our friendship away, and that was something that I would miss terribly.

Frustration and emotional exhaustion fueled my tears and I couldn't control them. Out of nothing, Rumpel appeared and wrapped his arms around me. I should have known he would follow us, but I couldn't be mad at him. I leaned into him as my body shook with sadness. He held me tight, stroking my hair as I soaked his shoulder with tears. He didn't say anything but let me cry in peace. Every few moments he would stroke my shoulders or my back; otherwise he stood still and strong as he held me.

All the while, I continued to cry. I felt foolish for doing so, having recognized for myself that my feelings for Aiden were not strong. But it still hurt to hear his words, and it hurt to lose him. My body ached with the stress of the past few months. I longed to be free of the King's reach, to be back at home. I longed to understand Conrad, instead of analyzing his intentions every time I saw him. I longed to free Rumpel from his curse. I longed to know my place in this world, and I longed to understand my feelings.

My mind was racing as fast as my heart was beating, but finally the tears slowed. My breaths still came in gulps, but I gained control of my shaking.

Rumpel kept his arms around me until my fit stopped. I once thought that Aiden's felt safe, but I was wrong. Being here, held by Rumpel, this was what safety felt like.

He stepped back and looked me in the eye, speaking gently. "You deserve the world."

With those words, my last tear fell. Rumpel wiped it from my cheek before he vanished again. I didn't even get a chance to thank him.

After a while, I rejoined the town, keeping my distance as everyone admired Conrad. His guards had organized a food cart for the people and were busy passing out loaves of bread and fruit and vegetables. Conrad rolled up his sleeves as he helped distribute the food, talking amicably to those around him. When he spotted me, he waved his whole arm, beckoning me to his side. I joined him in passing out food and watched as he continued to charm the villagers.

In so many ways, Conrad appeared the perfect leader. I kept observing him, trying to find a hint of the faults lying beneath his appealing exterior. So far, I came up empty. Rumpel's word was the only thing holding me back from putting my faith in Conrad as our next monarch.

Hours went by and the people didn't relent. Eventually, Conrad reached for my hand and put his other hand over his chest. His voice boomed so he could be heard. "I'm so sorry, but we have to get back to the tavern. All are welcome to join us there tonight."

Mama and Papa were going to make a lot of money. I hoped they were ready.

Conrad kept his hand in mine as we weaved back through the crowd, and I saw many eyes on us. My cheeks flushed, and I knew what they were thinking. I would have to talk to Conrad later about not giving the appearance that we were together, but it wasn't the time. I resisted the urge to search the crowd for Aiden to see if he noticed; I didn't need his judgment.

I spent most of the night in my family's company as I helped out at the tavern. It was strange, how much I used to despise working there and how much comfort I found in it that night. It was nice to feel something normal again. Just when the evening was settling down and customers were starting to wander home to their beds, Aiden appeared at the door with his hands deep in his pockets. I shook my head and quickly moved to the front to push him back outside.

"What are you doing here?" I asked quietly. The gathering dark cast shadows across his face.

"I don't want the prince to hurt you." He peeked inside the door, which I then pushed shut.

"I told you, I don't have feelings for him."

Aiden tilted his head. "Maybe not yet, but he's keen on you. You know he just wants the gold. If he knew... he wouldn't want you anymore." Apparently, he hadn't hurt me enough.

"Aiden, you've said enough. You don't even know him."

"I know enough. And if it will keep you safe, I'll tell him that you can't spin gold."

I sucked in my breath. The possibility of Aiden selling me out hadn't crossed my mind, but now that he brought it up, it terrified me. He could cost me everything. I peered through the darkness to see his expression better, and found it was stone cold. "Please don't. It's not Conrad I'm worried about, but his father. He's gone mad. When he finds out I've been lying, there's no telling what he'll do."

Aiden's voice was flat as he gave his ultimatum. "It's for your sake, Cosette. Come home soon, or else I'll tell him myself."

Chapter Twenty-Four

"I DON'T KNOW WHAT he's thinking," Rumpel said as he sat at his wheel. I held straw in my hands, but he wouldn't take it. Instead, he turned around and crossed his ankles, looking at me with a puzzled expression. "I just don't get it. Why is he involving himself in this?"

I sighed. "I can't tell if he's trying to hurt me or help me, but I can only hope he didn't mean it."

"I think he did. I can't say I like this chap," Rumpel said.

"He wasn't always so...manipulative," I said as I twisted the straw in my fingers and tried to give it to him again. "But I've thought about it and how could the King believe him when I produce gold each morning? He'll laugh Aiden off and send him back home, none the wiser."

Rumpel studied me for a moment as he continued to ignore the straw. "That's a calm response for someone whose life potentially hangs in the balance."

A nervous laugh escaped my lips. "You saying things like that doesn't help. But I have enough to worry about as it is; I can't see Aiden following through on the threat. Now will you take this straw? Or else we're going to be here all night!"

"Fine." He finally took the straw. "But I really am sorry about Aiden."

The pain hurt less today. At this point, my heart was mourning the loss of what it once desired. I allowed it to feel the sting; it was good for me to have something else to focus on besides what would happen when the King learned that I couldn't spin gold, which would still probably occur even without Aiden's intervention.

I couldn't understand the King. Papa spoke so well of him when I was younger. He was a charismatic ruler who made friends easily in different countries. I couldn't understand what changed since then that made the people dislike him, or why he was still King. Conrad said that he was changed by the death of his wife, then again by the war, but I think it all drove him mad.

I'd seen my share of drunk men. I didn't even bat an eye at them anymore. There was always a phase between rational and drunk where men could act normal, but their decisions were clouded. One moment they made a perfectly sound choice, and the next they did something ludicrous. That was where the king lived, on the line between realistic and manic. I couldn't bring it up with Conrad, but I feared the King's mind was long gone.

What sort of man threatens to kill a village girl so easily?

"Did you know the King's name is Bellifusa?"

Rumpel snorted as he laughed. "I did, in fact. Bellifusa Alfred. Quite the charming name, I think," he joked.

I giggled. "It is something. I was planning on naming my first kid that. Actually, I really like the name Alfred."

Rumpel chuckled before glancing at my face. "Oh, you're serious! That's an awful name!"

"Alfred? Why? I think it's strong!"

"For a horse, maybe."

I dropped my jaw and pretended to be offended. "What did you name your daughter?"

He grinned. "Posey."

Now I remembered the name from my research, though I couldn't make fun of that. Posey was a delicate name. I glanced at Rumpel, who was smiling as he spun, and dared to ask more about his daughter.

"Do you know what became of her?"

"She married a farm boy, and they had three daughters of their own, and one cute boy. I got to visit them often and saw each of them married." His face was distant as he remembered them.

"Are they still alive?" I asked as I handed him more straw.

"They are, though they are at the end of their lives." He frowned slightly.

I loved having Rumpel here with me, but it didn't feel right that he'd spent the last of his life and his grandchildren's lives with me, when he could have been with them. I said so, then held my breath for his reply.

He turned and gave me a small smile. "I could go see them, but they don't know me well. I'd rather spend my last months here with you." His words brought a hint of warmth to my heart. I was glad that he enjoyed being with me as much as I enjoyed being with him.

The next day Anna was sick, and I insisted on spending the day taking care of her for a change. I fetched her tea and soup and put her in my bed. She complained at first that I was trying to get her fired, but she didn't have enough strength to argue for long. After a little insistence, she crawled into the bed and let me fetch her some handkerchiefs.

I tried to clean the room while she slept, and barely found time to eat. I ended up being late to dinner with Conrad, then rushed to the room where I spun gold with Rumpel.

Rumpel usually began spinning before I came in, but today, the spinning wheel was pulled away from its usual place on the rug and set up closer to the window, which was open to let the late spring air into the room. Rumpel sat against the wall under the window with his feet out and a book nestled on his lap. When he looked up at me, his face was elated. He set his book aside. "I've been thinking. If there's any bit of magic inside you, I could teach you how to do this." He waved his hand toward the spinning wheel.

"I don't understand," I said as I closed the door behind me.

Rumpel's hand stroked his chin for a few moments while his eyes narrowed in thought. "See, I can't figure out why everyone would have a Gift but you, so my best guess is that the magic in you is lying dormant. We might be able to wake it up, and mold it into what we want it to be."

"So, people aren't confined to their Gifts?" I marveled. He stood up and rubbed his hands together.

"Theoretically, no. I don't think. This is all speculation. But I've been reading about it, and I want to find a way to teach you to spin gold for yourself, so you'll survive after I'm gone."

Rumpel's enthusiasm was catching, but he was forgetting an important fact. For a moment, he reminded me of Aiden, so determined to find my Gift as if that was the only way I'd have a place in this world. "I don't have a Gift."

He shook his head. "I don't believe that there's no magic inside you. We just have to find it."

"Let me get this straight. So, while I've been spending my days researching how to break your curse, you haven't been trying at all? Instead, you've been making preparations for when you go?"

"I'm doing it for you. You're welcome."

He did a funny little bow, and I had to laugh. Truthfully, I was grateful for the effort. Words couldn't express how worried I was for what would come in a few months when Rumpel's time was up. Neither of us was certain of what that would look like for him, and I knew I had to have a strategy for what I would do if he disappeared.

I'd still come no closer to breaking his curse.

The books that Old Mr. Walters gave me were stashed under my bed so I could read them the next day. Anticipation gnawed at me, and I couldn't wait to discover what stories would be told. I would have devoured them today, but I had foolishly put Anna to bed in my room, right above where I hid the books, and I didn't want her asking any questions. She was feeling better, and I would have time later. But first, I must get through tonight.

"I don't know how you plan to accomplish this." I held my arms open wide. "But you may try."

He rubbed his hands together like a giddy boy. "Sit, sit." He moved from his seat and patted the wooden plank in front of the wheel. I rolled my eyes at his eagerness, fanning out my skirt as I perched myself on the edge of the seat.

I watched Rumpel do it enough times that I knew the moves, but I humored him as he showed my hands where to start. "Oh, there, really? I thought I held it here." I moved my hand way down to the bottom of the wheel.

"No, you silly girl. Focus." Rumpel smirked as he moved my hand back to the correct position. I straightened my back obediently. "This will go through there, and gold will come out here." He moved his hand to the end of the spindle.

I shook my head. "It's not going to happen."

Rumpel took a step back and put his hands on his waist. "According to my books you need to have a positive attitude in order for this to work."

I laughed. "Really? I think you're making that up. I'd like to see this book."

In a flash, Rumpel was gone. I blinked. A second later he reappeared with a small, blue book riddles with loose pages and layers of dust. He rifled through the pages, pushing it toward my face. "Fine, I'll modify my attitude." I turned my body back toward the spinning wheel.

I'd grown accustomed to sitting behind the wheel when I spun for Seamstress Kira, though it was only for a short while. It had been several months since then, and the feeling was no longer natural to me. I shifted uncomfortably in the seat as I willed positive thoughts into my mind.

Fingers twisted the straw as I eased my foot down on the treadle. The straw approached the bobbin, but its rough exterior got caught and bunched up. I moaned.

"See, that is what is supposed to happen. Straw on its own can't be spun, it must be retted and heckled first. This won't work." I put the straw down and turned to get up from the stool, but Rumpel's hand stopped me.

"You've tried one time and you're giving up?"

"This isn't giving up. This is being smart enough to know that I can't do it."

Rumpel pointed to his book. "Well now we know why it didn't work. Wrong attitude."

I swatted the book from his hand. "That's not the problem."

Rumpel took my hand in his. His eyes held mine as he batted them. "Please? Try?"

I grumbled as I lowered myself back to the seat. I picked back up the straw and tried to twist it harder. I needed the crispy part to break off, leaving me with the soft fibers in the middle. That was the part that could be turned into thread. When Rumpel worked, the straw magically fit through the bobbin and wrapped itself around the spindle. If I couldn't even get the straw through the bobbin, then I had no chance of making thread, much less gold.

Again I tried, but to no avail. Time after time I pushed that straw forward, but not once did it fit. Rumpel came closer and put his hand on my back, leaning his head down and whispering encouragement to me as I tried. I was sure he was trying to help me achieve my goal, but all he managed to do was distract me.

Finally, I gave up. "If one of us doesn't spin gold, we are going to be in a lot of trouble in the morning."

"Ah." Another motion toward his book. "The art of desperation. The book mentioned that might be a motivating factor as well."

"Ha! Where did you get this book?"

"Literally the same place we got all the other books."

"That library has given us nothing helpful," I grumbled.

"I don't think your heart is in the right place. Maybe you're still too upset about Aiden," Rumpel suggested.

The sting from Aiden was fading surprisingly fast. I guessed that showed how little I cared for him to begin with. My heart still felt raw, but it wasn't broken.

Rumpel sighed. "I will finish tonight. But I want you to try again tomorrow."

"Alright." I moved off the seat and happily retook my place on the floor next to him. "But don't get your hopes up."

"I believe in you."

His words, though playful, were kind, and it warmed my heart to know that he was there for me. I vowed that as soon as I was released from this room, I would devour those books under my bed. Breaking the curse would mean that I would never need to learn to spin gold.

I must save Rumpel.

It was more than just saving Rumpel. If he left, I would be lost and at the mercy of the King. I needed to break this curse to save myself, too.

Chapter Twenty-Five

HAPPY BIRDS CHIRPED OUTSIDE my open window, singing me their songs while I rested on a mound of pillows and my hand floated by a plate of sweets. I enjoyed being home, but I had missed the sweets more than I thought I would.

My knees snuggled in the blankets and my book lay propped up against them. Today, I would solve Rumpel's curse.

I opened the book slowly, anticipation and hope stirring inside me as I thumbed through the pages and hoped this volume would give me something that none of the others had.

I don't know if I was expecting to see a picture of Rumpel, but I didn't see one as I flipped through the pages. Still hopeful, I nestled into the pillows and started at the very beginning.

Each page told a remedy for one ailment or another. Some were caused by magic, others were as simple as warts: normal and magic ones. Both remedies called for frog skin.

Then, located right after a troll's curse, was a page titled "True Love's Kiss." There was a lovely picture of a couple kissing and sparks flying around them. I read through the page quickly. It seemed that true love's kiss could break powerful curses.

I wondered if it could cure warts too.

Then I wondered if Rumpel tried that. He hadn't told me every single thing he tried, but if he'd considered true love's kiss, I wondered if he left it out of his story on purpose.

But did the object of the curse have to be in love for true love's kiss to work? Or could they kiss the person who was meant to be their true love, and it worked all the same? I doubted I could find a girl for Rumpel to fall in love with in four months. It wouldn't be hard to get the girl to fall in love with him, but he seemed rather put off from romance. He possessed the good looks and the personality, and he was free to go out and chase every girl that came his way, but instead he chose to spend his final months holed up in the back room spinning straw with me. That didn't sound like someone looking for love.

A silly thought flew through my head, but I dismissed it just as quickly.

But maybe...

No. It was crazy. I didn't love Rumpel. He didn't love me. My kiss wouldn't save him.

With Aiden, I had to think about if I was in love, until I'd convinced myself that I was. It wasn't instinct. The next time I was in love I wanted it to be so undeniable that I couldn't breathe. I wanted to know without a doubt that my heart was in it. There would be no questions and no reservations.

I wouldn't sit here and debate if I was in love with Rumpel. If I was, I would know.

Sometimes his smile made my heart flutter. Sometimes I would smile at the thought of him. Sometimes I found myself thinking about him.

Perhaps I liked him. I wasn't afraid to admit that. I liked Rumpel.

But I was afraid to let it go further. Rumpel was cursed, and in four months, who knew what would become of him. Likely, he would be gone, morphed into the power of magic. If we couldn't break his curse, which was a very real possibility, then Rumpel wasn't an option for me.

I didn't love him. But I didn't want to lose him.

For that reason, I made up my mind to kiss him, and hope that it worked anyway.

The book wasn't clear on what would happen when you tried an I-like-him-and-I'm-desperate kiss, but maybe Fate would grant us her graces and allow it to break the curse. At this point, I was willing to try anything.

That night, while Rumpel tried to teach me to spin straw into gold, I got frustrated. It just wasn't happening. There was a lot of yelling involved. I didn't even know how to initiate a kiss, but I figured that wasn't the time for it. I willed myself to be better the next night, or at least not to yell at him. I couldn't promise more.

The third night I set the mood. Anna twisted my hair that morning so by the time evening came it curled. I admired it in the mirror as I let Anna paint rouge on my lips and cheeks. She didn't ask about the new look but simply hummed as she worked. She liked performing beauty rituals, so I justified myself by saying that I did this for her.

The truth was that I was doing this for Rumpel. I still didn't love him, but I'd made up my mind to try true love's kiss, and I wasn't going to do that in my plain clothes.

I had foregone dinner with Conrad to prepare myself for the evening with Rumpel. I headed to the back room earlier than normal, surprised to find that I'd beaten Rumpel there. The straw was already piled up and the spinning wheel sat in its usual place on the rug. My head suddenly felt hot. *Probably nerves.* Fresh air would help me breath, so I pushed the window open and let the breeze calm me.

"You can do this," I whispered to myself. I'd never initiated anything resembling a romantic moment before, but I didn't think it would make me so nervous.

A familiar sound creaked behind me, drawing my attention. My body trembled with anticipation.

He was here.

I slowly turned around. There he was, positioned at the wheel, already spinning his gold. I moved toward him, aware just how unexperienced I was.

A new thought struck me, almost halting my steps. So focused on how to make my move, I hadn't considered his reaction to it. What if he hated the kiss? Or laughed at me? The thought of him mocking me was almost enough to convince me to abandon my plan.

But he wouldn't do that. Rumpel was too kind to mock me for my feelings. If it came to that, I'd tell him it was just to try to break his curse, and he couldn't fault me for that.

Rumpel looked up as I got closer, but his hands didn't stop spinning. "I thought I would start for tonight, give you a chance to watch. Then, when you feel ready, you can try. I'm still determined to teach you."

Another reason why I was determined for this kiss to work, I was tired of failing at spinning gold. I paused in front of Rumpel, tilting my head to the side. My most charming smile fluttered across my face. "I wanted to thank you for helping me, and I don't just mean trying to teach me. I mean all of it. Thank you for standing by me, even when you didn't have to."

"Well," he said with a smirk. "It's good to see you're in a better mood than yesterday."

"I'm serious. Thank you." My breath was shaky and shallow, and my throat felt tight. "I can't express how much it has meant to me. With words, that is."

There was the line I practiced over and over in the mirror, one that I'd read from a book once. I lowered myself to his lap, still holding most of my weight on my own legs. Rumpel stopped spinning at last and looked at me, clearly bewildered.

Before I could talk myself out of it, I slid my hand around his neck and kissed him.

Rumpel's lips froze for a second before relaxing and pressing into mine, and his hands moved to my back, holding me still. Every part of me tensed, afraid to move and break the moment. His hair tickled my fingers, and I resisted the urge to run my hand through it.

Too soon he pulled back, but kept his head bent close while his eyes searched mine. When he spoke, his breath warmed my face. "What was that for?"

I hadn't thought that far ahead. I stammered, "I thought that true love's kiss might break your curse. It was a long shot."

Rumpel broke into a loud laugh that made me jump up from his lap. "You thought you were my true love?"

My face flushed. He was going to mock me after all. "No, but I thought it was worth a try anyway."

Rumpel nodded slowly and I wished I could read his thoughts. My mind was already replaying that kiss, searching for a clue as to how he felt. He kissed me back, I knew that. What I didn't know was if it worked.

"How would you know if your curse was broken?"

"I think I'd just know."

"Oh. So this didn't...?"

"Work? No, I don't think so."

I rocked back on my heels, embarrassed. Why did I think this was a good idea? I desperately wished that I could take it back. The flutter in my heart told me I was starting to feel something for Rumpel and kissing him only opened myself up to rejection.

Rumpel brushed his curls back toward his ears and sighed deeply as he stood up. His light brown eyes were steady as they watched me. "Listen, I need to be clear about something. I know you just kissed me to try to break the curse, but I do have legitimate feelings for you."

Oh. Of all the ways I considered the aftermath of my stunt playing out, I hadn't expected that confession from him.

"But," he went on. "I don't plan to do anything about it."

Just as soon as my hopes got up, they went down again. Rumpel was using his hands as he talked, rolling them over so his palms faced the wide wooden beams lining the ceiling.

"It's not that the kiss wasn't nice, but I don't want you to get hurt. I can't promise that I can finish anything that we start." He touched his forehead to mine, and my heart fluttered. My feelings for him were new, but was it possible that he felt this way for a while?

An unexpected warmth swirled around inside me at that thought. "I know you can't promise me anything. I don't need anything. I just want you to be okay."

He sighed as if breathing me in, closing his eyes closed and keeping his forehead against mine. I savored the moment. His touch, his breathing, the flutter of his eyelids: I didn't want to forget this feeling.

If Rumpel never broke his curse, if in ten years he was only a distant memory to me, I wanted to hold on to this feeling.

"I'm sorry the kiss didn't work. But thank you for making me feel alive again," Rumpel whispered to me. Then he pulled away and sat back down at the spinning wheel, turning the straw over in his hand. My feet stayed still for a few moments more before I moved to help.

I wasn't in love with Rumpel. But I could no longer deny the effect he had on my heart. I had to pull it back before it broke.

Chapter Twenty-Six

"YOU ARE A LIAR!" I stormed into the room and threw the book at Rumpel. It slid toward his feet. He picked it up in surprise, blocking himself from any further attack. "You deceived me! You lied!"

I dug my nails into my hands as tears streamed down my face. The sight of Rumpel made my heart ache. I was so happy the day before. So naïvely happy. Now my blood rushed with fury. There were only a few times in my life when I had been this mad. Once, Anika had lost my favorite book. It had taken weeks to forgive her for that. Another time, my friend told one of my secrets to another friend, who let the word spread. I had been so upset that our friendship never recovered.

This anger surpassed both of those instances combined.

I would let Rumpel go through the book, find out on his own what I was talking about. With his eyebrows scrunched together he examined its cover, but I urged him to open it and he did, flipping through the pages.

It was the second one that Old Mr. Walters gave me. It told me the story, the whole story, of how Rumpel was cursed. Rumpel told me only part of the tale, about how after he saved Clarissa from the Black Sickness, a band of men came and killed her in hopes of setting the balances of life straight.

Then he had been cursed, and I hadn't fully understood why. But I did after reading that book. Rumpel hadn't told me everything.

The disappointment on Rumpel's face indicated that he identified the source of my anger.

"Let me explain." He put the book down and tried to approach me, but I backed away from him.

"I don't need an explanation. I already understand *why* you did it. But it wasn't justified. It was cruel and heartless." I spat the words at him. Heat rushed to my head and fueled my fury.

Rumpel's eyes were wild and he ran his hands through his hair. "Please calm down, it was a long time ago. I've changed." He stumbled toward me and this time I let him. I wanted him to clearly see the rage in my eyes.

"You know," my voice was raspy. "I never understood why you were cursed. It didn't make sense. But now? Now I get it. Now I know you deserved your punishment."

"They killed my wife!" Rumpel yelled. I choked out a humorless laugh.

"So you killed them, and their entire families? Children? You killed them all! You got drunk on your power and your grief and you murdered innocent people!"

The pain in Rumpel's face was evident, but I was too angry to let it sway me. He hid this from me. According to the book, after his wife was murdered, Rumpel chased the killers back to their village in a fit of rage. His power overcame him and he killed everyone who lived there. A whole town wiped out because he couldn't control his anger.

They killed his wife, and that was terrible. But they were right that without magic, Clarissa should have died. And those children? They shouldn't have died. Rumpel killed a hundred people who deserved to live.

"Cosette, please understand. Clarissa was my life. Without her I was lost and confused and angry. My powers were so new to me, and I couldn't control them. I did not consciously kill those people. It was a mistake, one that I have had to live with like an anchor on my soul ever since."

I shook my head at him. "You don't get to explain yourself now. If you would have told me this on your own, then I could have listened and understood. But you lied. You hid this from me. You can't expect me to pity you now."

"How was I supposed to tell you that? I can hardly live with myself because of it. I didn't want you to see me the way that I see myself."

His words sounded pitiful and dripped with desperation, and I saw tears in his eyes that matched my own, along with a quiver of his lip. I kissed those lips yesterday. I shuddered as I pushed the image from my mind, replacing it with my anger.

"That's why you aren't fighting hard to break your curse? You think you deserve to die?"

Rumpel nodded slowly.

"You're right," I said. Regret filled me as soon as I said that, but I didn't let him see that. He sucked in a sharp breath and closed his eyes. A tear slid down my face, but I wiped it away. My voice shook when I continued. "There's something else I never understood. I want to know the truth. Why did you start helping me? It never made sense why you would do it when it gave you nothing."

Rumpel opened his eyes again and I could see the sadness residing deep within them. "I thought it would break my curse. The King would have killed you. Because of me, he didn't. I thought saving your life would make up for the ones I took."

I pursed my lips and looked away, crippled by his deceit and my inability to see it sooner. Rumpel lied to me the whole time.

He wasn't selflessly saving me; he was always trying to save himself.

My body shuddered, and I turned to leave, but before I got to the door, I spoke over my shoulder. "How can I believe you now? How can I believe the stories you told me about Conrad when you haven't been honest with me?"

"Why would I burden you with the dark secrets of my past? I wanted to keep the shameful parts hidden."

My head turned further so I could shoot him one more angry look. "You should have let me in."

"Where are you going?"

"Back to my room. You can spin gold, or not. I don't care anymore." Slamming the door would have been too childish. Instead I held my head high and floated quietly from the room.

Chapter Twenty-Seven

ANNA WAS SURPRISED TO see me awake in bed when she came by in the morning. I didn't have the strength to tell her that I spent the night there, drowning in my tears. I was so angry at Rumpel for lying to me, angry with him for killing all of those people a hundred years ago, and angry at myself for developing feelings for him in the first place. On top of that, I'd cried for the innocents that died at Rumpel's hand.

Rumpel was my stronghold here in the castle, where I didn't belong. He was my light in a place shadowed with confusion. He was my breath of fresh air. Now that was tainted, my memories of our time together stained with his dishonesty.

How many hours did I spend trying to break his curse? How many times had I gone over ideas with him while he kept the real reason for the curse a secret? Learning the truth in this way was just the wake-up call that my heart needed to pull back and protect itself.

My pillow was stained with my tears, which Anna mercifully ignored as she set my tray of food next to the bed. It was customary for me to sleep in through the morning after being awake all night, so she let me be without question.

I waited to see if the King would come.

Rumpel might not have spun gold for me, after all, I'd been so mad at him that I told him he deserved to *die*. He had no reason to continue helping me. It was only a matter of time before I found out if Rumpel covered for me; the King would come in if he hadn't to demand why the room only held straw this morning.

Every part of me shook with nerves. What would I say to the King if there was no gold? Would he believe me if I told the truth? What would Conrad say?

Nervously, I nibbled at my food before pushing it away. I tried to get myself ready for the day but found myself back in bed, hugging my knees.

The guards might not check on the gold until it was time to refill the room with straw, which could be any time before this evening. My feet swung over the side of the bed, determined to do something with myself, but I ended up simply putting on my day dress and pacing about the room. How long would I have to wait?

Hours passed as I found little ways to preoccupy my mind. Reading books, organizing my clothes, taking a bath. Time inched by as my mind went mad.

The door creaked open slowly as I peeked my head out to see if any guards were coming my way to arrest me. Nothing but sheets of sunlight from the window filled the halls, as well as distant footsteps on marble floors, growing quieter with every pace. Sighing, I pulled my head back in and closed the door.

I remade my perfectly fine bed. I braided my hair then let it out again. I fluffed the pillows and sorted the desk. I settled into the bed and tried to read a book. I had to get my mind off the possibility that Rumpel hadn't spun gold, that my life would end soon. The King's face kept appearing in my mind, red and angry, threatening to kill me.

No. I wouldn't think about that. I focused on reading instead.

Over the top of the book, something caught my eye—a small piece of paper had been slid under my door. I threw the book down and rushed to the door. Flinging myself on the ground, I picked up the paper and read quickly.

Cosette,

I spun the gold. I couldn't bear the thought of anything happening to you. But I would like a chance to redeem myself in your eyes. Come tonight to the back room. You don't need to say anything to me. I will spin gold for you each night as long as you come.

-Rumpel

Relief rushed over me. Rumpel came through. I hated needing him, but it was easier than dealing with the King. The wooden door supported my weight as I leaned against it, debating the request.

There was nothing more to say to him, but I could sit in the room while he spun gold. I could give him that much.

Knowing I wouldn't face an angry king after all, I became quite productive, braiding my hair and finishing my breakfast, then grabbing a shawl and heading out to find Conrad. If I had been wrong about Rumpel, then I could have been wrong about Conrad. He deserved a second chance.

I spent the afternoon with the prince and joined him at dinner. These political dinners became more bearable as I got to know people. Their interest in me had faded, leaving behind mutual respect and light friendship. I no longer needed to stick to Conrad's side all night, as I was able to hold my own in conversations.

The only person who I hadn't found common ground with was the King. We orbited each other, exchanging pleasantries and tense smiles. Our conversation never went deeper than general inquiries or well wishes. From what I saw, he was like that with most people. There were a few with whom he seemed to connect, but more often than not, he could be seen at the edge of the large room among the protective shadows, quietly watching the court in a way that I found unsettling at first. But as days went on in this manner, it appeared to be more social anxiety and quietness that kept him at bay. When he spoke as a king, his voice was filled with power and authority, but in social circumstances he was timid and removed.

It eased my worries to see him as something other than the unyielding king that I'd met that first night. Someone more human who gets nervous around crowds.

He was quite the opposite of his son. Conrad's laugh could be heard from everywhere in the room. His smile was the widest, his voice the loudest, and his hair the brightest. He was filled with charm and energy that pulled everyone to him, making it obvious why the people wanted him to take his place as king.

On this particular night, I was quieter than usual, content with staying in Conrad's shadow. My mind was still on Rumpel and the hurt that I felt after finding out he lied to me. A strange, unsettling mix of feelings coursed through me, both a longing to see him and a desire to never see him again. I ignored them for as long as I could, until it was time to go to the back room. The familiar hallway felt longer to walk this time, each step bringing me closer to an uncertain evening and conflicted heart.

With a shaking hand I opened the door and peered inside. Rumpel, familiar Rumpel, sat at the wheel, spinning gold. In my procrastination I came late, and he'd weaved several spindles full already.

He looked up at me and smiled gently, but I didn't return the gesture.

"Are you going to throw anything at me tonight?" There was a curious amount of humor in his voice.

"I'm unarmed."

"Good." He returned to spinning and I watched for a few moments. It all looked so familiar, the flicker of the lantern light casting unpredictable shadows across his face. The pile of straw over his right shoulder. The fraying rug under his feet. The barred window and old table, sitting next to the bed that Rumpel graciously acquired for me so long ago. It was all so familiar.

Yet, it was all so different.

This had been my favorite part of the day. Being with Rumpel made leaving home worth it. He made me feel okay as I wandered about the castle, holding on to our little secret. He was, quite literally, the reason I survived these past months.

The sight of him now made my heart ache and my mouth run dry. I wanted our friendship back, but I couldn't trust him. I couldn't get the haunting image of him killing those people out of my head.

He only had four months left, but I was afraid it would take me longer than that to forgive him.

Stricken with sadness in his presence, I moved to the stairs. Over our time here, we'd never used the loft, as it was poorly lit and filled with old furniture. It wasn't a comfortable seat, but it was furthest from him. I sat on those stone stairs and watched Rumpel spin, waiting to see if he would say anything. He never did. I eventually moved to the bed, and though I had slept in for much of that morning, I found myself lulled to sleep by the sound of the wheel.

I only briefly woke when Rumpel finished spinning. Before he left, he stopped by the bed and leaned over me.

"I'm sorry," he whispered.

And with that, he was gone.

Chapter Twenty-Eight

MY DAYS OVER THE next two weeks fell into an unusual pattern. I spent the mornings sleeping in, my afternoons with Conrad, and my evenings in stilted silence with Rumpel. I asked that he not check up on me during the day, and as far as I knew he gave me my space. Conrad didn't ask why I was suddenly so free to spend time with him but took my companionship in stride.

The castle hosted a talent show, where citizens from around the kingdom came to showcase their Gifts. I had heard a little about it from the village but hadn't known anyone with a Gift elaborate to be showcased. Conrad and I attended together, marveling at some of the Gifts.

It seemed everyone in the castle, whether uniquely Gifted or not, wanted to show off. As we walked through the hallways the window washer cleaned several windows in unison, the rags moving according to his will. Anna filled the hallways with flowers, while another young lady could snap her fingers and instantly clear the passages again. It was humorous to watch her and Anna together, as they made a game out of their differing Gifts.

The throne room was where the real entertainment was happening. The King sat on his throne looking giddy as visitors performed around him. Tables were set up with the finest sweets I ever tasted, each made by someone's Gift. A man with greying hair was there who could control fire. Another controlled water, and they had a routine together. A few people could fly—*fly*—and they spent their time soaring near the ceiling.

Several translators came, and Conrad got to show off his Gift of language. I clapped for him after each sentence, and he bowed extravagantly with a huge smile plastered to his face.

Never before had I seen Gifts showcased in such a manner. Back home, each person's Gift was used in the most practical way possible. If your Gift wasn't practical, then it wasn't valuable. We didn't treat our Gifts as shows.

We continued on our tour, watching each person's Gift. One person could read minds, though I was too nervous to go near enough to see for sure. I didn't want anyone seeing inside my mind.

"I have to go talk to someone there," Conrad pointed to a tall man standing near the wall in the main room. "Will you be okay for a moment?"

Though curious about what he needed to talk about that I couldn't be around for, I nodded, saying I'd be out in the gardens. Conrad squeezed my hand before strolling away, and I pushed through the crowd to get some air. The fire shows were staining the air with smoke.

An open invitation was issued for the festival, and though I never heard of it until this year, it seemed popular with others. It was a strange feeling, walking around among villagers who were visiting, giving them directions in a castle as if it was my home, and all the while feeling like I didn't fit in with either world. I was so eager for my time here to come to an end and to return to normalcy.

A small part of my head reminded me that my time ending here would mean my evenings with Rumpel were over, but I pushed aside the emotions that came with that.

The gardens offered more space to walk without bumping against other guests, and I soaked in the fresh air. It didn't take long to find a bench near the front doors to relax on, close enough that Conrad could find me when he finished his conversation inside.

No sooner had I closed my eyes for a moment of peace than a hand appeared on my elbow. My eyes opened quickly, and I gasped. "What are you doing here?" I asked sharply.

Aiden sat next to me, dressed up in his nice clothes with his face washed and hair trimmed. He wore a frown on his face as he looked me over.

"You fit in with everyone else." There was something in his voice I didn't recognize, and I struggled to name it. Sadness.

"Aiden, what are you doing?" I blinked twice and looked toward the door, expecting Conrad to come out any moment and recognize Aiden from the Riverfront Tavern.

"I'm worried about you here; I don't trust the prince." Aiden's eyes shifted to all the people in the garden as he scooted closer to me and lowered his voice. "Don't you think it's time you came home, back to reality?"

I put my palm against my forehead. "That's not your decision to make."

"I know we left things badly, but I want to help you come home. I know you've never been good with confrontation, but the King needed to know the truth if he was ever going to release you."

My breath caught in my throat and my head felt dizzy. When I spoke, it was barely a squeak. "You didn't..."

He shrugged, unaware of the problem he was creating. "He didn't believe me, so it was a waste of a trip."

I felt like yelling at him, but I could hardly get the words out. His betrayal stabbed me in the stomach. "I can take care of myself!" My eyes shifted to the door to see if Conrad was coming yet. I needed to get Aiden out of here fast and talk to Conrad before his father did. If he was going to hear anything, I needed it to be from me. The King was unstable, and I couldn't guess what his reaction to my deception would be. Conrad's loyalty to me remained my best bet.

Aiden was defending himself, but I wouldn't listen. I put up my hands as I stood up. "I want you to leave, now." He stood up as well and opened his mouth but I stepped back. "I mean it. You have no idea what you just did." I shook my head, my thoughts running frantically through my mind. I took another few steps back. "Please, leave."

I didn't wait for him to leave. Instead I turned and walked away from him. I needed to find Conrad.

He was about to walk outside when I found him and steered him back. "Conrad, there's something we need to talk about."

"Okay, what's wrong?"

"Can we go—?"

Before I could lead him to a quieter place, the King's voice boomed from his throne.

"Ladies and gentlemen!" The King stood up in the front of the room as he called for our attention. I tried to get Conrad to follow me, but he held my hand steady as he looked toward his father. It took several minutes for the King to get everyone's full attention, but the one who could control fire cast a flame around the room, drawing all of our focus in. He bowed to the King then folded his hands.

My breathing was fast as I waited to hear the King's words. All I could think of was Aiden betraying me to that man.

"Thank you. Now, I am so glad you have all made it for the celebration of Gifts. The Gifts are the one thing that have distinguished us from the kingdoms around us for years. They make us stronger, bind us closer together. They have also given us an edge in the war." At the mention of the war, the people seemed to shrink as if the topic cast a heavy cloak on the room. The King shook his head. "I have good news! We have met with representatives from Vernes and Osmelee, and the end of the war is coming!"

The room erupted in cheers, and I remembered our agreement; I was only obligated to stay here until the end of the war. If that came before Rumpel's curse was up, then I could return home easily. If I was lucky, the King didn't believe Aiden and would never learn the truth.

The King beamed as the cheers continued. After a while they died down and he spoke again. "It seems fitting that while we are here celebrating Gifts, that we acknowledge the one whose Gift has made it possible to end this war."

A sickening feeling slunk to my stomach.

The King continued. "She came to us a few months ago, offering her talent. She has been working night after night to provide us with the means to buy off our enemies."

No. No.

The King motioned, and from behind him came two men with a spinning wheel. They set it down beside him on the platform. Two more men came forward with a box of straw.

No.

"Did you know about this?" I whispered to Conrad.

He looked genuinely surprised. "Not a clue, but is it okay? You don't have to if you don't want. I know you prefer to spin in private."

I didn't have the option of saying no. The King was standing next to the wheel, scanning the room. He found me, and a wide smile came to his face. I felt weak to my stomach. He might not believe Aiden, but he was prepared to test the theory.

"Please welcome the Lady Cosette of Westfallen!"

The room cheered: not as loudly as when they heard that the war was ending but still loud enough to make my ears pound. Though, maybe it was fear doing that.

"Cosette?" Conrad squeezed my hand and I held on to him for stability while he led me up to the platform where I shakily sat down. There, I risked a peek around the room. Close to the back of the room stood Aiden, looking stunned. No doubt he hadn't planned for me to be shamed so publicly. I wanted to glare at him but didn't want to be seen while all eyes were on me. Hoping for comfort, I instead looked into Conrad's eyes, but they offered me no consolation. He looked at me proudly as he stepped back and waited for me to perform.

Rumpel's gaze would have comforted me. But I had pushed him away. I never needed him more than I did then.

Shaking, I brought the straw up from the basket. Rumpel's words played over in my mind. A confident attitude was the key to making this work. Still trembling, I tried to muster confidence, but it was impossible with all these eyes on me.

My breath shook and I fumbled with the straw.

I could do this. I had to do this.

I rested the straw near the bobbin and took a deep breath. I felt more comfortable with my eyes closed, where I could pretend I was alone in the room. Even with my vision blank, my ears still rang with the sounds of the room, multiplied by my nerves. Shuffling feet, muffled whispers, tapping toes.

I could fake fainting. I read about a character who did that once, and it worked for her. But could I pull it off? If I fell to one side, I would topple off the platform. If I fell the other way, I would land in a basket of straw. Falling off the stage would guarantee that I wouldn't be shaken awake and put right back on the spinning wheel. I sucked in my breath and prepared to execute my escape plan.

Before I could, I felt a tingling in my hands, then a voice in my head.

"Let my magic flow through your hands."

Without warning, I lost control of my arms. My eyes flew open. As if controlled by someone else, my hands turned the straw.

Rumpel.

His magic flowed through me and out my hands. I straightened my back and let him take control as he worked the straw through the bobbin. I tried to look natural as he moved my hands for me. I had no idea that he could do this.

The straw turned, entered the bobbin, and came out, winding itself around the spindle. The room filled with gasps. People shoved at each other, trying to get closer to the platform to see for themselves. I continued to work, winding the gold around the spindle until it was thick enough for everyone to be sure of what they were seeing.

"Gold! She makes gold! We are rich!" The room exclaimed happily. They cheered and applauded and clapped each other on the back. My face flushed with the praise, though I knew I didn't deserve it.

Conrad's face stood out among them all. His shoulders were dropped, and his mouth was slightly open. He watched, mesmerized, as my hands moved. Soon a little smile came across his face.

I wished I knew if that smile was for me or for the gold.

In the back of the room, I saw Aiden duck his head and slip away, and I felt both the grief and relief that came with his departure. I doubted we would see each other again for a long time. I lowered my head back to the wheel.

When the straw was used up, my arms started to tingle again and I slowly regained control of them. Flexing my fingers, I pushed myself off the spinning wheel and stood up.

The room roared as they all called out my name. I still felt sick, but I bowed obediently. The King clapped loudest of all.

"Thank you Cosette, you have served your country well."

I blushed again, wondering how fast I could get off that stage. Conrad came up to me and offered his hand, which I took eagerly. I let him lead me down into the crowd of eager people.

So many questions came my way as the music picked back up and festivities resumed. I tried to answer them to the best of my ability, guilty that my deceit was spreading to so many people. There would be a mess to deal with once Rumpel was gone.

Some people asked me to spin gold for them. They offered to pay me, then realized that I would already be giving them money, then offered me more money than I would spin, then realized that would put them at a loss. Eventually they offered something other than gold, such as jewels, clothes or suitors. I declined it all, saying I wished to retire back to my home. They would huff at this and toddle away.

When the crowd let up, Conrad pulled me to the side and out into one of the hallways. There were still people there, but fewer than there were in the throne room. With the doors closed and muffling the music, I was able to hear my own breathing again.

"That was incredible," Conrad exclaimed. I laughed as his giddiness.

"I've never spun in front of anyone before."

"You should. You look magical doing it."

My stomach churned with my lie, as I remembered that lies were the reason I was so upset with Rumpel.

What would Conrad think when he found out that I lied? Would he be as upset as I was with Rumpel? I didn't mean to hurt him by lying, I was only trying to save myself—Conrad had nothing to do with it.

Yet, that was the exact reason that Rumpel lied to me. He was trying to save himself. He spun gold for me, thinking that the selfless act would break his curse, and he kept his violent past hidden because it didn't concern me. Rumpel keeping his secrets had nothing to do with me, and everything to do with his own desires. My choice not to tell Conrad I couldn't, in fact, spin gold had nothing to do with our friendship and everything to do with protecting my life from his unpredictable father. And yet, if he found out that through all the days we spent together that I chose to keep this secret from him, wouldn't he be mad?

There was one difference, though. I hadn't killed a village full of people. That alone was enough to keep me guarded around Rumpel.

My throat felt dry and my head felt light. Today took more out of me then I thought it would. Hoping he would understand, I excused myself from Conrad, who looked disappointed but let me go. I thanked him as I retreated to the safety of my room, where I threw myself on my bed and buried my face in the blankets.

How had my life gotten so complicated? How had I gone from the quiet girl serving drinks at the tavern to the girl in a silver dress spinning gold in front of the king, being courted by the prince, and researching how to break an old king's curse? Today, Aiden almost cost me everything. If Rumpel hadn't saved me, the King could have killed me for my lies.

I'd had enough.

For the past six months, I had complied as Fate handed me twists and turns, choosing to not fight the King hard enough and instead letting him bully me into spinning gold for him. Then, I'd let Rumpel save me time and time again instead of fighting for myself. While I'd been so concerned with pleasing everyone else, I had lost my sense of identity.

That was about to change.

I wouldn't wait for Rumpel's curse to end before I figured out how to take care of myself. I was going to fix my problems on my own.

Chapter Twenty-Nine

MY FIRST STOP WAS Rumpel. He didn't deserve my trust, but he did deserve an apology. "Keeping your secrets had nothing to do with me, and I'm sorry that I tried to make it so."

His body relaxed and he let out a breath. We stood facing each other in the small back room with the spinning wheel beside us. The moon blanketed the room from the window over Rumpel's shoulder, casting dim silver beams through his hair and over the fibers of his shirt.

"So, are we good?" He motioned a finger back and forth between us.

Now it was my turn to let out a deep sigh. "I still don't trust you. But you've saved my life over and over again, so I owe you," I explained. "Plus, I miss your friendship."

He crossed his arms and smirked. "My friendship? Is that all?"

I laughed despite myself, thinking of our kiss. "Yes. That is all."

"Alright. We better get started on this straw then. I still need to teach you to spin on your own."

"Actually, you don't. I have a plan."

Rumpel looked interested. "Does it include you spinning gold?"

"No. That was a terrible idea and it was never going to work."

Rumpel eased himself down to the spinning wheel and propped his feet out. He brushed his curls back from his face and looked at me intently.

I sat beside him in my usual place. "I'm going to make a deal with the King. I will spin gold, or rather, you will, for two more months. At that point I am to be released and never called upon again. It guarantees that there is a timeline to all of this and that I get my freedom before I lose you. It also gives you the last six weeks of your life to do whatever it is you wish."

Rumpel looked thoughtful. "And if the King says no?"

"If he says no, I walk out. He has no control over me."

Amused, Rumpel said, "He's gone mad, there's no telling how he'd react. He could send his guards after you. I doubt you could take them."

"Then I sit in his cell and refuse to spin. Eventually he will get bored with me and send me home."

Rumpel picked up some straw and started to spin. "He could kill you, you know."

I knew. That thought went through my mind hundreds of times. "But I don't think he would. I think Conrad would spare me."

"I wouldn't be so sure. If he can't get gold out of you, I don't know that he'd want you."

That was the second person to insinuate that Conrad was only interested in me for the gold. I'd already guessed as much, but I didn't enjoy hearing it. "I'm prepared to take that risk."

"If you're sure. For the record, I think it's crazy. But I also think it's brave."

My heart swelled and I reminded myself that I was still a bit angry with him.

Rumpel stopped spinning and turned toward me. "I need you to know, I didn't mean to do it. It was an accident. I was so mad, then I blacked out. When I woke up, they were all dead. It was never my intention to hurt them."

"But you wanted to hurt *someone*," I said meekly.

He nodded. "Yes, the men who killed my wife. I wanted them to pay. But it was never supposed to go further than that. It's important to me that you know I didn't consciously kill anyone."

I twisted my mouth. "I believe you, but it's still a hard thing for me to swallow."

"I can accept that."

Now that we'd moved on from our dispute, we spent the rest of the night talking. We started on the festival, and all the crazy Gifts that people had. That led us to the food that was there, then food that he used to love as a child, then about what his childhood and parents were like. By the end of the night, it was as if the past two weeks never happened.

As easily as that, things felt normal again. As normal as they could.

There was a moment before leaving when Rumpel stood close to me, his eyes asking a question that I couldn't answer. It wasn't good for my heart to get invested in him again, but I didn't have the strength to tell him so.

My eyes gave me away, and he nodded understandingly as he pulled back. The moment I could no longer feel his breath on my skin, I wished for the closeness. I almost asked him to kiss me, but I stopped myself.

I had more important things to think about than Rumpel's lips, no matter how soft they were.

Chapter Thirty

I ASKED ANNA TO dress me in something regal.

"You ask as if I've been dressing you as a chimney sweep!"

I laughed. "No, the dresses have been lovely. I just need something that makes me look as confident as a queen today. Ah, there's the door. Come in!"

A skinny guard popped his head in the room. "You called for someone?"

"Yes," I said as Anna watched grew even more confused. "I need an audience with the King this afternoon."

"I'm not sure that'll be possible, miss."

I put my hands on my hips and wished that I was already in the dress that Anna would find. It was hard to look in charge when I was still in my nightgown. "Well, if I don't see the King today then I won't give him gold tonight. It's his choice."

The guard looked uncomfortable and I almost pitied him. I kept my stance strong until he bowed and left the room.

Anna was staring at me with wide eyes. "What is going on?"

I smiled casually at her. "Nothing, I just need to speak with the King about our arrangement, which is why I need a dress."

With newfound energy she bobbed a curtsy and scrambled out of the room. I tidied up until she came back a few minutes later with a thick bundle.

"This is from the queen's old clothes," she said as she pushed the door shut with her heel.

"Oh!" I hadn't expected Anna to take one of those. The queen died years ago; I was surprised they still had those or that Anna had access to them.

The color of the dress matched sandy shores, and I envisioned the blue silk that lay overtop trailing up from the bottom of the skirt and stopping just below the billowed sleeves and laced neckline, was the ocean rising to meet the land. Intricate pearls were stitched into the bodice. Certainly, that dress was worth more than I was.

If I wanted to look like a queen, this dress would do it.

"Will the King mind if I wear his late wife's dress?"

Anna smoothed out the dress on my bed. "It was made to wear at a celebration when she got better, though she never did. The King has never seen this dress."

I felt strange being buttoned up into the late queen's dress, but I didn't have time to change my mind, because no sooner had Anna tied off the last clasp than we heard a knock on the door. With permission to enter, the same guard as before came into the room, and his eyes got wide at the sight of me. I allowed myself to savor his stunned expression before he came to his senses.

"Ahem. The King has agreed to see you. You may come when you are ready."

"Thank you, that'll be all."

After he left, Anna burst out laughing. "Did you see his face? You look like a queen for sure in this! He was so surprised!"

I laughed with her. "Let's hope the King is as impressed."

"Are you really not going to tell me what it's about?"

I didn't know how to explain to her. "You can come with me and find out for yourself."

I hadn't thought it would, but that offer sent light to her eyes. "I've never been invited to the throne room before!"

"As my trusted maid, you are welcome wherever I am," I said. I tried to think if I ever saw maids in the throne room before and realized that I hadn't. I wasn't sure if I had the authority to invite her there, but she looked so happy that I was glad I had.

"Thank you, miss! You know, you're a favorite around here." She settled me into a chair and got to work on my hair.

"What do you mean?"

"Well, most nobility around here don't see people like me. But you do. You don't treat me any differently. We've all noticed it."

Her compliment made my eyes water. "You know, I'm really not different from you at all. I'm from a small tavern in an outer village."

She laughed. "You can spin gold! You can call audiences with the King! You have the prince's favor! You are nothing like me."

I know she meant it all as a compliment, but I contemplated her words. I thought of myself as being just like her, and the people at those fancy dinners were all above me. I saw myself as a village girl among nobles. But she saw me as one of them. Did that mean that I fit in with both worlds, or that I didn't belong in either?

"I hope you become our next queen. I could be the queen's maid!"

Now it was my turn to look surprised. "That's not why I'm here!"

"Don't think I don't see the two of you walking through the halls together day after day!" Anna said with giggles. "I think it's just splendid. You're going to be a beautiful queen."

Beautiful and queen were never words that I used for myself.

"Let's just finish getting me ready." There was enough on my mind without the maid's gossip.

With my hair piled on my head and my dress weighing on my hips, I went to see the King. People admired me as I passed by, and some followed me to see what the occasion was. The guards before the throne room bowed to me and reached for the handles.

This was it. There was no going back now.

I straightened my back and held my head high.

The doors came open with a small gust of air. The room inside looked vastly different from yesterday, with fewer people and the decorations removed. Still, it held more people than I expected.

In my head, I'd practiced my speech in front of the King and maybe a few advisors. The room before me looked like it held all the advisors and some of their friends. Anna gasped behind me as every head turned almost in unison to look our way. The guards stepped forward to ask her to stay behind but I held up my hand.

"She comes with me," I ordered. Fearfully, I waited to see if they would allow it. They looked between each other and nodded, letting Anna through. We both sighed.

I returned my focus to the King, who made his way to his throne. Conrad sat by his side. I hesitated. I didn't think he would be in the room.

My feet carried me forward with as much grace as I could muster. Anna stayed along the wall behind me, as though she couldn't bring herself to stand any closer. The faces of the people around me were mixed. Some held confusion, some awe, and some upset that I was interrupting.

I ignored them all as I curtsied deeply before my king.

"Lady Cosette." I couldn't read the King's voice. "To what do we owe the honor?"

I looked up to his face. Next to him, Conrad was bewitched, staring at me with a smile in his eyes.

The King was looking at me intently, waiting for me to speak. I cleared my throat.

"I have a proposition for you," I began as rehearsed.

"Then tell us, daughter of Westfallen."

The title made me pause for a second, but I shook it off. "I have spun gold for you night after night for five months. I have asked for little in return and have been honored to serve my kingdom in this way."

He smiled at me, but I could see the distrust in his eye.

"But I will not stay indefinitely. I have given you enough gold. I will continue for two more months, at which point you will grant me the freedom to return home and never call on me again."

I tried not to look at Conrad's face as I said this. I didn't want to see him hurt.

The King stood up. "Will you not stay to see this war over?"

I gulped. "I feel I have done more than what is fair."

He nodded, pursing his lips. I ignored the chatter of the people behind me. The King paced while Conrad sat there looking stricken. "And what will you do if I demand you stay until the war ends?"

My knees wobbled but I righted them. I needed to look tough. "I will walk home today."

That got a reaction from the crowd. I steadied myself as the King raised his eyebrows. "Walk home? Interesting. Well I have my own proposition for you."

"Father," Conrad stood up, but the King hushed him. He turned to me, squaring his shoulders.

"One alternative is to have you executed as a traitor to the country for refusing to help us in a time of war. I don't think you want that option. The other," he stopped and looked at Conrad. When he turned back to me, there was a sly smile on his face. "The second option is that you spin gold for two more months, at which point we will reward you for your time and Gift."

"Reward?"

He grinned, gesturing to his son. "You will be given the hand of the heir of Westfallen."

That got the biggest reaction yet.

"Father!" Conrad jumped up.

"Sit down. You could do worse than the girl who spins gold."

I turned to scan the crowd. They were talking to each other and staring at me. I thought I caught a glimpse of Rumpel's golden curls but when I looked again, he was gone.

The queen's dress didn't feel so luxurious anymore. Instead, it felt like a prison.

"If I don't want either of those options?"

The King slowly stepped down from the platform and approached me and I had a flashback to my first night at the castle. I would hold myself proudly this time.

He drew near and narrowed his eyes. It was safe to say that our evening routine of stifled pleasantries and polite greetings were over. "I have given you two options. By the end of the month, you will accept one of them."

Conrad abandoned his chair and came to stand by my side. "Leave her be."

I was touched that he stood up for me, though his father looked annoyed. "I'm making a business deal. A kingdom can never have too much gold, and you'll soon learn how fast resources can be depleted. She guarantees eternal wealth."

Conrad looked to me with a tilted head and raised eyebrows, but the look in his eye differed from his father's. His father saw me as a tool for the kingdom, someone he could force into submission to provide all the wealth that his greedy mind could desire.

A slave. He saw me as a slave.

I was no one's slave, least of all his.

But the glint in Conrad's eye sent warmth curling through my chest.

He saw me as a person, and his eyes were asking if I was okay. I gave him a small nod before addressing his father. "I assume the previous offer of spinning until the war's end then going home is no longer on the table?" I asked, still holding my chin up.

"It was your choice to push this," the King whispered.

My eyes scanned the room. Feet shuffled closer in to hear what we were saying. All eyes remained on us, and no one uttered a word.

This had not gone as planned. Before leaving, I needed to reestablish some strength. I pulled my shoulders back and my neck up. I tried to imagine how a queen would hold herself in a room of advisors and a cruel king. I didn't feel the part, but I hoped I looked it.

"You do not control me," I said bravely, anger seeping through my tone.

As I turned to exit, the King got a strange smile on his face. "I control everything."

A shudder went down my spine and I hoped he didn't see it. With as much dignity as I could muster, I paraded out of the room, beckoning Anna to follow, who slunk along the wall with her head down. I doubted her first time in the throne room had been all that she hoped for.

Chapter Thirty-One

WHEN I RETURNED, I half expected to find Rumpel in my room to give me encouragement. He wasn't there. I dismissed Anna, wishing to have a few minutes to myself. She left without arguing. I sat myself down at the desk and began letting the pins out of my hair as I reran the scene over in my head.

Where had it gone so wrong?

If I hadn't marched in there, determined to win back some control over the situation, I would be free to go home once the war was over. Instead, I felt the need to make a mess of it. Now I had to marry Conrad or die.

How was the King still in charge with demands like that? Didn't the advisors have an opinion as to who Conrad should marry? Didn't anyone else think that him threatening to kill me was an abuse of his powers as king? Surely there was someone who would protest his demands.

My mind flashed to the coup that Conrad was planning, and I could only hope he would go through with it soon. He could overturn the King's demands.

Conrad.

I buried my face in my hands. That look on his face when I said I didn't want to stay here; I would never forget it. He looked so rejected, and I was the reason his face looked like that.

A knock came at the door, startling me. I shook off my surprise and went to answer it, hoping to see Rumpel. It wasn't him. It was Conrad. He was still wearing his blue suit coat with buttons in the sleeve collars.

We stood looking at each other for a moment without talking. Finally, he raised his shoulders and let them drop. "What was that?"

"I'm sorry," I said, grabbing him by the sleeve and pulling him into the room. He stumbled in, leaving the door open behind him. I pulled the last pins from my hair and pushed them into a pile on the desk. Conrad stayed in the middle of the room watching me. How could I explain this to him? "Listen, I didn't mean to hurt you. I just got so sick of doing everything by his terms that I wanted to assert some control over the situation. I couldn't live with myself if I just went along with everything."

Conrad nodded, but I could see the questions lingering in his eyes. "I get wanting to be in control and wanting to be seen as confident. But no one thought any less of you for agreeing to stay here and spin gold for months."

I buried my face in my hands and moaned. "I'm sure they think less of me now."

Gently, Conrad placed a hand on my shoulder. "Nonsense. If anything they see that you have courage inside you. It's a valuable trait for a queen. And this dress! You're stunning!"

I blushed and twirled for him. "It was supposed to be for your mother. I hope you don't mind."

A sad smile came to his face. "Then it's perfect that you have it."

He moved to the desk beside me, fingers playing across the carvings on the chair. "I'm sorry about my father. He can be dramatic sometimes, especially when challenged."

I breathed a sigh of relief. "So, he didn't mean it?"

"Unfortunately, whether he meant it or not, his words stand. He's the King, and there were several witnesses. He can't change his mind now."

I pulled my hands through my hair, flattening it out. Then I leaned against the desk and crossed my arms. "He would actually kill me?"

A stricken look came across Conrad's face. "He's killed for less."

Someday I'd ask him to tell me the story there, but we had more important things at hand. With shaky steps, I closed my door, then turned to face Conrad. "You told me you were planning on taking over. When?"

Conrad sighed deeply, rubbing the back of his hand across his forehead. "Soon, but not that soon. I can try to push it up, but we need every advisor on board for this to work peacefully." For the first time I saw the strain of his job hiding behind his face. He looked tense, with stiff shoulders and a clenched jaw. "There is a chance it can still be an easy transition even without Silas on our side; he's a stiff old man that few people like. He will be one of the first to be replaced, as soon as the buzz settles. But I'd like to have Nathaniel with us first. There's a chance, after the spectacle today, that he will be more amenable to joining us. I haven't seen my father behave like that in public in a long time."

I tried to understand, but princely coups were beyond my comprehension. "I don't know if it means anything, but you have my support."

He smiled at me. "It means the world to me. We should talk about my father's offer. You'll still need to accept it."

I sighed. I didn't want to hurt him, but I needed to be clear. "Conrad, I'm not interested in marrying you. I like you, but not that way."

He took it in stride. "You don't have to be ready yet. I'm not asking you to be in love with me right now. But I hope I'm a more attractive offer than death?"

He was right. Almost anything was more appealing than that. I nodded slowly.

"Good! Then agree to marry me. We drag this engagement on as long as we can. I take over the throne, and if you haven't fallen in love with me by then, I end the engagement. You'd be free to leave."

Hope fluttered in my chest as he spoke. That could work.

"Do you think you could be happy with that?"

Despite myself, I smiled. "Yes. I can do that."

Conrad straightened. "Great. Take the whole month to get back to my father; it'll help drag this situation out. In the meantime, I'll go see about Nathaniel."

He stepped forward and kissed my head. Then he gave me this smile, as if I made him the happiest man in the world despite having asked to leave earlier that day. His face was lit with joy.

I almost told him right there. I almost told him everything. From Rumpel to the curse to my inability to spin straw into gold, I almost told him the whole story. But something stopped me. I still didn't trust him with my life, and if he knew that I didn't spin gold he might not protect me from his father.

So, I kept my mouth shut and watched my almost-fiancé as he strolled from the room, leaving me as confused as ever.

I blamed it on the dress. I should have known better than to put on the late queen's dress. I brought this chaos upon myself.

Chapter Thirty-Two

"WELL, THAT WENT WELL," Rumpel joked. I tossed straw on him.

"That couldn't have gone worse."

Rumpel shrugged. "You're still alive. So yes, it could have gone worse."

I sat barefoot in my long navy dress on the ground next to the straw. "I made such a fool of myself, storming in there and demanding things."

"It was bold. I like that," Rumpel said.

"You're not the only one. Conrad liked it too," I joked. He made a face, but he knew I was making fun.

"So," he tied off a spindle and reached for another one, sliding it in its place. "Are you going to marry His Highness?"

I groaned. "Not really. I'll wait a month, then accept the King's offer to marry his son. Another two months of spinning gold, then Conrad and I will try to drag the engagement out longer. In that time, Conrad will try to carry out his coup and replace the King. Then he's king, and he can end our engagement."

"Something tells me he won't end it," Rumpel muttered unhappily.

"He has to." There was tenacity in my voice. "I won't marry him."

My legs were stretched out and my feet played with Rumpel's as he spun. I wondered what it was like for him to talk about me being engaged to someone else, even if it wasn't real. It must be hard it was for him, knowing that he can't give me those things.

"There's one thing that you're forgetting," Rumpel said.

I threw my hands up, tossing straw everywhere. "I'm sure there are a million things I'm forgetting."

Rumpel laughed, but his voice remained serious. "In three months, my curse is final. So right about when you are supposed to marry Conrad, I'll be gone. I know you want to drag the engagement out, but you might be safer as his wife."

My chest constricted. The whole point of me marching into the throne room was to guarantee that I was free before Rumpel's curse was finalized. Instead I was more trapped than ever.

"I don't want to be his wife." My voice sounded whinier than I intended.

"Trust me, I don't want you to be his wife either. But he'd have more grace for you if you were."

I was quiet for a long time. There must be a way out of this, I just wasn't seeing it. Rumpel's offer still stood to take me away before he left. I'd be alone and in hiding, but I'd be safe from the King's or Conrad's anger.

I didn't want that, though: to hide or run away. I wanted my life back. "I hate this."

Rumpel rubbed his foot over mine. That was all the touching we would do. Rumpel wanted to protect my heart from the pain of losing him, so he was holding himself back from me. Occasional touches ran between us through our fingers, our feet, but never anything more. He sighed. "I hate it too. I hate that I can't give you the things that Conrad can. I hate that he can parade you through the halls during the day while I'm stuck hiding with you at night. I hate that I can't give you the life that you deserve."

Warmth and pain filled my heart together. I hated that I cared more and more for him each day, while he was running out of time. I hated that we hadn't broken his curse yet, that I ever believed that we could.

I hated that I was falling in love with Rumpel, and that I was going to lose him. I hated that more than the thought of losing my life.

Without expecting it, tears began to stream down my face. Rumpel saw, and quick as a fox he was on the ground next to me, pulling me close. I continued to cry into his shoulder, holding on to him.

"I'm sorry," I said, wiping my face in an unflattering way.

I loved Rumpel. But he wasn't mine forever. I only had three more months with him, and before that time was up, I needed to get engaged to a prince.

I walked back to my room after Rumpel finished spinning gold that night. A maid caught up to me with an envelope in her hand. "I was just on my way to your room to give you this. It's from your family."

I eagerly reached for the paper in her hand. She curtsied and scurried away as I ran back to my room to open it.

I sat at the desk and tore into the paper. There was only one person in my family who knew how to write.

My Dear Cozy,

I hope this letter finds you. I wasn't certain if we were allowed to contact you during your time at the castle, but Conrad seemed so nice that I assumed he would allow it.

Your visit meant so much to us. We assumed you were well when we were given a title and money, but seeing you set our hearts at peace. It is one of my greatest joys as a papa to know that my children are safe and well.

It is also a joy to see my children grow, and you, dear Cozy, have grown into a wonderful woman. I don't know all that has gone on while you have been away, but you are stronger than ever. You have a new confidence inside you that we had never seen before.

We can't imagine all that you are going through there, but we know that you will be a beacon of light to those around you. We have selfishly kept you to ourselves for the past twenty years. Anika is ready to attack the world with gusto, but you have always been more cautious then her. You see the world with realistic eyes and you don't lose yourself in it. For that reason, we know that wherever you are you will be okay.

It appears the young prince has feelings for you. And, if it's not too forward of me to assume, you don't feel the same way for him. I'm proud of you for not feeling pressured toward anything. But, if your feelings change, you have our blessing. I know you've had a hard time seeing yourself as more than the tavern girl because you don't have a Gift, but you have more than you know. You have spirit, you have gentleness, and you have courage. That will lead you to many places in life, and if it leads you to be queen then we are proud of you. But if it leads you back home, then we will be overjoyed.

I couldn't be more honored to be your papa.

I love you.

My eyes welled up with tears as I reread the note over again. He always knew just what to say. Somehow, without knowing what was going on, my Papa reached across the distance and gave me the strength needed to go on.

Chapter Thirty-Three

"LADY COSETTE, HAVE YOU reached a decision?"

He knew I had, that's why we were gathered there that morning. It was only the King, Conrad, and a few advisors in the room. I hoped there would be more people, but this should work too. The sweet scent of breakfast found me on my walk here, and I regretted passing up on mine to prepare myself. I wanted to look as comfortable and confident as I could when I stood before the King with my decision.

"I have, sire." I curtsied deeply. Anna found me a deep blue dress for today with a high neckline and slender skirt. It wasn't as extravagant as the dress I wore last time, but I still felt pretty in it.

I decided not to wait the full month to tell the King my decision. I knew what I wanted. I was going to take charge of my future, and I didn't need Conrad to help me.

My hands were sweaty but I resisted rubbing them on my dress. Instead, I straightened my posture and looked the King directly in the eye. "I have decided to decline your offer of marrying your son."

The King's eyes went wild while Conrad lowered himself into his chair. I tried not to focus on his face. The King breathed deeply. "You know this means you will be put to death for refusing to give your country gold to end the war?"

"I have offered to spin gold for you for two more months. I would take that deal if I were you."

"Ah, so you're testing me?" the King sneered. I gulped but didn't reply. He knew my decision, now it was his turn to decide how far he was willing to go.

The way I saw it, he could relent and let me spin for a few months, then set me free. Or he could stick to his word and have me killed, a decision that would hopefully grant Conrad the support he needed to overthrow his father and therefore void my sentence.

The King waved his hand to the back of the room. "Very well. Death it is. Put her in the dungeon."

I had really hoped it would go the other way.

With tight grips, guards seized my arms and pulled me back. "I can walk, don't drag me!" I exclaimed, getting my feet under me.

Conrad stood up to speak to his father, but the King wasn't paying him any attention. His gaze was fixed on me. He wanted to see if I would break.

I wouldn't give him the satisfaction.

The guard's grip on my wrists remained harder than necessary. I yanked on my hands, but they held tight, digging their nails into my wrist and crippling my hand. A cry filled my mouth, but I blocked it from escaping, determined to not let the King see my weakness.

They dragged me from the throne room, while my feet scrambled to gain control. The King watched me leave with his arms crossed. I regained my footing once we were out of the room, but the guards' grip didn't relent. They pulled me down back hallways and dark stairs. I grew frantic but kept it inside.

A thick wood door separated one last stairwell from the rest of the castle. Down the stairs, a pungent smell grew. I was regretting my decision already. A series of tunnels came after the stairs. A large key ring hung on the wall, which one of the guards grabbed.

The dungeon cells were unpleasant spaces. A man pressed against his bars and cursed at us. I hoped I wasn't placed near him.

We moved past him and down the tunnel. Some of the rooms had small windows near the top, while others drowned in darkness. Small squeaks drew my attention to the ground, then I instantly wished I hadn't looked. Rats scurried in and out of the cells, poking their noses in corners and sniffing at our feet. I bit my tongue and tried to ignore them. The guards looked equally disturbed.

"This one will do." The guards halted suddenly, almost making me trip. They fiddled with the keys until they got the door open, casting me inside. I stumbled to the ground, bashing my knee on a stone.

The doors were locked before I stood again.

Without a word, they tipped their heads at me and left, eager to be free of the vile atmosphere.

My surroundings were a far cry from my bedchambers upstairs. I hadn't been lucky enough to get a room with a window, but it was far enough away from others that their curses and mutterings were muffled. A small cot lay on the back wall with no more than a thin blanket. The ground was sticky, and I dreaded thinking what from.

The smell was the worst, and I pulled my dress's neckline up to cover my nose. After inspecting the cot, I cuddled up into it. Shamelessly, I allowed tears to stream down my face as I contemplated the decisions that led to my being here.

There was a chance that tonight would be my last, if the King let me live that long. How long did death sentences take to carry out?

A scurrying sound caused me to jump. Rumpel's voice came quickly, calming me down.

"You shouldn't sneak up on me like that," I complained, yet I was so grateful that he was here.

"What is that smell?" he asked. His side brushed against mine as he joined me in my misery on the bench, and he scrunched up his nose.

"I don't want to know." I cuddled myself into his side. He put one arm over me and slid his other hand into mine.

The room didn't seem as bad with him there.

I was breaking his rule about physical touch, but he didn't protest. Apparently, the rules didn't apply in the prison.

"So that could have gone better," Rumpel said flatly. An echo of another prisoner's shout ran down the hallway. I hoped they'd quiet down soon.

"I'm so sorry I didn't tell you my plan. I received a note from my father, and it gave me this strength. So, I just decided to stand up to the King."

"I don't think your father wanted you to do this."

I laughed. "No, probably not. Think he'll actually kill me?"

Rumpel stroked my thumb. "I'll save you before that happens. I can snap my fingers and whisk you away."

"Where would you take me?" I leaned further into Rumpel and imagined how nice it would be to be whisked away by him.

"Anywhere you want. We can go see the ocean. Spend my last few months together, just you and me."

I admitted that sounded nice. But it would mean that I could never come back home. I would have made an enemy out of the King, and in turn, my kingdom. He might take it out on my family. I couldn't stand the thought of me by the ocean with

Rumpel while my family suffered. I would only use Rumpel's offer of an escape as a last resort.

"If it comes down to it, then yes. Take me away."

Rumpel kissed my forehead. "Just say the word and we will go."

My stomach growled and I deeply regretted missing breakfast. I didn't want to think of the disgusting food they probably served prisoners. I was grateful that Rumpel was there to distract me from the wretchedness of this place.

I looked over at him as a new thought came to mind. "Can you make gold?"

Rumpel sat up straight and cupped my face in his hands. "Are you okay? Because if you don't know the answer to that..."

"No, I mean can you make gold out of nothing?"

"Oh. Yes, I can do that."

"Then why on earth did you spend so many hours spinning straw through a wheel when it could have taken you a few seconds?"

Rumpel smiled, still holding my face in his hands. "Darling Cosette, don't you know? Even from that first night I wanted to spend every second that I could with you."

His words always melted my heart, and I leaned forward to him, hoping he would break his rule. Thankfully, he ducked his head down and kissed me with all the tenderness of a flower. I never knew I could feel so loved in a prison cell. Despite my happiness, though, I found tears streaming down my face again. Rumpel pulled back, surprised.

"Silly girl, why are you always crying?" he asked gently as he rubbed my cheeks dry. I reached up and clung to his hand.

"I don't want to lose this. I don't want to lose you," I sobbed. Rumpel rubbed my nose with his.

"You have me for as long as I live." He kissed my cheeks. "As long as I live, I am yours." I let him kiss my face until he breathed in sharply. "Someone is coming. I must go, my love."

He disappeared then, leaving me clinging to that word, *love*. I hadn't told Rumpel yet that I loved him. He wouldn't want it; he would tell me I needed to guard my heart.

Once Rumpel was gone, I pulled myself up and approached the bars, wrapping my hands around them. A figure came closer, their feet making a rhythmic sound on the floor. I recognized his shape before I could see the details of his face. He sighed as he stood in front of the bars, looking down at me.

"Cosette."

"Conrad."

"Come with me."

Chapter Thirty-Four

"I DON'T UNDERSTAND."

Conrad was quiet as he led me out from the prison and back into the light of day.

"I thought the King was going to kill me."

Still no answer.

I asked again what was going on. Conrad huffed as he looked around. He stopped walking and turned to face me.

"What are you doing?" he yelled.

"I don't even know what *you're* doing."

Conrad crossed his arms. "We had a plan. It was going to work. You would get engaged to me, we would take the throne, then break the engagement. But instead you had to go make my father mad and try to get yourself killed! Is the idea of being with me that horrible?"

I drew myself back. I had never seen Conrad mad before, he always wore a huge smile on his face. That smile was gone now, replaced by thin lips and scrunched up eyes. I cleared my throat. "I will not be a pawn in his game. I don't think he will go through with killing me."

Conrad laughed and grabbed my sleeve, pulling me so I would continue walking. "Then you're crazy. My father has no rationality." He dragged me back toward the throne room.

"Will you at least tell me where we are going?"

"Well," Conrad's voice was still louder than it needed to be. "Since you seem so intent on making a spectacle, father wants to announce your decision to all the advisors at once. He's called a meeting."

That seemed unnecessary to me, but I wasn't in a position to argue. Conrad was furious with me. I looked over my dress. It remained fairly clean in the dungeon, but I knew the smell clung to it.

I didn't have time to worry about that. Conrad pushed open the doors to the throne room and pulled me in by the hand. I tried to keep up with him, so I didn't look like I was being dragged. I had been dragged through this room enough.

Conrad stopped next to his father and turned me around. I looked around the room at people who I shared dinner with over the past few months. Would any of them stop the King from killing me?

We stood on the platform, a few steps above the rest. The men straightened their suits and stood in a rough formation in front of us, waiting to hear the announcement. They waited patiently, but when the King spoke, it was to me alone. He turned his face to whispered in my direction. "You tested me. Now I will test you. You don't want to die."

I tried to assess his meaning while he turned to the room. "Ladies and gentlemen of Westfallen! Today is a wonderous day. Today, my son has won the hand of Lady Cosette!"

Oh. That's what he meant.

My jaw dropped as the room roared with applause. At my side Conrad looked as shocked as I was, and I was pleased to know that he hadn't orchestrated this. The King clapped loudly and stepped back to give us the stage. His eyes were on me, challenging my next move.

Very few people knew I had already told the King that I rejected the marriage proposal to his son. And they couldn't know that I'd come back and changed my mind. The King was making it look like this was my choice. He was choosing for me.

And he bet that I wouldn't fight, because I didn't want to die.

My first instinct was to clarify the situation, explain that I was not marrying Conrad, but the thought of going back to that vile prison intimidated me. I wasn't going to fight right here, but I wasn't going to marry his son. I would find a different way to fight.

I calmly walked toward the King and said, "I will continue spinning gold tomorrow night. Tonight, I need to wash this stench off me."

With that, I exited the room, leaving the cheers of the people behind me.

Anna was surprised to see me. She was folding up the sheets from my bed while dabbing her red cheeks. She dropped the sheets in surprise when I came in the room.

"I thought you were going to die!" she wailed as she flung herself across the room and into my arms, weeping. I had shared my decision with her this morning, as well as my assumption that the King was bluffing. Apparently, she hadn't shared my confidence. I patted her on the back, sorry to have caused her pain.

"No, evidently I'm engaged to Conrad now."

She perked up instantly. "I knew it! You'll be such a good queen!"

I hated to let her down, but I didn't want anyone to think that I would be the next queen. "I don't love Conrad, so I won't marry him."

Her face fell again. "But you aren't going to die?"

I grinned. "That's not in the plans." I moved to help her remake my bed, then she asked if she could draw a bath. I was going to take a bath anyway, but she suggested it first. I guess I smelled more than I realized.

"Are your reservations about Conrad, or about being queen?" Anna asked. I stopped to consider the depth of the question.

"I never thought about being queen. I don't know what I think about it. I wouldn't mind being queen, but I'd feel like a fraud. There are so many people better suited to that role than me."

"That's true," Anna replied honestly as she repositioned some of her hair in her bun. "There are better people out there for the throne. But there are also worse people. I think you'd do just fine. Now, I'm going to go and I'm not coming back until you smell decent."

I laughed and watched her go. Then I slipped out of my dress and into the warm tub. The water greeted me favorably, soaking away my worries. I leaned my head back, closed my eyes, and daydreamed about being queen.

A noise startled me, and I threw my arms around myself. Anna shrieked.

"I'm so sorry, I was sure you would be out by now!"

"You're fine, I should have gotten out already. My skin will be pruned for the rest of the evening. Turn around so I can get out."

"You should get dressed quickly; you have a visitor waiting."

I shook my hair into my towel. "Who?"

"Your fiancé." Her voice carried an apology with it. I sighed loudly. I wanted an evening to myself.

I took my time as I dressed in a plain shirt and flowy skirt. I left my hair down to dry as it was. I didn't feel the need to dress up for Conrad.

Anna fussed over my appearance, but I shook my head at her. I would see Conrad, then I would be right back for my warm bed and a plate of treats. My stomach was already growling at the thought of them.

Conrad was sitting in the hallway when I came out, looking like a lost puppy. My heart softened a bit. Perhaps I needed to take his feelings into greater consideration. He had displayed nothing but kindness to me and I had, in return, been cold and inconsiderate.

Papa would be disappointed in me.

Conrad had taken off his suit coat and jacket, leaving him with a loose plain shirt tucked in carelessly. He held his hands on his head and his eyes were red.

I sat down next to him, lacing my arm in his. We sat quietly for a few moments until my stomach ruined it by growling obnoxiously.

"Do you want to go get food with me?" Conrad asked in a voice no greater than a whisper. I nodded in reply.

He pulled himself up and offered me his hand. "Come on then, I heard the cook made cinnamon cookies and duck soup that I want to try."

Chapter Thirty-Five

IN A TOTAL CHANGE of mood, Conrad showered me with compliments that I didn't deserve, telling me how brave I was, how strong-minded and beautiful. They were just the things that someone I rejected publicly shouldn't be saying. He understood, he claimed, how I couldn't get engaged to him when I didn't love him. He was sorry that his father pushed it, but he was glad that I wasn't in that filthy dungeon anymore.

I was glad too. That had been the grossest few hours of my life.

Still, his pleasantries confused me. He should hate me.

I enjoyed his company with a cautious mind. We ate our early dinner and walked in the gardens while the sun was starting to descend. Bit by bit, I let my guard down as I assured myself that I was in control of the situation. My confusion, however, was reignited when he started speaking about his mother.

"I'm sorry, I'm confused." I put up my hand and shook my head. "I rejected you, twice, publicly. I know that you are happier than the normal person, but you are supposed to be mad right now. Instead you're acting like everything is normal. Great, even!"

Conrad didn't reply but searched for a flower instead. Bewildered, I watched as he meticulously chose one, then plucked it. He turned to me, twisting the flower in his fingertips. "I was hurt, yes. But I sense your dislike for me comes from hatred for my father, and not anything I've done. Beyond that, I recognize that we are trying to end the engagement between us, but this is still my first time getting engaged. Everyone is thrilled for me, and I'd be lying if I said I didn't want to enjoy it a little. So, will you, as my fake betrothed, grant me pleasant company so that I can find some joy in the situation?"

He held out the flower at the last words and waited for me to take it. I felt like I was being unfaithful to Rumpel simply by being with Conrad, but he was right. He was my friend, and there was no reason we couldn't enjoy each other's company in an innocent way. I took the flower, feeling foolish for my actions.

"I really am sorry. I know you didn't plan any of this."

Conrad chuckled. "I didn't want this at all. I like you, that's no secret, but it was never my intention to bully you into companionship."

"I know, and I'm sorry for taking out my anger on you. From now on, I will be nothing but pleasant. As long as you know that I have no interest in marrying you."

"Trust me, message received." He turned and held out his arm, inviting me to continue walking with him.

Conrad shared his heart with me that night. He told me about his mother and the songs she used to sing while she tended the garden when he was a boy. He told me about his father and how different he was then. He shared his dreams and fears freely, holding nothing back. In turn I tried to share my own heart but found it difficult. So much of my life, my dreams and fears and interests, had to do with Rumpel. I wasn't willing to let Conrad see that part of me. Still, I shared what I could.

I never realized how easy it was to talk to Conrad. His laugh was contagious and his voice inviting. It was easy to feel safe with him, like any secret you told him would be kept safe forever. He didn't make my heart flutter like Rumpel did, but I realized I missed out on a great friendship.

Conrad picked a different flower for me from each patch that we walked by, until I could hardly hold them all in my hands. I laughed as he stacked flower upon flower until my hands were overflowing with beauty. Conrad threw his head back to laugh too.

His back stiffened when a guard came around the corner.

"Sorry, I heard noises, I was coming to investigate."

"All is well here." Conrad smiled at him, but his eyes weren't as happy anymore. When the guard left, he turned to me and sighed. "They ruin things sometimes. I'm sorry you have to deal with guards everywhere. I know it's not what you're used to."

"I've never been this watched before. But I don't hate it like I thought I would."

Conrad shoved his hands into his pockets. "Could you live like this the rest of your life?"

I hated having to tell him this so many times, but I couldn't play with his heart. "I don't want this life."

Conrad looked around before steering me toward a bench. Some of the flowers fell into my lap as I sat down next to him.

"Is there someone back home who has your heart? Is that why it's closed off to me?"

I ducked my head. "It's something like that."

Conrad nodded. "If you didn't have him, do you think you could ever want me?"

He must have amazing confidence to willingly set himself up for rejection so many times. It brought me no pleasure to continue hurting him, so I softened my answer. "Maybe. But I love him."

"Your actions make more sense now. Still, I think you could love me, if you tried." His eyes looked at my own, peering as if looking into my very soul for the information he sought. I wanted to give him some relief, some glimmer of hope that I could perhaps love him, but my heart was so full of love for another that there was no room for him. Even knowing that Rumpel's love was not one that I could have for life, I couldn't imagine another beyond it. My heart very much belonged to him, and I wasn't willing to share it with anyone else.

Either Conrad couldn't see this, or he simply didn't want to. Either way, he remained hopeful for the rest of the evening that my feelings could change, ending the night with a kiss on my hand and a brisk walk away as if his spirit danced in his feet.

"This contract is to officially declare..." The King stopped to cough. "The engagement between Prince Conrad of Westfallen and Lady Cosette of Westfallen." Another cough.

My hands were sweating, and my head felt heavy. Anna had piled my hair up and set an elaborate crown upon my head as if I was queen already. She found another one of the queen's old dresses and altered it for me. It was deep purple with gold lining, and it was majestic. Anna had hung jewelry on my neck and arms and went as far as insisting that we pierce my ears. I told her that no such thing would be done.

Anna was there, somewhere in that room, watching with bright eyes.

I had been encouraged to get a few more maids, as the future queen, but I thought Anna was enough. She, though, had been taken off her other duties. I felt so embarrassed; I didn't even know that she still served anyone but me.

All the advisors stood near the front of the room, and the rest of it was filled with the ladies and the gentlemen of the court. It appeared that announcing an engagement was quite the spectacle.

My family had been invited, but I purposefully didn't send their letter. I didn't want them to witness this. With luck, this engagement would end soon, and I didn't want to have to explain that to them. I just prayed that word didn't spread to them before I had a chance to clarify.

I wondered if Rumpel was here too, hiding in the shadows. The thought made me want to pull my hand from Conrad's, but duty held me still.

Conrad was dressed finer than I had ever seen him. His suit was pinned with medals that caught the sun and reflected brilliant colors. In a way, he matched the decorations on the wall, bearing the country's colors. I don't know why I hadn't thought to wear those symbolic colors. It was just another thing that showed I clearly didn't belong here.

Conrad squeezed my hand gently while keeping his chin up and eyes rested on his father and the scribe. I turned my head ever so slightly to glance at him. He didn't look nervous at all.

I took a shaky breath and hoped that my body wasn't trembling hard enough for the whole room to notice. My muscles didn't listen to my desires as the shivers extended to my very toes.

"If you will sign." The scribe held up a large quill. I thought he meant the King, but it was Conrad who stepped forward, bringing me along by the hand. I stiffly ascended the stairwell, praying that

I didn't fall. The King stepped back and folded his hands over his stomach, looking as if he had gotten his life's wish. He coughed again, ducking his head into his shoulder. His shoulders shook with the force of it.

Conrad looked over the document that had just been read out loud. I peeked at it, but the handwriting consisted of so many swirls and large words that it would take me an hour to get through it all.

"I didn't know we had to sign something." My face leaned in close to Conrad as I voiced my concerns. To anyone looking on, which was a room full of people, it would look like a tender whisper to my love.

Conrad leaned back. "Don't worry about it." He peeked at the scribe, giving him a nod, before bowing down to sign his name. He signed his full name, curling the end around the bottom. The quill was then passed to me.

I had written my name a few times, and it was the only thing I knew how to write. I was suddenly grateful that Papa had made me learn how to sign my name. He hadn't taught me how to write Lady, or Westfallen, and I hoped that simply Cosette would do fine. Embarrassed by both my handwriting and how long it took me to complete my signature, I tried to curl the end like Conrad had to make it look fancier. It looked like a child's scribbles compared to his name.

The scribe didn't bat an eye as he took the document and rolled it up. It was then sealed with wax and the King's ring.

The King held up the document and Conrad and I turned to face the room. His hand slid into mine and held them up for the audience to see. From one wall to the other, the throne room exploded in cheers.

The King showed a deep smile as he applauded for us. "Congratulations on your engagement."

Chapter Thirty-Six

I DIDN'T FEEL RIGHT accepting gifts, but my ill wishes did no harm to the relentless pile growing against the wall. My feet hurt and my cheeks were sore from the fake smile I plastered on for the advisors to see.

Conrad stayed close to my side, shaking hands and accepting congratulations. He answered all the questions that we encountered, for which I was grateful. Even so, if I had to hear someone ask where we would honeymoon one more time, I was going to hurl something.

The prince answered graciously that we hadn't planned that yet, without looking bothered at all. It took a little extra strength to keep my smile in place. The thought of sharing a room with

Conrad made my skin crawl. I distracted myself with the sweet aromas of the dinner that I hadn't had the opportunity yet to taste.

Dinner was served in a buffet style, with round tables set up along half the room for us to eat when and what we desired. I desperately wanted a break to rest my feet and shove my face in a strawberry cake, but there never seemed to be a moment.

Anna slipped away after the ceremony, leaving me with no other allies besides Conrad and the few diplomats that I met over the past few months at dinners.

"We knew it would only be a matter of time before you got engaged," one such diplomat gushed. "You two are always so cute together at dinner."

I strained a smile as my stomach rumbled. The overly dressed diplomats went on. "Just think, this will be the rest of your lives, here together. You'll be king and queen, oh, and babies! There will be little princes and princesses running around before too long! I hope you have plenty of little ones!"

"I'm sorry," I blurted out, then quickly tried to recover. "I'm famished, I'm going to try some of the roast, if you'll excuse me?"

Conrad kissed my hand gently. "Of course, I'll join you in a moment." An apology hid in his expression for Lady Bringham's brashness, but I wasn't in a forgiving mood, I was in an escaping mood.

I piled my plate high, so if I couldn't escape then I could hide myself behind it for a good hour. I found the furthest table and plopped myself down, audibly sighing as my feet throbbed with relief. It wouldn't be long before my table was flocked with well-wishers.

Music played from a band in the corner. A few couples danced, but most people were merged into groups, speaking amongst themselves. I recognized only half of the room. Nobility from neighboring countries had been invited to the ceremony, and they filled the other half of the room with thick accents and foreign perfumes. Most sounded like they were from Vernes or other countries not involved in the war, but I recognized a few pins from Osmelee as well. I hadn't seen anyone from Tames.

Conrad joined me before I finished my roast. He lowered himself into the seat next to me with a plate of his own, generously loaded with meat. "I'm sorry for the spectacle. Even I couldn't have predicted how big of an event this would turn out to be."

It was easier to hear him in this far corner of the room than it had been a few minutes before. The diplomats had to practically shout at us to be heard.

I tried to remember that this wasn't his doing, but the King's. "It will make it harder to break the engagement, after so many came to celebrate us."

"Let's not break it then! Let's get married and have all those babies," Conrad said. I would have been upset with him for pushing the matter, but one look at his face showed me he was joking. While I didn't find his sense of humor particularly funny in this matter, I was glad that he wasn't serious. He seemed to finally accept that I wasn't going to marry him.

"Any further word on the coup?" I asked as I stacked vegetables on my fork.

Conrad grunted and finished his bite before answering. "I wish. Still a little pushback from Silas and Nathaniel, but the whole group feels that it will be easier to move forward now that I am engaged and they will be getting both a king and a queen out of the deal."

I stuck up my nose. "Perfect. More people to let down."

Conrad shook his head. "Don't worry about it. When I'm king, we can drag this engagement out as long as we need until the kingdom is secure in my rule. No one can force the king to marry. We will come up with a good reason to end the engagement, so it doesn't cause a scandal."

The way he said it made it sound so easy, but the thought of dragging the engagement out made my stomach queasy.

Eventually, I would need to tell Conrad that I couldn't spin gold.

I wondered if now was a good time. We were in public, so he couldn't make a scene about it. He seemed happy, sipping his wine and conversing with nobles. Perhaps he would go easy on me.

Perhaps. But perhaps not. I wasn't ready to risk his reaction yet.

The sharp sound of a chair sliding across the floor interrupted my thoughts, and when Conrad and I both looked up to see who was joining us, my jaw fell open.

Rumpel. He was dressed in a blue suit with a green and white pin stuck to his chest, and his golden curls were pulled back in a knot, making him look more formal than I was used to. His collar pointed up, and a clock chain hung around his waist. His appearance made him fit in among the other diplomats, and Conrad didn't bat an eye. I blinked twice.

"Sir, join us." Conrad hopped up quickly to pull out his chair. Rumpel thanked him in a thick accent that I didn't recognize.

"It'z an honor to bez here to witniz the ceremony." Rumpel's voice slurred with the accent. He shot a wink as Conrad sat back in his chair. My eyes were wide.

"The honor is ours. Where are you joining us from?" Conrad squinted at his pin.

"Ah. I am Duke Bjorn of Guava. I waz visiting friendz in Osmelee when your invitation reached them. I thought I would come by to see the fabled beauty of Lady Cosette."

Conrad smiled at me and took my hand. "We are grateful that you came."

My back was stiff and eyes fixed on Rumpel, who looked more comfortable than a sleeping cat. He leaned forward as he chatted eagerly with Conrad, asking him all sorts of questions about our relationship. I shook my head at him, but he ignored me. I looked around to see if anyone else noticed Rumpel, but no one was looking our way.

The King caught my attention, coughing into a napkin. That wasn't the first time he coughed today. I'd take extra caution to stay away from him and protect myself from any sickness he might have, so my last days with Rumpel weren't spent wheezing.

"Cosette?" Conrad drew my focus back to him.

"This is a favorite jingle of mine, would you carez to dance?" Rumpel stuck out his hand toward me as amusement danced in his eyes. "If it'z okay with your prince, of courz."

Before I could raise my eyebrow, Conrad waved his hand. "Of course, see if you can teach her more rhythm than I can."

Rumpel laughed with Conrad as if they were close friends, an odd sight to see. I got up slowly and joined hands with Rumpel in an act so strange and so familiar all at the same time.

"What are you doing?" I whispered as soon as we took a few steps away.

"You looked like you needed a friendly face," Rumpel said, squeezing my hand.

"What if you get caught?"

"No one else knows me."

We reached the dance floor and he turned me around to face him, drawing his other hand around my back. Still stiff, I let him lead me through the basic moves. A few people watched us, and I squirmed under their gaze.

"Relax, Cosette, you look like you hate this," Rumpel said.

"I'm just nervous. Today has been a lot." I tried to relax in Rumpel's arms, but I couldn't get too cozy there. I just got engaged to Conrad, and I had to maintain that image. Still at the table, Conrad spoke with another diplomat who'd taken my seat. At least he didn't watch us.

Sunlight streamed in from windows, and we danced in and out of its rays. I'd be trapped in this room until the sun went down, several hours away still. And today wouldn't be the end of it. Tomorrow the guests would still be here, along with the intimate questions, and the giddy, watchful eyes while I'd be expected to fawn over Conrad each night.

"You know," he spoke. "You can, if you want. You can marry Conrad. After I'm gone, I don't want you to be alone."

The very idea seemed ludicrous, and I pulled my head back to see if he was serious. "I have no interest in Conrad. Not now, and not ever."

"Think you'll go back to Aiden, then?"

Was this the sort of thing that went on in his mind? Who I would love after him? "I haven't thought about it," I said, and then, because that sounded too close to a yes, I added, "but no, I won't. Of course I won't." I moved myself closer to him as we danced. "I know this isn't forever, but I am all in, and I'd like to pretend that this is going to last, until the day that you leave."

Those were the kind of words that we used when we talked about him dying. We said leaving, or when he was gone, because both of those phrases sounded better on the tongue then death.

Rumpel pulled his head back and looked me over. "Would you marry me, if I stayed?"

I almost tripped. Truthfully, I'd imagined him asking me that many times. In my dreams, we would have just broken his curse, and he would be so happy that he would pick me up and spin me around the room. Then, he would set me down and lower himself to the floor, asking me to be his bride. I would say yes, and we would laugh and cry together, overcome with joy and the possibilities of a future.

That was the image that I often played in my head before bed. Sometimes we were in the castle, other times we were in a field. Sometimes Rumpel would give a monologue about love, other times he would jump right into the question. There was one thing that didn't change, though. Every single time I said yes. In my head, it was a romantic moment that we would cherish forever, knowing that we had forever.

It wasn't real, and it couldn't be real. In a few months, I would lose Rumpel, and it was becoming painfully clear to me that I couldn't stop that from happening. There was one thing still in my control, however, and I couldn't let him go without him knowing how much he meant to me. He was my whole world.

"Yes, Rumpel. I would marry you in a heartbeat."

He had an intense glint in his eye, and I almost looked away at the tenderness of it. But instead I stayed in his gaze, feeling my heart swell in my chest. I wanted to pull him close, but I kept him at an appropriate distance. I would hold him close later.

Rumpel's voice cracked as he spoke. "I know it's selfish, because I've gotten my share of life. I've lived, I've loved, and I've existed longer than a normal man should. I've had my chance. But I'd give anything to have a life with you. I'd give up everything to be able to give you the rest of my life."

Now it was my turn to cry. I blinked away tears, knowing I couldn't adequately explain them to Conrad. So instead of tears, I let the sadness out in a long sigh. My mouth almost formed the words, *I love you*, but I stopped myself. I hadn't said that yet to Rumpel, and I didn't want the first time to be in a room full of people. I wanted to be able to kiss him as I said it.

So instead I stared at him as we danced, and we didn't say any more.

Too soon the music stopped, and duty pulled me away from Rumpel and back to Conrad. My feet moved, but I left my heart behind with Rumpel. I loved him.

Chapter Thirty-Seven

"FROG FOOT FIXES EVERYTHING, apparently," I said. Rumpel and I giggled as we flipped through the book. Finished spindles of gold lay besides us while we passed the time looking through the book that Old Mr. Walters had given me about breaking curses. I thought of Old Mr. Walters often, mostly wondering what became of that note I wrote for him to give the sorceress. Foolish of me to believe he knew her, but every once in a while, I let myself imagine that he did and could contact her. Dangerously, I let myself hope.

"This remedy requires dragon breath. How do you even get that?" Rumpel wondered, holding his finger over the page.

I squinted. "Are dragons real?"

"Shortly after I became cursed, a baby dragon terrorized the Northern Mountains. They don't breed naturally but can be conjured up by magic. They are surprisingly timid, though, so not worth the hassle."

"Can you make one?" Almost every day I discovered a new ability Rumpel could do and had become fascinated by it.

He smirked at my enthusiasm. "I could, but it would take me a day to accomplish. Would you like that? I could make a dragon for you, to protect you while I'm gone."

I pretended to think about it. Then I shook my head. "No, you don't know this but I'm surprisingly bad at keeping things alive. I had mice once, but they died at the paws of a cat. So I adopted the cat, and she died too. No idea why, one morning she just didn't wake up."

Rumpel laughed. "A dragon is different than a cat, who probably died of old age, by the way."

"It's more than the cat and mice! Any living thing I've ever owned, from pet to plant, has died. I'm not good at keeping things alive, myself included."

"Fine. No dragons then."

"No dragons."

We continued flipping through the pages, and his hand found mine. It was the most he had touched me since we danced at my engagement party, to protect us both from the growing feelings. Time was going by too quickly. If Rumpel's calculations were correct, he only had a month left before the curse was finalized. One month before he was gone.

"Remember when you tried this one?" Rumpel pointed to the page. I groaned and buried my head into his shoulder. His shoulder shook with his laugh. "True love's kiss. I'm not sure what surprised me more, the fact that you kissed me, or that you thought you were my true love. At least you turned out to be right about one thing."

It took me a second to realize that he'd said that I was his true love, but when I did, my heart stung with emotions. Our eyes met while I tried to wrap my mind around the fact that he loved me. *Rumpel loved me, the poor village girl with no Gift.* I didn't deserve him.

"Promise me that when I'm gone you'll forget about me."

"You know I can't promise that."

"Promise you'll try?"

I understood the sentiment behind it, but I wished he'd stop asking me to protect my heart. He'd be gone soon, and there was nothing I could do about it, I knew this. We could never get married or have a life together. These things were my first thoughts every morning. There was no future here, but for the time we had, I wanted to live with my heart open and feel everything, the joy and the love, while I had the chance. And when he died? I wanted to feel that too. I wanted to feel the sorrow of a lost love, not the sorrow of never telling him that I loved him.

I should say it. I should say it now.

After almost telling him at the engagement party, Rumpel had reminded us that we needed to guard our hearts, so I'd kept the sentiment to myself, unsure if I'd ever tell him. If he died before I told him I loved him, I would regret it, and that realization alone was enough to convince me to tell him then. After a slow swallow, I opened my mouth, ready to share my heart, but his eyes darted from me toward the door. Mine followed.

Before another moment passed, Rumpel vanished, leaving the book to fall on the empty floor next to me as the handle of the door turned and it creaked open. Conrad stood in the doorway, peering into the dimly lit room.

"Cosette? I'm sorry to bother you. Oh, you're finished already! What are you still doing in here?"

I brushed off my surprise at seeing him and held up the book. "Reading. I don't like to wake Anna, since she goes to bed early. I was just going to go." I stood up, bringing my book with me. Conrad crossed the distance between us.

"Can you come with me? It's my father."

The thought of the King made me squirm, and my mind instantly started going through everything I had done to upset the King. As far as I knew I hadn't done anything lately, but the King was unpredictable.

The distain was obvious in my voice. "What does he want?"

"He's dying."

"What?" Coldness washed over me, and guilt at my thoughts of dislike. Only then did I notice the slump in Conrad's shoulders, the darkness in his voice, and the redness in his eyes. He took a shaky breath as he stepped back toward me.

"Have you noticed him coughing?"

I nodded. Everyone had noticed. It started around the time of our engagement party and persisted through the month.

"Well, we've had several doctors come, and they agree that he's getting worse. He's coughing up blood. We don't know how much longer he has."

Every bad thought I'd ever directed toward the King suddenly felt selfish. I took Conrad's hand and went with him toward his father's room. Conrad led me up a set of stairs that I had never been on, and down a new hallway. He tapped on the door before easing it open.

The King's room was ginormous. There was a bed bigger than any I had ever seen sitting in the middle of the room. Not along the wall, but right in the middle of the room so you could walk all around it. A long table was pushed against one wall, set up as an endless desk. Behind the bed there looked to be a siting area, though off to the side was an entrance to another room that could have also been a sitting area. A large piano was to the right, and I wondered if the late queen had played. I couldn't picture the King bent over the keys, making music.

A doctor stood near the desk with his open bag next to him. A worried expression stained his face.

"How long have you known?" I asked Conrad. He gulped.

"I just found out the extent of it a few days ago."

"A few days! Why didn't you tell me?"

He looked at me with sad eyes. "I know that this thing between us isn't real. I didn't want to burden you with my troubles."

My heart ached at the sight of his pain. "I would have been there for you as your friend. Why tell me now?"

"My father beckoned us to come to him together."

My heart stopped for a moment, fearing this would be one of those moments where the father said that he didn't want to die before seeing his son wed, and we would be married at his bedside. I scanned the room for a priest, and while there was none, my worries didn't settle. I timidly approached the bedside with Conrad.

The King looked small in the large bed. The room was dark, with only candles lit in a few places and the pale light from the moon coming in. Shadows hid the details of his face, but his breaths came out raspy and a shaky hand wiped sweat from his brow. Seeing him like this, it was hard to believe that I was once so terrified of him.

He slowly extended his hand to Conrad, who took it with both his own. A tear slid down Conrad's cheek, and turned my gaze away from it.

"My son," the King's voice was soft. "Thank you for coming."

"Of course, Father."

"I don't know...how much time I have left," the King said. Oh no. Here it was. "I want... I want to see you married before I die...so I know that you will be okay."

I knew it. I knew he would ask this. I lifted my eyes to Conrad to see his thoughts, but he kept his on his father. "Of course. Anything for you."

No. Conrad continued to comfort his father while I stood like a frozen pawn. The open door called from behind me, and I debated running. How far could I get before someone caught me? Could I make it all the way home?

The King sighed as if we just granted him eternal peace. "Thank you. It'll do my heart good to see you married."

That couldn't be true. Couldn't a father tell when his son wasn't in love, and when his son's fiancée was being forced into the marriage? More likely, he just wanted to see his orders carried out before he died.

That wasn't going to happen.

I stood quietly as Conrad grieved his ailing father. Then, when he wiped his face free of tears, I walked with him back into the hallway. "I'll be back in the morning," Conrad called to the King before he closed the door. I was glad he hadn't said *we* would be back.

Once in the hallway, Conrad leaned against the wall, tilting his head back to rest it against the stone. I tucked my arms around me, unsure what to say in that moment.

After a few breaths, Conrad spoke. "We can get a divorce."

I wanted to be sympathetic in the moment. I really did. If I had found out that my father was passing it would be so hard on me, and I would turn the world around to make his passing easier.

But I wouldn't marry Conrad.

"Do you understand what you are asking of me? Do you know how difficult it would be to find someone to marry me after a divorce?"

"Cosette, it would be quite the opposite. In the town, yes, if you had a failed marriage then it would be difficult to find another husband. But as the former wife of a king? People would be lining up to have your hand. We can say that your tender heart led you to serve underprivileged villages, keeping you away from me, and we felt we could serve our country better apart. The divorce wouldn't have to be shameful. And don't you have some boy from back home who wants to marry you anyway?"

"I only said that I was in love, not that he wanted to marry me. That...it isn't an option." I would let Conrad make of that what he would. "I can't do this, Conrad. This would ruin my life."

"Being with me isn't ruining your life. We won't consummate the marriage; your honor will remain intact. I'll vouch for you. But who knows, maybe you'll fall in love with me."

"Do you hear yourself? This is crazy. I can't do this."

Conrad stepped off from the wall. "It's late. We don't have to talk about this now. Can I walk you to your room?"

Perhaps he was right, and my sleepiness was preventing any sensitivity to him or to the situation. I needed a night's rest and more time to come up with solid reasons why marrying me was not in his best interests.

"I'm sleeping in tomorrow morning; you can find me in the afternoon."

Chapter Thirty-Eight

CONRAD TOOK HIS TIME finding me. I told Anna how the King was sick, and my marriage was getting pushed up, but since I couldn't explain to her exactly why I didn't want to marry Conrad, she couldn't understand my distress. I gave up and turned my attention to a list of reasons why we shouldn't get married.

The biggest reason was that I didn't spin the gold. If he knew that, I was sure my case would look a lot more reasonable. But, while it was my strongest point, it was also my riskiest point. There was no telling what the King would do if he found out I lied to him and the whole kingdom for months.

My other points were weaker, but still valid. I did not love Conrad. That should hold more weight, but it didn't seem to matter to either the prince or the King. Another reason was I wouldn't have time to plan the wedding. I knew that I wasn't expected to be involved in much of the planning, but it meant that diplomats and nobility from other kingdoms wouldn't have time to travel and attend the ceremony, either. With the war still on going, we weren't in a position to be angering neighboring countries.

The war was part of my third point as well. We should wait until the war was over, so the country could really celebrate. It'd be wrong to make merry while a war was going on.

Those were all my points. I could have come up with more, had I not shamelessly slept the morning away.

In the late afternoon, Conrad came knocking at my door. Anna had been given the day off, so I answered the door myself.

Conrad stood outside the door with his hands in his pockets and bags under his eyes, dragging his feet into my room as he undid his tie.

"I'm sorry I'm so late. It's been a crazy day."

"Things with your father?"

"Of sorts. It seems the advisors are more reluctant to go through with the coup now, when it looks like the King will be dead in a month anyway. No one wants to deliver a death blow." Conrad sat down in my chair and peeked up at me. "Are you still upset about the marriage?"

"Yes, but I'm willing to talk about it more rationally now that I've slept."

That perked Conrad up. "Good, because I'm prepared to bribe you into it."

"Bribe me? With what?"

"Simple. Originally, I'd planned to offer you and your family enough money to live comfortably, but you make gold, so I don't think you need my help. Instead, I will give you all the books in the library. They can all be yours. We will still end the marriage when the time comes, and wherever you chose to go beyond that, the books can go too."

The thought of bringing all those books home with me made me swoon, and Conrad saw that hesitation. He lowered himself onto his knees. "Please Cosette, I need this. I need you as my wife to appease my father and make me look like a strong king. Everyone knows that a king's strength comes from his wife. I can secure my rule with you by my side." He rested his hands in his lap, staring up at me with a lost look in his eyes. "Is there anything else you'd want?"

I thought for a moment. "Could you send cakes to my family each month? The cook here makes excellent cakes and pies and tartlets." Contrary to what he believed, I couldn't spin gold, so I would be little use to my family back home besides sweeping floors. But those cakes could be eaten or served in the tavern. They wouldn't do much, but they could help.

Hope flickered across his face. "I can send them by the bucket every single month."

I sighed. I hadn't expected to say yes, but something in his expression changed my mind. Grief mixed with desperation. It mirrored an exact look I once saw on Anika. She was so young at that point, and we were so hungry. Papa had promised to keep her safe, and though I had nothing to offer her, I had promised the same thing.

I could keep her safe now by sending food each month and keeping the tavern afloat in ways that only a queen could.

It could go beyond them. As queen, I would be in position to serve my country and the people in ways that I never could before. Conrad's broken expression stayed on me, the look of a man who would do anything for his kingdom.

This wouldn't be for Conrad, but like him, I would do this for those that I loved. For the sake of my family, and all the times they'd cared for me, I could care for them.

It was with a heavy heart that the words came out. "Alright. I'll be your queen."

Conrad jumped up and grabbed me in his arms, swinging me around. I let out a cry as I clung to him. He set me back down and pulled me in for a tight hug. "Thank you, Cosette. Thank you. We will be married in three weeks."

"Three weeks?"

"I must go begin preparations." He practically ran from the room, perhaps an effort to deprive me the opportunity to change my mind.

A royal wedding required more preparations than I could have envisioned. The flowers, where we put the flowers, how long the flowers would stay out, what food we would serve, who we would invite and where we would seat them. What rooms we would open for company and how we would decorate these rooms. Which glasses would be used for dinner, which forks, which plates? What dress would I wear, and what symbolic jewelry?

These were only the decisions that I was a part of, though I knew many more took place without my aid.

Rumpel voiced his dislike of spending his last month watching the castle be redone for my wedding, though neither of us could do anything about it. Conrad and I would be married, then sent off to a summer home on the border of Westfallen and Vestalin for a vacation, which meant that these next three weeks with Rumpel would be our last. Beyond that, he only had about a week left, if his calculations were correct.

I prayed his calculations were correct.

Each day, I dreaded the thought that he had counted wrong and that he wouldn't be there the next day. I made every goodbye count. But he still showed back up, sometimes in the early morning, sometimes at night after I sent Anna away.

I sent Anna away every chance I got, but it was getting harder and harder to find time alone.

"Are you listening, my lady?"

Her sharp voice pulled me from my thoughts. I stayed up late talking with Rumpel the night before, and was then woken up by

Anna early, so I didn't get a chance to sleep well. The bed called to me, and I looked at it longingly, but was too aware of Anna's tapping foot to give in to the temptation.

"I'm sorry Anna, tell me again."

"I need to start on your dress, so I need to know what color you want."

"Umm, white?"

"Yes, obviously, but what kind of white?" There was more than one white? Seeing my confusion, Anna sighed. Her patience with me grew thin. "Look at these swatches, pick one."

She pushed fabrics toward me to peer at. Some were softer whites, some darker. One was bordering yellow. I didn't want that. I picked the plainest white I could find.

"Finally. Now, we want to incorporate some of the country's colors in the dress, so I was thinking either a blue sash or blue lace at the bottom, or blue stitching in the back."

If I thought about all my options for too long it would make the whole process unbearably long, so my new strategy was giving the first answer that came to mind. "Do the lace. We can do a blue ribbon in my hair too, if you need more blue."

Anna, looking pleased, went on to ask my about what style of dress I wanted. I groaned and settled back into my chair. We could be here for hours.

A knock at the door caused me to sit up. Anna dropped her things to answer it. "Your Majesty."

I craned my neck, thinking she was referring to the king. Perhaps he was better, and I didn't need to get married so soon. Instead, Conrad strolled in. "Ah, more wedding plans, I see."

"That's all I've been doing for a week," I complained.

"Well would you like to take a break with me?" He held out his arm. In truth, I did want a break, but I wanted one by myself. Still, this was something of a win, so I would take it. I told Anna she could make all executive decisions on the dress and left her to work.

"Thank you for saving me."

"I'm not fully saving you, I'm afraid. I do have a few details that I need your input on."

I tried not to let my disappointment show too much, knowing that he was dealing with worse than I was. The King hadn't gotten better, and while he wasn't worse, the doctors were certain that he had a few months at best. Conrad was planning a wedding and a funeral at the same time.

Conrad led me toward the stairs we took to get to the King's room a week ago. Before I could ask him if we were going to see his father, he told me our destination.

"Your room?" I hadn't seen his room before, and I didn't feel comfortable being alone in there with him.

"Yes, soon to be our room. There are a few changes that need to happen before it's ready to host both of us."

"Conrad, I like you as a friend, but I don't like the idea of sleeping in the same bed as you."

The prince blushed. "I'm not asking you to. Unfortunately, it won't be an option to continue staying in your current room. To keep up appearances, we will have to stay in the same room. But there is a sitting room to the side that has a very comfy couch, I can sleep there for the duration of our marriage."

I felt relief at his words. I was glad this wasn't a topic that we would have to argue. "So, what am I needed for?"

Conrad stopped outside a set of double doors. "There are a few feminine touches needed, and since it'll be your room, I figured it should be decorated by you."

He pushed open the door. My jaw dropped.

The room looked like not one, but several storms had come through it. The bed wasn't made, clothes were everywhere, books and papers scattered across the desk and floor and bed.

"You're a slob!" I exclaimed. Conrad put up his hands.

"I am a prince, and I am a busy man. I don't have time to clean my room every day."

"You don't have to do it every day, but maybe once a year?"

Conrad laughed. "My father is dying; I have more important things on my mind then the state of my room." If it wasn't for his smile, I would think he was hurt. I walked toward the bed, pointing at the papers.

"Did you sleep with those in there?"

Conrad laughed again. "Yes, and they survived just fine."

I shook my head. He needed more than a few feminine touches. He needed to see the floor. "Don't you have a maid?"

"I asked them to stop cleaning things when I started losing everything. I know it looks messy, but it's an organized sort of mess. I'm going to have to ask you don't disrupt it."

I tiptoed around the room with wide eyes. Even Anika wasn't this messy.

"When I live here, there's going to be some order to the chaos."

"That's fine by me, I'll clean up before the wedding. I have to, they are painting the walls and redoing the sheets."

I turned around the room and tried to imagine what it looked like without the mess everywhere. "Maybe if there was a small bookshelf by the window with flowers in a pot, and a comfy chair by its side. That would make a sweet haven for me. And a soft rug, so I could go about barefoot. If we took down these hideous paintings, put up something softer. Why on earth do you have paintings of previous monarchs hanging in your room watching you sleep?"

He shrugged sheepishly. "It motivates me to be the best I can be."

"I don't think motivate is the right word. This person has murder in his eyes. I think scare is the word you are looking for."

Conrad laughed so hard that he doubled over. He straightened up, placing his hands over his stomach. "This is why I need your help redecorating the room."

My walk around the room continued as I tried to picture myself living here. There were a few windows on the outside wall, one of which led out to a balcony. The space overlooked the back of the castle, with the river and forest to one side, and the training grounds to the other. It was a tranquil image.

It would need to be cleaned before I could live here; there was no way I'd sleep in a room this messy. The disorder of it would drive me crazy. The desk alone, which currently overflowed with endless papers, would take hours to sort through. Some of them looked extremely important, with dark red seals pressed into the ink, and I wondered if the advisors knew that important documents were scattered around the prince's room along with what looked to be a list of birds.

A different list caught my eye. Held in place by a short candle and empty cup, pushed up to the wall, a paper titled Boys at War lay with crumpled corners. Rumpel's voice flashed through my mind from when he told me that Conrad forced boys to be soldiers. I gulped, turning slowly to study Conrad. He didn't look nervous about me being near the papers, as one might be had they been hiding a secret. His was not the look of a man who forced young boys into a cruel war.

I trusted Rumpel, but I knew that he could be mistaken.

I also trusted Conrad.

The idea of sifting through Conrad's things while he was away, watching him and trying to figure out if Rumpel's claims against him were true, exhausted me. I didn't want to do it. That wasn't the sort of relationship that I wanted to have with Conrad.

"I need to ask you. Do you force boys to fight?"

Conrad's eyes got wide and he crossed his arms. His voice was gruff as he replied, "What do you mean?"

I fumbled the page with my thumb. "I heard a rumor that you go to villages and drag boys back to fight for you, leaving behind a note for their families saying that they chose to go."

Conrad's head tipped in a slow nod. "Who told you this?"

"That's not important. Is it true?" I watched him carefully, trying to evaluate his reaction. He didn't seem offended at the accusation. Instead he moved his hands into his pockets and strode toward me with his eyes on the ground.

"I'm sure it's not as your friend explained."

That was as good as a yes.

Conrad explained, and I took a step back from him as I listened. "The war has been dragging on for years, and we hadn't had new recruits in a long time. I traveled out to villages to see if the hesitation was because the people didn't want to fight, or they didn't know how to join. I found that many boys wanted to fight, but they didn't think it was possible. Either they didn't have the ability to come to the castle to sign up, or their families depended on them for an income. A lot of boys wanted to fight, and I knew if we had them on our side we would win. So, I helped them write letters to their families if they needed, and I send what money I can to their homes to help them get by without their sons."

"But you didn't force anyone to fight who didn't want to?" I asked. That was the crucial part of the tale. Conrad tilted his head.

"I encourage them, but I don't force them." I saw no lie in Conrad's eye, but his story didn't line up with Rumpel's.

I suddenly wished that I was back with Anna, picking out dress designs. That would be better than being here, trying to make sense of this.

I was just about to let the matter drop when I saw it. Conrad pulled back his lips and shifted to his left foot. It was small, but Conrad always held himself confidently. His stance never looked weak. I replayed his words in my head. Did they sound forced?

All the guessing in the world wouldn't give me clarity. I didn't know Conrad well enough to analyze his behavior. All I had was my instinct, and that told me he was lying.

Fear crept up on me, though I knew I was safe here. Still, my body told me to flee, so I listened to it, making small excuses and leaving him standing in that messy room with his hands still in his pockets.

The fear dug deeper as I pondered what sort of person I was marrying.

Chapter Thirty-Nine

"DID YOU HEAR HIM?"

"I did."

"So," I asked, "is he lying to me?"

Rumpel looked right in my eyes. "Yes. His story started out true. For the most part, he brings back the boys who want to fight. But a few, like the ones that are especially strong or fast, are forced."

I tucked my feet under me on the bed. A small cup of tea rested in my hands and crackers sat on a plate next to me. The sun set less than an hour ago, and I had sent Anna away an hour before that so I could spend the rest of my evening with Rumpel.

Wedding preparations had worn me out, and I had eagerly pulled on warm socks and sunk into my bed.

Rumpel had, unsurprisingly, been there to hear my conversation with Conrad. I should have known he wouldn't let me go into another man's bedroom alone. I skipped dinner that night to ponder things over in my room, giving the excuse that there were too many things to prepare to formally dine that evening.

"Alright, you made it sound like he prowled through villages kidnapping boys in the night."

Rumpel scoffed. "He might as well. Even taking one boy against his will is too many. He's taken fifteen."

I felt horrible for thinking this, but fifteen was much better than the hundred that I had been picturing. Still. *Those poor boys.*

Gently, Rumpel sat on the bed next to me and took my hand. "A diplomat went out yesterday with signed papers from Westfallen. Vestalin has already signed, and if Osmelee and Tames follow suit then the war will be over, and the boys can go home. Already the fighting has stopped as all soldiers wait in anticipation. No more lives are in danger."

I hadn't realized I needed to hear that, but my chest felt like a boulder had been sitting on it that was gone. The war was almost over. The soldiers could all go home.

Even though I wouldn't be queen for long, I was glad that I would be coming into the title at the end of a war, instead of the beginning.

"Can you see me as a queen?" I asked Rumpel.

He didn't hesitate before answering, "Yes. I think you are untrained, but that can be fixed. I don't think your mind is clouded by vanity or tempted by riches. You'd rule with a clear head, and that's one of the most important things."

The idea of being queen scared me to my core, and I was glad that someone believed in me. I doubted I would have any responsibilities besides hosting dignitaries who came to visit, but the fact that Rumpel believed I could rule made my heart happy.

"I know you don't want it right now," Rumpel said as he stroked my hand. "But if you become queen and you find that you love it, I don't want you to leave it for me. I don't want you to feel an obligation to me to break your marriage with Conrad. If you find that you love it, or love him, then I want you to be happy."

My body twisted toward Rumpel. "That won't happen. As soon as I can, I will end the marriage. I'll move back home and continue working at the tavern and for Seamstress Kira. I'll save up my money and buy a shop where I'll open a bookstore and serve tea. Maybe someday I'll meet someone else, but I don't need to. You've given me enough love for a lifetime."

I saw a tear form in Rumpel's eye, and I longed to kiss it away. It seemed every time we got together, one or both of us cried. The number of days we had left were fewer, and while I tried not to think about it, it was all that filled my mind.

The Fates blessed me by giving me Rumpel. Even though they would be taking him away soon, I was a better person for knowing him. I would hold on to that fact after he was gone.

Rumpel wasn't the first one to tell me he thought I could be queen. Papa believed in me too. Even with both of their blessings, I still knew that I didn't want it. I had no desire to be queen. I was honored that they felt I was up for the job, but I felt wildly unqualified and considerably uninterested.

"I wish I could stay around to see how beautifully you do in life."

I smiled. "Yeah, me too." And in that moment, the smallest part of me felt sure that everything would be okay. I knew he wouldn't let me kiss him, but I hoped he would let me rest my head against his chest. I put down my cup and brought myself closer to him, asking with my eyes. He raised his arm up for me and I tucked myself safely into his side. As I wrapped myself up next to Rumpel, I wished the castle away, along with all its problems. All that would be left was Rumpel's arm around me, protecting me from the dangers of life and reminding me of his love. In that moment, I allowed myself to forget my worries and breathe a little deeper. I allowed myself to dream, until sleep claimed me and brought vivid ones of its own.

The tears flooded my eyes as soon as I woke. The night before I had fallen asleep next to Rumpel while he stroked my hand, despite how hard I fought to stay awake. *To stay with him.* At some point in the night he must have left, because the sheets beside me were flattened and smoothed, eliminating any trace of him. As always, he'd slipped away right after I fell asleep.

The light hadn't reached the foot of my bed yet, so it was still early. I pulled the silk sheet over my head as a cold tear slid down my temple. I didn't want to move. *Please, don't make me do this.*

The white dress loomed in the corner, taunting me. I called out to Rumpel but only hallow echoes replied. The doorknob jiggled and Anna crept into the room, apologizing as she reminded me of the task at hand. As a reply, I sank further into the bed.

My head was foggy, and my bones felt weak. My heart felt like it had been shattered into small pieces, too delicate to ever be put back together. I wanted to run or hide, but I had nowhere to escape to.

Anna accepted, though she couldn't understand, my sorrow, and her hands moved tenderly to get me ready. As she worked, tears slid down my cheeks, which she kindly ignored.

She helped me into the dress, pulling the intricate fabric up to my shoulders. Where once I might have marveled at the design of the fabric, today I found no joy in its beauty. Instead, I loathed the tight shoes on my feet and the heavy jewelry around my neck. A thin tiara was pinned into my hair, the final piece of the image. I couldn't look at my reflection in the mirror. It was the bitter reality of what this day would bring.

Once finished, Anna left me alone for a few final moments of peace, and I had never been more grateful to her for giving me those minutes.

I drew away from the mirror, feeling the weight of my attire on my body as I trudged toward my bed. My eyes held no more tears left to shed, so I stared at my hands and tried just to breathe.

A new, folded paper lay on my bedside table. With more energy than I'd displayed all morning, I reached for it. *Please be from him.*

He had given me one last gift. I opened the note, greedily soaking in the words.

My dearest, darling Cosette,

I love you with all of my heart. You have given me more in this last year of my life then I could have ever asked for. For so long, I thought that I had had my love, but then you came around and opened my heart. Now there is no doubt in my mind that you are the one I was meant to find. Do not think that true love's kiss didn't work because you aren't my true love, because, my darling, you most certainly are. You are the truest thing in my life. I give my whole heart to you so that it will live on long after I am gone. I love you, Cosette, and I would give up everything to be with you.

Yours forever,

Rumpel

My body crumbled as I clung to the last piece of him that I would ever hold. I smelled the letter, trying to catch one last whiff of him. One tear fell on the page and I wiped at it feverishly, desperate not to blemish the letter. It needed to stay looking this perfect forever, just as he was.

My body was still shaking with sorrow when Anna came back in the room. Silently she approached me, wrapping her slender arms around me without question. I leaned into her, grateful for her presence.

When I could avoid it no longer, I wiped my eyes clean. Anna dutifully repainted my face and polished my eyes. My fingers clenched the letter, not willing to let go. Anna seemed to understand and held up the shoulder of my dress.

"It can slide it in here. It won't be comfortable, though."

I was already beyond comfort. Grateful to her, I slid the letter into the shoulder of my dress, keeping it tight against my skin. Anna repositioned the dress, so it was perfect again, then held my hands in front of me.

"Are you ready for your wedding?"

Just when I thought I had no tears left to cry, another slid down my face.

Chapter Forty

THE ROOM SMELLED LIKE lilies and death. I kept my shoulders back as I walked down the aisle, ignoring all the people in the room. I knew I should have been smiling, but I couldn't feel my face. I felt numb all over.

I should have let Rumpel take me away when I had the chance. I had been so convinced that staying was the right thing to do, but standing under those tall ceilings, surrounded by painted faces, it was hard to rationalize my decision. All I could feel was unbearable grief. I would never see Rumpel again.

Conrad looked like a proud groom. He deserved a glowing bride. I couldn't be that girl for him.

The King looked better today, but I could still tell that he was weak. His body hunched more than usual, his hand shook, and his forehead was creased with the strain of trying to sit up straight. Any strength he had left was fading quickly.

It didn't seem fair to me that an old king who was losing his mind could still hold so much power. Especially since a sickness had claimed him, he should have been relieved of his duty. He shouldn't have been able to threaten me into a marriage. He shouldn't have been able to rule. But there was nothing I could do about it. I was just the storyteller's daughter.

With luck, this marriage wouldn't last more than a few months. Then I could go home.

Conrad met me at the end of the aisle, taking one of my hands in his. We settled on our knees in front of the priest. He was a heavyset man with a smooth face, but a rough smile. He held a staff in one hand and a big book in the other. I lowered my head so he wouldn't see the grief in my eyes.

I wondered if Rumpel was here somewhere, watching me commit myself to another man. I hoped he wasn't anywhere nearby. I didn't want him to see me this way. If he had to see me in a wedding dress, it should have been for him.

The priest launched into some long speech about Westfallen and marriage. Conrad kept a gentle grip on my hand, stroking it with his thumb. Every so often we would hear a noise from behind us, a sneeze or a muffled clatter, but other than that I tried to ignore the room full of people that I should have never met. I wondered which ceremony would be bigger, this one or the coronation after the King's death. I cringed at the thought of having to go through this again. I couldn't hide this from my family forever; word would reach them that I was queen. I dreaded telling them what happened almost as much as I hated going through it in the present.

The priest stepped to his right, revealing a small table behind him. Three large candles sat on top. Conrad and I were to light ours and then light the middle one together, something about our fires never going out for each other. With trembling feet, I followed Conrad over to the table, taking hold of one of the candles. Somewhere, someone was playing a piano.

"Are you alright?" Conrad whispered to me.

I looked him over. There was nothing but kindness in his eyes for me. "I will be."

"He's a lucky guy, whoever has your heart," Conrad said. I pushed my emotions down my throat as they threatened to come out. I wouldn't cry again, not in front of all these people.

I pursed my lips as I tipped my candle forward in unison with Conrad. Right as the wick took the flame, the back door was pushed open.

I peeked up to see who it was and almost dropped my candle. Rumpel was walking quickly down the aisle, dressed as a prince. He wore a red suit coat on with a white sash around it, decorated with pins. His pants looked pressed and he wore nice black shoes. I stared as he came closer. Others turned to look at the man coming down the aisle, no doubt thinking he was simply a latecomer.

I didn't care what they thought. I got to see Rumpel again.

The candle dropped from my hand and almost caught fire to the tablecloth. I patted at it quickly to put it out. Conrad muttered something under his breath, but I couldn't make it out. My head was spinning.

"Stop everything," Rumpel called out once, then again. He came to the front of the room and dropped himself next to the King. I almost tripped over my dress as I flew down the stairs toward him. Conrad followed suit, and several guards approached us.

The entire room started to shift as people turned to ask each other questions. All I focused on was Rumpel's face. He said something to the King, who slowly brought his eyes up to me.

"Is this true?" I barely caught the King's words and halted my approach. Conrad passed me and brought himself protectively to his father's side.

"Yes." I could hear Rumpel clearly then. "Cosette cannot spin straw into gold. I can."

Everything happened so slowly from there. The gradual turning of heads from the few people close enough to hear what was happening. The narrowing of eyes from the King, the furrowed brow from Conrad. Rumpel looked at me over his shoulder and gave me a steady smile and simple nod. My feet didn't allow me to move. I stood frozen in that spot as I waited for the royal reaction.

This was what I dreaded during my entire stay at the castle. Every day for the past six months, I feared what would happen when the King found out that I was a fraud. My mind pictured this moment a thousand different ways. I never would have guessed that moment would come while I stood in a wedding dress in front of the whole kingdom.

The King was going to kill me.

I doubted more than a second had passed. Rumpel twisted back toward the King. "If you let her go, I vow to stay here and spin gold for you and for your son every day for the rest of my life."

That was sneaky of him. The King didn't know that Rumpel only had a week left to live.

"Why should we trust you?" Conrad asked. He had his hands around his father's shoulders.

"Cosette never lied when she told you she can't spin gold, yet you told her you'd kill her if she didn't. Do you know what you've put her through these past six months? I didn't have to stay to give you gold, but I've done so every single night. I've already proven that I'll do that for her."

I wanted to go to Rumpel, but all I could do was watch the King's face to see if he would show mercy on us.

It was Conrad's expression that showed remorse as he looked right at me. "You could have told me."

I brought my shoulders up then let them fall again. "I was afraid."

The guards stayed close but let their hands fall from their swords. Some brave people wandered up the aisle to try to see what was going on, but other guards held them back. I was grateful for the space. The priest rubbed his forehead as he watched the spectacle.

The King slowly leaned forward in his chair. "She can go, if she passes my test."

I wasn't sure that I heard him right. Conrad looked at his father in surprise. "Father, we have no use for her anymore. She should be allowed to return home."

The King waved him off. "She's signed a contract agreeing to marry you. She belongs to you now." His voice crackled as he spoke.

Conrad scoffed as he pointed at Rumpel. "She doesn't belong to me. We can have this man instead."

I didn't like the thought of them owning Rumpel. I didn't want Conrad or the King anywhere near him.

"I'll need you to sign a contract saying that you will let Cosette be in peace. Then I will start spinning gold immediately." Rumpel was still crouched down on one knee next to the King.

Though we waited for the King's reply, it was Conrad who spoke in a light voice. He studied me, then Rumpel. "So, this is the man you love."

I nodded to him while Rumpel raised his eyebrows and smirked, looking back at me as he did. I hadn't told him that Conrad knew I was in love with someone else.

"It seems we should know who this man is."

Rumpel shook his head. "All you need to know is that I'm a man of my word. In addition to giving you gold, I can heal your father."

That sent a new murmur through the people around us. Their whispers carried the tale back toward the far edges of the room.

Conrad gawked. "Can you do that?"

Rumpel lifted up his hand and placed it on the King's knee. The guards stepped closer, but Conrad raised up his hand to stop them. He watched intently as Rumpel kept his hand there for several moments. The King's back gradually straightened. A touch of color returned to his face. He still looked weak, but there was obvious improvement.

"I can't keep him from death, but I can heal him from the sickness that has him now," Rumpel said. Conrad's eyes were wide as he moved in front of his father.

"How do you feel?" He breathed the question as he clung to his father's hands.

The King licked his lips. "I think he's telling the truth." He coughed, but it wasn't a thick, long one like before. "But we will look weak if you don't go through with the wedding. We've already informed every country of the engagement and thrown a party in your honor. Now it is your wedding day. Imagine the scandal if she walks out in front of all these people? No one will stop talking about it."

"You suggest I marry her so that people won't talk?"

The King cleared his throat again before settling his eye on his son. He grasped Conrad's hand in his. "Gossip is a king's ruin."

For a moment, Conrad looked like he was debating it. I knew how strong of a king he wanted to be. How far would he be willing to go to maintain his reputation?

I found my voice. "I won't marry him."

"Then you agree to my test?" The King looked delighted, as if this is what he'd wanted all along. "You pass my test, you go free. If not, you marry Conrad."

I felt he was missing the important part. I was no use to his son. "But I can't spin gold."

"Father, you've lost your mind. You're not well."

The King waved his hands again at Conrad, pushing him back. He found more strength now and he shifted in his seat. "She signed a contract agreeing to marry you. I am the only one who can declare said contract as void. If she wants to leave, she has to pass my test."

As soon as he was done speaking, Rumpel turned to me. "Cosette, you don't have to do this." He moved back to the King and held his hands out. "Sir, I'm offering my life in exchange for hers. She is of no value to you. I will give you gold and save your life if you let her go free."

The King laughed. It sounded bitter to my ears. "I still plan to hold you to your word. The gold, my life, and her freedom. If she can pass my test."

"You're playing games, Father. Let her go."

"Test me. See if I'm playing a game. I guarantee you that I am serious. If she can't pass my test, she marries you."

"But then we get no more gold." Conrad tried to reason with his father. He ran his hands through his hair and looked around wildly, only realizing it for the first time. "You've lost your mind."

All the people were out of their seats now, moving about the room, hiding their faces behind their hands as they whispered, trying to get the full story. If the King thought the wedding could resume as normal, he was crazy. The people were already talking, and I had no faith that the story would remain inside these walls.

Suddenly I felt ashamed of myself for letting it get to this point. I should have fought the King harder that first night. I shouldn't have let Rumpel spin for me. I should have told Conrad sooner. For six months, I'd dodged the truth and let Rumpel cover for me, while the pit in my stomach grew along with my fear of what would happen when the King found out that I couldn't spin gold, and I let that hold me back from telling the truth. I rationalized my actions by convincing myself that I was saving my life and that the situation was out of my control. I spent so long caring what others thought of me that I didn't stand up for myself.

I stepped forward. "Tell me your test."

A slow smile spread across the King's face. Fear took hold of my heart, but I kept my chin up. His voice scratched my ears. "It is a simple question, with a simple answer. What is my name?"

"Father, you've lost your mind. She doesn't need to play your games," Conrad said, but I put up my hand.

Fates had passed me over for a Gift, denied me good looks, gracefulness, or charm, and deprived me of the one thing they'd given to everyone else. But they blessed me today, because I knew the answer to the King's riddle.

I read his name in a book when I was searching for Rumpel's story. The bizarreness of the name stuck with me, so much so that I remembered it clearly.

Now it was my turn to smile, first at Rumpel, then at the King. "Your name is King Bellifusa De'mentaro."

His face fell into a scowl. Rumpel breathed a sigh of relief and sprang to his feet, embracing me at last. I breathed him in as I wrapped my arms around him, feeling his note move in the fabric by my shoulder as I did. It made me smile; I had been so distraught this morning, convinced that I would never see Rumpel again. Now I held him in my arms.

"We should have thought of this sooner. I could have set you free so long ago," Rumpel spoke into my hair.

"She played your silly game. Can she go home now?" I heard Conrad ask.

The King grunted. "Yes, but the gold man stays."

I clung to Rumpel, realizing that I was about to say goodbye all over again. "I'll come visit you," Rumpel said quickly as my eyes looked around wildly. The King was motioning for guards to take me. I dug my hands into Rumpel, not wanting to be parted from him again.

"Take her back to her village," the King commanded. "And bring straw for our new friend."

My breath caught in my throat as I looked over Rumpel's face. I could see all his love through his eyes. I wanted to kiss him, but I felt my arms being tugged away.

"No." I pulled against my captors, but they were stronger. My hand slid from Rumpel's arm until we were separated and my breath caught in my throat. "No, I don't want to leave him."

Rumpel snapped his head around to the King. "Do I not get to say goodbye?"

"My generosity has been extended enough today. I have no more patience for the girl."

Conrad's expression held no generosity either. He stood in his wedding attire, rejected as I got pulled away. The room was in an uproar now, and it was hard to hear anything. Rumpel turned his head back toward me. The guards had brought me almost to the side door.

"I love you!" I called out in vain, unsure if Rumpel could hear me. My only reply was a shut door.

Having no desire to be dragged off, I cooperated in my removal from the castle. I was led directly to the stable, where horses were mounted to a carriage. The mud squished beneath my shoes and dirtied the end of my wedding dress as the horses whined around me. *Rumpel will visit soon,* I repeated to myself. Maybe he would come that evening.

We planned on not seeing each other during his last week, because I would be on my honeymoon with Conrad and I wanted Rumpel to find some sort of peace before he was gone. But as I headed home while he stayed at the castle, I had no doubt that he would slip away every day to visit me until he couldn't anymore.

I feared what the King would do when Rumpel left next week, but Rumpel was smart and Conrad was kind. Rumpel would get the King to agree to my continued freedom, and Conrad would leave me be.

I was loaded into the carriage with two guards, and we started the long trip home. I stuck my head out the window to watch Westnut Castle get further and further away.

When it was out of sight, I breathed deeply at last. It was over. I was free.

But I was broken.

Chapter Forty-One

WE ARRIVED AT SUCH a late hour that the tavern was empty. The guards did little more than stop on the tavern road and let me out. Reluctantly, I offered them room for the night, but they declined. We'd already endured a painfully long ride together, and I was eager to be rid of their company anyway.

Quiet as a mouse, I snuck toward my room, but Anika heard my noises and came to check. After that, the whole family was woken up and gathered in my room to hear my tale. I was quite a sight in my wedding dress stumbling in after dark. They kept asking if I was home for good, and I reassured them several times that I was.

I tried to tell my story with as little emotion as possible, but I teared up as I told them about Rumpel. I couldn't capture my emotions in words, nor could I explain to them how deeply I had fallen in love with him. I could only tell them how he was cursed and would die next week. It was the first time I said that word out loud, and it felt like poison on my tongue. They comforted me through my tears, but I reassured them that I would see him again before he left.

Truthfully, I had hoped he would be waiting for me when I got home. I supposed he knew how late it was and that I would need my sleep. I told myself that I would see him in the morning, and there was nothing to worry about.

My family promised me more of their questions in the morning, but they let me have my night. The heavy dress slid off my shoulders as I replaced my life in the castle with my life at the tavern, and the itchy clothes that came with it. Rumpel's note got tucked into a drawer with my few socks and shoes. His words would comfort me in the morning, and soon he would be here too.

But Rumpel wasn't there when I woke. He didn't come all day. I tried not to fret as I explained to my family why I didn't invite them to my wedding, but by nightfall the worries consumed me. Anika comforted me, saying he was probably busy, but my fears persisted.

When he didn't come the next day, I started to fear the worst. Chores were the only thing that eased my mind, and I threw myself relentlessly to them. Seamstress Kira agreed to continue seeing me, but I needed time before I could face her house and the spinning wheel that lay within, reminding me too much of Rumpel.

The one good thing I brought home was news that the war was almost over. It spread quickly, resulting in a celebration at the tavern that night. Many lost sons would soon be coming home. Aiden was at the tavern the second night, and his body went stiff when he saw me. Dressed in one of my plain dresses and sitting on my usual stool in the corner, it was almost as if nothing had changed.

Almost.

He crossed the room to me and I gulped. The last time I saw him, he had told my secret to the King and almost cost me everything. Now home safe, those feelings of anger toward him began to simmer down, but my heart wasn't ready to forgive. Still, I cordially shared my tale with him while he shook his head in wonder.

Finally, he threw up his hands. "I still don't understand, but you're home for good now?"

I nodded.

He rocked back on his heels. "I'm really sorry about everything." His voice was low but I felt the sincerity in his words. I pulled my lips back as I shrugged.

"It happened, it's over now." If I stayed in this village, I'd see Aiden often. There was no use holding a grudge when no one got hurt, but I would never let him back in my heart.

We stayed in the main room with people gathering at tables around us. It all looked so normal: the smell of ale, the cheers from tables, the sight of Aiden, the grins from my parents. This was home, yet I didn't belong anymore. The long months had gone and taken me with them, leaving behind someone I hardly recognized. It would take me a while to get to know this new person.

I prepared myself for Aiden to ask about our relationship, and if we could pick it back up again, but he never did. I think he finally recognized it was over. He moved away soon to talk with other folks, who could no doubt hold a conversation better than I could right now. All I could think of was Rumpel.

Anika approached me a few minutes later, shaking off her hands and plopping herself down on the stool next to me. She followed my eyes to Aiden and made a little sound. "Ah yes. Poor lad will never get over you, I'm afraid."

I prayed that wasn't true. I hoped that I hadn't turned him off to finding love. He deserved it, and I knew several girls who would be happy to find it with him.

In a very un-Anika-like gesture, my sister reached for my hand. "Come with me."

"What?"

"I haven't wanted to bring this up while you are mourning your lost love, but I want you to come with me when I leave for the manor. I don't like the thought of you wandering around here alone. You can start over. The manor is near the Vestalin castle, and we'd be welcome at court. It'll be a great sister adventure."

I dreaded thinking of all the trouble that Anika could get into living on her own and attending court. They had no idea what was coming for them. I pulled my eyes away from Aiden to study her. It was a tempting offer. "I don't want to leave Mama and Papa alone."

Anika waved her hand at them. "They'll be fine. They deserve a life away from us, and I think we're old enough to take care of ourselves."

"They're hesitant to let you go without me, aren't they? I'm your chaperone?"

Anika grinned. "Yes. But I meant what I said about the sister adventure. I think it'll be good for us."

She had a point. Looking over the tavern, I realized that I didn't want to live in the shadow of my old life.

"Alright."

"You mean it?" Anika sounded surprised. "Because I had several more arguments ready."

I laughed. "I'm sure you do."

She leaned back against the bar, her eyes on Papa. "It's good to have you back. They were overbearing while you were gone. I got my way a lot, though. Do you know I was this close to getting a gambling table put in?" She held her fingers an inch apart.

"You know how to play cards?" Her mischievous smile answered that question. I laughed. Of course she did.

She slid off the chair, turning to give me one last grin. "We are going to have so much fun together."

Chapter Forty-Two

MY TEARS KEPT ME company all through the night. It was the fifth day, and Rumpel hadn't come to visit me. It was all too clear why. He had been off on his calculations. His curse had ended, he was gone.

Rumpel was gone.

If the King wasn't a madman who would likely kill me if I showed back up, I would have run all the way to the castle by now to look for Rumpel. A small part of me held out hope, but as each moment passed that hope flickered dimmer, until it was too small to comfort me.

My sorrow felt like a deep hole carved into my chest, pulling at my insides and making it hard to breathe. My promise, on leaving the castle, was that I would see Rumpel again. Our last interaction replayed in my mind. I wish I would have known it would be the last time I saw him; I would have held on to him longer. I would have kissed him. *Why didn't I kiss him?*

My one consolation was the note that he wrote me, which I reread until it was memorized. The edges of the paper were rubbed soft and I was worried the note would fall apart at the rate that I was handling it.

I had to limit myself to keep the grief from swallowing me up and would only allow myself to open the note once a day. I couldn't drive myself mad that way.

I was slow to pack and get all my things ready to leave. Mama and Papa agreed that going to the manor was the best thing for me, and our timeline moved up. Anika was ready and waiting for me by the front door, but I took my time. This room looked foreign to me now, while it once kept me so safe, and it felt strange to abandon it now. My leather bags loomed in the corner, waiting to be picked up.

I broke my rule and opened Rumpel's note again. I wanted his words to comfort me as I left my childhood home.

I love you, Cosette, and I would give up everything to be with you.

His words never failed to bring tears to my eyes. I tucked them into my pocket before picking up my bags. It was time. I needed to leave.

I grabbed one bag and pushed the other over to the door with my foot, where I reached with my free hand to pull on the handle. Anika appeared in the doorway with her arms crossed. She donned a riding jacket on over her dark dress, and her hair was braided and wrapped around her head. Though only seventeen, she looked incredibly grown up when she put effort into her appearance.

"I'm sorry I took so long, I'm coming now." I huffed as I hauled my second bag up over my shoulder.

"I'm glad you know I want to leave. Keep that in mind. There's someone at the door for you."

Anika must have been too free in telling people we were leaving. Perhaps Aiden caught word and wanted to talk before we left.

"I'll make it quick."

Anika didn't offer to help with my bags as we walked. I wondered if the horses were there yet. Some neighbor had heard where we were going and offered two of their horses for the journey. The horses belonged to their cousin, who lived near our manor, and we were saving him a trip by bringing them ourselves.

We stepped into the main room of the tavern, in view of the front door. Papa and Mama came into view first, sitting in a booth by the east wall. Their backs were to me and Papa's head moved as if he were talking, but he wasn't looking at Mama. With a few more steps my angle shifted, allowing me to see our visitor.

The golden hair came in to view first, then the thick eyebrows and long nose. I gasped, dropping my bags.

Rumpel was here.

My head whipped around to Anika who stood behind me with a smirk on her face. She knew! "Anika, why didn't you tell me?"

She shrugged, not giving me an answer. I didn't wait for one, turning to Rumpel instead.

"And you, why didn't you come sooner? Do you know what you've done to my heart?" I clutched my hand to my chest.

"I'm sorry about that, but I'm here now."

He slid out from the booth and stood up with a big smile on his face. He was dressed in a plain shirt and riding pants, with his hair wild as if he had in fact ridden a horse to get there. There was cracked mud on his shoes, chipping off as he strode toward me with his arms up. "I tried; I couldn't come right away."

Emotions were flooding through my veins. I spent the last week crying each night, haunted by visions of Rumpel dead. I drove myself mad thinking that he was gone, replaying our last times together and wishing I had more moments with him. I thought he was gone. And he was there, in my parent's tavern, coming toward me.

"I thought you were dead." My voice came out in a gulp. The distance between Rumpel and I closed, and he wrapped his arms around me, letting my tears fall on his shoulder. The familiar scent of him filled my lungs, calming me.

"Those darned horses are taking their time," Anika said, tapping her foot at she stared out the window. I ignored her, pulling back from Rumpel so that my eyes could drink him in.

"How long can you stay?" I asked. If his calculations were right, he should only have a day or two left at best. My hands clenched his arms tight, unwilling to let go, as if the second I did he would vanish forever. My eyes blinked rapidly as they held back tears. Was he really there in front of me? How long did I have before he was truly gone?

"Forever."

I wasn't sure that I heard him correctly. That couldn't be right.

Rumpel beamed with pleasure as he loosened my grip on his arms and cupped them in his, kissing my fingers gently. "It's a long story, but the short answer is that I'm yours forever."

My hand flew to my mouth as tears slid down my cheeks and I choked on my words. "I don't understand. How?" My head spun, wanting to believe him, but I spent so long thinking his time was limited, I couldn't understand what he meant when he said forever.

His forehead found my own and he breathed deeply, letting his breath warm my cheeks to remind myself that he was real. I pulled back and looked at his eyes, begging for answers.

"Sit, I'll explain everything to you." Rumpel motioned to the table and led me to the seat across from Papa. At some point, Mama had gotten a glass of water, which she handed to me. My throat felt dry, but I was hesitant to let go of Rumpel's hand, even to drink something.

"I'll start with what happened right after you left. Conrad ordered me into a side room, where the King and a handful of guards joined us. That's when the sorceress appeared. There were sparks and music and mist; it was quite the spectacle. Oh, you should have seen the King's face! He looked terrified! Conrad too, but he hid it better. The guards threw what weapons they had toward her, but they went straight through, and since she was in the middle of the room Conrad ordered they stop so they didn't injure anyone."

"The same sorceress who cursed you?"

"The very one. She looked exactly as she did a hundred years ago. Anyway, while the King stared dumbfounded, Conrad was shouting orders at her and those around him and ended up annoying the sorceress so much that she took away his voice. I really wish you'd been there to see it all. Then she hands me this—" Rumpel took something out of his pocket and handed it to me. I unfolded it before recognizing what it was.

It was the note I asked Old Mr. Walters to write for me and send to the sorceress. He actually did it. Curiosity hit me and I wondered what his story was, but it was masked by my need to know the rest of Rumpel's tale.

"The sorceress got your note."

My heart felt like it could burst with joy. Surely this was a dream. This was my greatest wish come true, and my mind struggled to accept it was real. "So, we didn't do anything to break the curse?"

"That's the thing. Apparently, the original way to break the curse was to feed a frog foot to a swan at midnight under a full moon. Though, how I was supposed to know that is beyond me. She's a little bit crazy." Rumpel laughed.

"Frog foot: it really does fix everything."

I could see my parents still sitting in the booth as they minded our space. Papa's arm was over Mama's shoulders and they smiled at us. Anika was still anxiously peering out the window, drumming her short fingers on the pane.

Rumpel chuckled. "It really does. Obviously, I didn't do that, but she said she was moved by my offer to stay so you could go free, and then by my offer to heal the King, who I don't care for. But, more than that, she was moved by your letter. It turned her heart and she took pity on us. We got lucky. If she had been in a bad mood, I doubt it would have worked. But we caught her on a good year."

I hated the thought that if she was in a different mood then Rumpel would be dead. I didn't like thinking something as random as that could have taken him away from me, and I would spend the rest of my life grateful that she showed mercy.

Rumpel continued without taking a breath. "The curse ending came at a price, though. She took my magic away. That's why I couldn't come sooner; I had to acquire a horse first! Plus, there were other things to attend to. After the King and Conrad discovered I'm the king of old, as soon as he was given his voice back, he started going on about how I couldn't take his throne from him. The sorceress took his voice away again with a snap of her fingers. She went in hysterics, saying she would curse everyone if we put Conrad on the throne, and anyone who wanted to challenge her could do so. None of the guards dared say a word, and Conrad couldn't even if he wanted to. A few advisors had wandered into the room by this point, but they stayed quiet as well.

"She took away his title right there, as well as the King's. He spoke up at that, but she told him if he kept his title, she wouldn't heal him, and his sickness would kill him within a month. Everyone could see he was losing his mind anyway, so I don't think anyone cared that he wasn't king anymore."

I tried to keep up with the story, and I could picture Conrad's face as he lost his throne. I shouldn't, but I almost felt bad for him. "So, what did he do?"

"She made him an advisor instead. He will still play an important role in Westfallen politics, but he won't have any power."

"So, we don't have a king?"

Rumpel cleared his throat. "Actually, they offered to let me take his place."

All of our jaws fell open. I closed my mouth first. "Is that what you want?"

Rumpel smiled at me. "I want a life with you, that's what I want. So, it's up to you. What life do you want us to have together?"

I tried to think about it, but I knew my answer right away. I didn't know exactly what life I wanted, but I knew what I didn't want. "I don't want to be queen."

"I figured you would say that. I already declined the offer. The throne will go to Gerard, Conrad's cousin. He's a decent man from what I've seen, with a kind wife and a little boy."

I felt like this was all happening so fast. Five minutes ago, I had been ready to leave with Anika to travel to the manor. If we had left a few minutes sooner, we might have missed Rumpel. "So, this is it? We're free from the curse and the castle?"

"We are free."

"Finally," Anika said. I turned to her, but she wasn't looking at me. One hand was on her hip and the other was shading her eyes as she looked through the glass window.

"You're going on a trip?" Rumpel asked, looking down for the first time at my bags.

"I know I am, not sure what she'll do," Anika said. I explained the situation to Rumpel.

"We can still go, if you want. I convinced them to let you keep your title. We could start a new life there."

Gratitude swelled in me. I hadn't realized that they might take our title away, but Rumpel was always looking out for me. It was hard to believe that I would have him looking out for me for the rest of our lives.

This decision of where we would live deserved more than an impulse choice, but Anika was tapping her foot as she waited for us to choose. The horses hadn't reached us yet, but I knew she would want to take off as soon as she could. The birds were finishing their morning songs, meaning we would have to leave soon if we wanted to get to the manor before the sun set.

"Let's go," I said with surprising certainty. I wasn't sure if we would stay at the manor or not. It had been uninhabited for some time, and I was not eager for cobwebs and the musk of dust. But we could go there with Anika to see her started and kept out of trouble for a time. The task of caring for my sister would be almost as great as getting the manor into shape.

After that, who knew where we could go. After six months of stolen moments in the small straw room, the world suddenly opened its arms to us and presented all its opportunities.

"Yes! Let's do it!" Rumpel picked me up and swung me around the room. Laughter escaped my chest as I clung to him. He set me down gently, then leaned down to kiss me, and my head tilted back as he pressed into me. His kisses were always sweet, but it felt different knowing I could kiss him for the rest of our lives. The futility of our romance had left, leaving behind joy and hope. Our kisses before left a bitter sting, as we both knew we were playing with our hearts by allowing them to feel for each other. But this kiss? This kiss with different. This kiss held the possibilities of a life together, and it made my head dizzy with glee.

He pulled back and his eyes shone like stars as he looked over me. I held his gaze as a sigh escaped my chest. This moment felt fragile, and I wanted to hold on to it for as long as I could. There was something so special about it, and I knew I would remember it forever: from the bright light coming through the windows and casting a glare on the floor, to the clean, familiar tables and my loving family gathered around. For the rest of my life, I would remember this moment as the one in which everything fell into place. A feeling flooded my heart, and I labeled it. Peace.

"If you two are done snogging, the horses are ready," Anika said. Her backpack slumped over her shoulder as she picked up two smaller bags in each hand. My parents slid out of the booth and looked at us with both joy and sadness in their eyes. They had already informed us that in a month they would shut down the tavern for a few days to come visit us, so we would see them soon.

I nodded to Anika, who let out a whoop. She yanked the door open and marched out of the tavern.

Rumpel turned to me. "Actually, do you mind if I get something to eat first? It seems my stomach needs nourishment now."

I grinned at the humanity of his request. What would Rumpel be like without his magic? "You can't sneak up on me anymore. You'll have to knock like a normal person."

He threw his head back and laughed. "I don't mind. For you I'd knock a thousand times."

I don't know why, maybe it was the joy or the relief that was still crowding my mind, but I was sure that no sentence had ever sounded more perfect.

"Before we do that," Rumpel let go of my hand and knelt on the floor as I sucked in my breath. He smiled up at me. "Cosette, you are the best part of my heart, and I'm convinced yours is made of gold. I know you wish you had a Gift, but I will spend the rest of my life grateful that you don't, because without it, you were led to me. You gave me back my life, and I want to spend the rest of mine with you."

Tears streamed down my face as I remembered all the times I'd imagined this moment, knowing that it would never happen. I almost laughed thinking of when he had asked me as we danced, while he pretended to be a visiting diplomat. This moment surpassed that one by far.

A tear slid down his cheek, melting my heart.

"Marry me?"

I settled myself on the floor next to him, kissing him gently. "Yes."

I always thought that if I had a Gift, I wanted it to be big or extravagant. I wanted something spectacular so I could provide for my family in some way. I was certain that if I had a Gift, I wouldn't need anything else.

I'd never know why the Fates didn't bless me with a Gift, but I did know that I had been wrong. Being here with Rumpel with the rest of our lives ahead of us was all that I needed. That was the greatest Gift.

Other books by Victoria McCombs

<u>The Storyteller's Series</u>

    The Storyteller's Daughter

    Woods of Silver and Light

    The Winter Charlatan (Dec 2021)

    Heir of Roses (May 2022)

<u>The Royal Rose Chronicles</u>

    Oathbound (Feb 2022)

    Silver Bounty (Jan 2023)

    Savage Bred (Jan 2024)

<u>The Fae Realm</u>

    Mortal Queens (May 2024)

    Shattered Kings (Jan 2025)

A note to my readers

Welcome to the Storyteller's Series! Fairytale retellings were my first obsession in books, so it was the natural place for me to begin when writing my own.

Something you may not know if that reviews mean everything to an author's career. The more reviews a book has, the more success it'll see from booksellers. I'd love if you left me a review on amazon! I'll read every review posted so I can hear your thoughts on my book! I love hearing from readers and am grateful for your time. You are also welcome to find me on social media (Instagram: victoria_mccombs) to connect further! My inbox is always open to readers!

Thank you! Your support means the world to me.

-VM

Acknowledgements

There are so many people who go into the process of writing, and even as I'm not indie, that list keeps growing. First, thank you to my kids who play semi-nicely while mommy writes. And thank you to Jonathan for always listening to my ideas even when you don't know what's going on. Thank you to my parents who help out so I can write and who always encourage me to keep pursuing this. And huge thanks to Oma. Without you, this book would only be half of what it is.

Thank you to the amazing community on Instagram where I've found so many friends to go on this journey with me. Ruth, for always being there for me to talk about books with. Caitlin and Stephen who I ask a million questions to about how publishing works. Danielle and Kassie for your steady friendship. Gretchen for your editing. And Tabby for being a constant well of encouragement. Above all else, thank you to Jesus for being my savior and for granting me the time and ability to create stories.

About the Author

Some of the things I love most in this world are peppermint hot chocolate, peanut butter ice cream, golfing dates, Jesus, and game nights with family. And of course, books.

Fairytales were my first love. I became obsessed with the idea that if one was brave enough, they could defeat dragons, and that true love was real. I met my true love in college, and together we raise our boys. I have my dad to thank for my love of writing, and my mom to thank for allowing us to keep a wall of medieval weapons in the house, which cultivated my love for that time period. My dream is to write vivid worlds and charming characters that will leave an imprint on my readers hearts, the way that so many books have done for me.

Made in the USA
Middletown, DE
01 December 2021